I want to dedicate this work to the women in my life, M,A,E,E,and S. Your support in this effort has been invaluable.

-Benton

Nigel Day 237

The silver BMW glides along the road, staying within posted speed, not weaving or changing lanes. The radio is somewhat difficult to understand, playing pop music from someone who thinks that looking pretty and singing well are the same things. A quick click to search and ABBA's "Does Your Mother Know" fills the air with melodic Swedish tones. Nigel's calm appearance belies his internal status. This trip has not gone as expected. First, the courier was late. Then there were too many people around when he changed briefcases. Third, traffic has been heavier than he anticipated, and he has always hated traffic, too many idiots on the road. In the back of his mind, these were just the surface reasons. When you are standing on the edge of a high space, it's your inner voice that tells you to back away from the edge. It's the same voice that tells you not to believe the pretty girl in the pub. While she might just have spectacularly great taste in men by flirting with you, it's not bloody likely. Sure, you have a certain style and manner about you, but you aren't that good looking. It was just like back at university, when that girl wanted to have you, then before you can complete the deed, she starts asking you how many kids you want and do you want to meet her

Jolly Nice Angriness

Benton Brockliss

**Published by Badger & Canary Press.
Copyright 2011 Benton Brockliss.**

Cover by G.M. Sager

ISBN: 978-1-937277-02-4

**Discover Nigel's extended story
at BENTONBROCKLISS.COM**

parents. This is precisely the sort of thing that would make the inner voice scream.

The inner voice was not so much screaming, as it was nagging. Nagging like a whiny bitch. Nothing specific, but working at a heightened sense of agitation. The inner voice wasn't always right, but it was always looking out for you. Why? What was it pissed off about? *"You've missed something Nigel,"* it said. Nigel scanned ahead watching everything. What should be there, what shouldn't, what was coming, and what was behind. BEHIND! Looking in his mirror, he kept getting a glimpse of a black Chevrolet SUV, just ten or so cars behind. When the lights changed and it got left behind, it always made a turn or sped up to keep pace. Nigel could see two guys in the front, no; check that, a woman and a man, but he couldn't see beyond the front seat. It has heavier tires than stock, but not aftermarket rims. Skid plate under the oil pan and what appeared to be a heavy sway bar underneath. Each time it came over a hill, he could note these features. Government issue surely. Why would an American heavy SUV be in jolly old England? Surely they would want to blend, and not be noticed? They couldn't be that thick could they? It would be about as obvious on the M4 as it would be for a brothel to have a neon sign on top, "Gonorrhea here, 20 quid."

"Call Kingston" he said out loud. The cars

integrated Blue Tooth connected with his phone and called the stored number. After three changes in the ringing tones, he could tell he had been routed back to Langley. The voice on the other end was robotic and unemotional. "Identify yourself," it said methodically, and he responded. "This is Aardvark. Route me."

"Stand by," came the metallic response.

"Go ahead Aardvark," announced a new voice, a computer generated one, even though strangely enough it had an American accent.

"I wanted to update my status. The pizza will be a little late, but still hot and under the 30 minute limit."

"Good, we are hungry. Why is the pizza late?"

Nigel said "Traffic, but nothing too severe."

The voice on the other end offered, "We were getting concerned; you missed your route check point."

The man driving the BMW noticed the SUV dropping back and turning left, but a Mercedes squeezed in where it had been. Something about it seemed too deliberate, too focused. He was able to discern four people in the car, all men, all dressed in suits. Then he got it. The SUV is supposed to be seen, so that a less obvious car or cars can maneuver closer. Well they just had a bit of a cock up, Nigel mused, because he had seen through their little charade and was keyed in on their game. Still with so many resources in the field, best to check.

"Kingston, I wanted to thank you for the shadow, but I find your lack of faith a bit hurtful. I have always finished my tasks." Nigel said in a mockingly hurt tone.

"We didn't send a shadow. Are you sure you have one?" came the alarmed query from Langley.

The inner voice screamed *"TOLD YAH!"*

Damn. It is a definite tail. "Ok Kingston, thanks for the notice. I'm going to take the pizza to the alternate address."

"Follow protocol. We will have a Sheppard there in 30 minutes."

During this exchange, the SUV had moved up from ten back to two back, and the Mercedes appeared in front of him by two cars. *Bugger.* "Gotta go Kingston, looks like they want to play."

"Confirmed Aardvark. We are activating extraction team. Go to the library. Kingston out."

Bloody lot of good Kingston was. He'd never make it to the alternate site before the two cars made their move. Traffic was thinning slightly and time was running out. The men in the Mercedes seemed to have a fixed stare ahead, definitely not a group out for a business lunch. Watching the road ahead, Nigel was looking for the trigger, the event that would allow the cars to close up, and then spring their trap on him. *Ok, if you want to play, let's play follow the leader.* He signaled to get around a lorry on the right as they passed an exit so that the front SUV couldn't take the exit, and he was momentarily obscured from the rear car. Nigel stabbed the brakes and yanked on the wheel, sending the car down the embankment grass to the exit. This move caught the Mercedes off guard, and they indicated their lack of anticipation by braking hard and trying to go down the other side's onramp. The SUV could only view these events when it cleared the lorry, and it's now agitated occupants saw that their quarry was very much aware of them. With a huge lorry in their way, they couldn't go to the right and catch up. Meanwhile, the poor bastard in the delivery lorry nailed his brakes, further interfering with the SUV and blocking it from engaging Nigel.

One down, one to go, he thought, but there was no time to enjoy his sudden advantage. His maneuver has caused them and their plan, whoever they were. Nigel nailed the accelerator, making the tires break contact slightly with the road, but he had no problem controlling the car; the traction control wouldn't allow the BMW to get squirrely. He quickly turned left, cut under the bridge and drove immediately up the entrance to the opposite direction of the highway. He could see in the mirror that the SUV had not yet entered the ramp to follow him; maybe it wasn't going to. Two seconds later, a familiar shape popped up from the entrance ramp and was in full pursuit of him.

Well, so much for the concealment and stalking routine. "Oh look, the Mercedes is crossing the grass and going to bring up the rear." he said to no one in particular. Doing a quick scan of all the other cars, he detected no other vehicles behaving strangely, so it was just those two. OK. *Gotta lose them now.* Watching the upcoming exits, he took the first one, which put him back in the city. A quick turn to the right and he momentarily lost both vehicles. Nigel slowed down quickly and drove between two buildings with a grassy strip between them, then behind the one on the right, and made another quick left behind a dumpster. He could just see a narrow gap between the dumpster and the building it belonged to, where much to his amusement; he saw both the SUV and the Mercedes pass by.

Like shooting fish in a barrel, and then realized

what a stupid expression that was. *Who shoots fish in a barrel?* He'd rather go to the fish store and just buy one wrapped. Nigel reversed the car from behind the dumpster, went back the way he came and made a right turn where he saw a divine sight. It was an automated car wash. He drove in, paid the man to do a full wash/wax/detail, grabbed the attaché from the passenger seat and walked calmly to the service desk. Noting that the car emerging from the end that the attendants were detailing was a Jeep, he grabbed the keys from the hook board with a Jeep logo, walked over to the Jeep, told the towel monkeys that he needed to go, tossed in the briefcase, and drove off in someone else's car. He was always gratified when a vehicle had the wheel on the correct side, as opposed to the left where the yanks put them. *What rubbish, can't even design a proper car.*

Easy peasy, he mused as he drove west; trying to put some distance between him and the two friends he just left. Knowing that he was likely seen on the CCTV, he pulled in to a flower shop. Nigel grabbed the case with his left hand and the door release with his right, and emerged briskly and strode to the door, pulled the handle with a yank, and walked in. Looking around, he saw that the shop was thankfully larger than it appeared. Nigel went to the tropical section and found a massively beautiful palm, over six feet tall. As he stood there admiring it, a helpful, pimply faced youth asked in a squeaky

8

voice, "Ahh, I see you like the palm. Would you like to take it home?" Grinning and smiling, Nigel answered, "It's just what I need to add that natural touch to my office. Do you have any pots?"

"Pots, sir?" the boy said with his squeaky voice, which was already beginning to become annoying.

"Yes, you know, those large ceramic things, often shiny. I would like one large enough for my new palm tree," looking at the boy's uniform, he added, "Gavin."

Embarrassed at being so thick, Gavin offered "Yes sir, we have several shapes and colors, over there past the potting soil."

"Be a good lad, and fetch me one large enough for this, and bring four bags of soil, I want to put my tree in it."

Looking a little unsure, Gavin inquired, "We can do that for you if you would like."

I so like doing this. Scrunching his face up in his best angry glare, Nigel raised his voice and said harshly, "Gavin! I've become quite close to my tree, Sally, and I want to make sure she is happy in her new pot. Now fetch me one, preferably green, and four bags of soil. Off with you, and be quick!"

Completely cowed, Gavin raced off to find a dolly and do as he was told lest he make this customer even angrier. He returned in ten minutes pushing a flat dolly loaded with four pots and four bags of soil. "I'm sorry for my delay, sir; I wanted to give you some choices."

Nigel responded, "Good lad, don't get customer service this good. Fetch me a watering can."

Gavin raced off, seemingly encouraged that this cranky customer had stopped yelling. When the errand boy was out of sight Nigel selected the largest pot to see if the briefcase would fit in the bottom. *Damn near perfect fit.* He opened the first bag of soil, and poured it over the case, then with a grunt, hefted the palm tree out of its plastic temporary container, and placed it on top of the soily case. He quickly opened and added the rest of the bags, to keep the tree vertical and cover the case. Then he tamped it down with his right leg. He had just finished when a visibly startled Gavin returned, staring with a bug-eyed confusion at the now potted palm in its new ceramic pot. "Sir, we could have done that for you, now your shoe is dirty."

"No worries. Sally was eager to get on with her new life," he said with as much emotion as he could muster even forcing a tear out of his right eye. This did not go unnoticed by Gavin who was utterly convinced that the man before him was a complete nutter. "She looks happy, doesn't she?" Nigel said almost so low that it bordered on being a whisper.

"Yes, she does," Gavin replied uncertainly. Gavin was starting to become concerned and alarmed at the behavior of the man who continued to gaze at his palm tree. "Well, right then. I need you to deliver Sally to my office," said Nigel as he handed Gavin a business card, "and I need her to be there tonight."

Gavin was even more convinced that the man before him was just plain wrong till he was handed five hundred pounds. Unable to take his eyes off of the money he said "Sir, the palm is about one hundred pounds and the pot is another hundred. The soil would only be twenty pounds; delivery would only be fifty pounds, so I will come back in a moment with your change."

"You will do nothing of the sort. I need this delivered tonight, Sally is eager to see her new home and spread her life giving oxygen to my environment. I expect her to be delivered tonight and to be well cared for. That's what my extra money is for. Can you do it Gavin? Or should I go elsewhere and cast Sally aside? That would only bring her grief and despair, as we have become quite close."

11

Crazy or not, that was real money in his hands. "No sir" said Gavin with a burst of confidence, "I will see that Sally gets to her new home safely. Do you still want the watering can?"

Stepping forward to look the boy in the eyes, no more than a foot from him, Nigel said "no" and turned on his heels and walked back the way he came, out the door and taking a left, hailed a taxi, opened the door and got in telling the driver to take him to this address as he handed him a piece of paper. Sitting back in the seat Nigel relaxed as the cab sped off into the afternoon sun. Nigel smirked as the cab drove past the SUV and the Mercedes at the car wash, his BMW being swarmed by grim men in suits and sunglasses. *Going to miss that car.*

Nigel realized he was in trouble. No car, no longer in control of his package, delivery to his drop might not be on time, and no idea who he can trust. *Being a spy seems like fun till someone shoots you.* He was going to try his best not to get shot. He took out his camera phone, and took as much video as he could while they passed the car wash. *Need to find out who they are. Turned my assignment into one big cock up till I found a way to make my delivery.*

The woman who was riding in the front of the SUV pulled out her mobile phone and made a call.

"He has eluded us," she said into the phone. Her driver watched her face tense up and could tell the conversation wasn't going well. "We'll pick him up again. We know where he is going." The SUV driver mused out loud to his now angry passenger, "Gotta give him credit, he did manage to lose us. Well timed, clean, clever. We may have misjudged him."

"Yes," she said as she hung up the phone. Maria had a very stern look on her face. He knew that look, but felt he needed to voice his concerns.

Maria had her school teacher look going and told him "We will get him."

"We should," he said, "but what if his profile is actually a cover and he is more than we thought he was? He did spot us and lose us with a perfect bit of driving and ditching."

Narrowing her vision, she sternly told her driver "When I want your opinion, I'll give it to you. Report back to the motor pool Agent Logan. I'm done with you."

It wasn't personal; he had failed. She was one of their best scouts, but he still felt that she was overly critical. *Fine. Let her get another driver.* He had seen this guy in action and thought he knew something about his personality from what he had observed. "As you wish," he said and turned away, walking toward the street where he hailed a cab and got in. As he closed the door he thought to himself, *once a bitch, always a bitch,* and the cab sped off to the south.

Enslow Unemployed Day 1

Enslow was awakened by his alarm clock. Buzz-buzz-buzz it went. His sleepy mind commanded his hand to reach out and hit the off switch. Sometimes that worked, other days it didn't. Today was one of those days. He just didn't want to get up. Today was the big day, when the overly political and accomplishment challenged class would give one of those speeches where they talked about the business cycle, becoming leaner, doing more with less, concentrating on core competencies and how today's layoff were hard for them too. Just like he had the last five times they gave the speech, Enslow would nod his head and praise the leadership for their bold vision and marvel at their management acumen and tell his teammates how glad he was that they had finally turned the corner, and all would be happy ahead of them. He went through his morning routine, ate a quick bite, kissed his wife goodbye and drove to work in the usual way.

He still didn't have his unicorn that pooped skittles. While he was not specifically promised one, the management class at his company always blew sunshine up his ass and promised him if he just focused on the team then they could all get through this. Enslow wondered what was more insulting, that they thought he was stupid enough to fall for the same tired patently obvious lie or that he actually was stupid enough to fall for the same tired patently obvious lie.

"After this, I'm definitely going to look for a job. I hate this place," he thought to himself. Enslow was forty five, getting a bit of a gut (he called it his father figure), was a devoted husband and father and was regarded by his peers as being very capable at what he did, but perhaps a bit quirky. Just a little too quick on the draw, one of his friends put it. As the years passed and he never got the promotion he felt he deserved, he would sometimes get a little bitter. His basic plan was to make himself indispensable by creating new and wonderful enterprise tools, but when he did, his superiors would take credit for them, that these fabulous creations were the result of their management brilliance, and that he was merely the lowest rung on the ladder and was granted the privilege of implementing their grand vision. When they had an idea of their own (which they likely stole from someone else) they would task him with implementing it. Quite often, he would explain that a particular idea was not feasible and inevitably when it did fail, it was always his fault, not their ideas that were bad. So he was doomed either way. If he won, they took credit; if they forced failure, he lost, but they still won.

16

"You worried?" Gene, his cube partner, asked.

"No, this is just a game they play, sacrifice a few loyal minions to scare us and tell us how lucky we are that we have jobs, give us no raise and then cut our benefits again. Same old, same old."

"I don't know man, I'm worried this time. Jeanie in accounting said the numbers are bad. The latest stupid advertising campaign just plain sucked. Late night comedians even mocked it on the top ten reasons why we suck."

"Dude, they can't run this sucker without us." Enslow reassured his friend, "These asshats know deep down that they are only in charge because they kiss a lot of ass. They know they don't know what they are doing."

Gene still seemed worried, but managed a smile. "You are always right, so I'm going to try to calm down".

Enslow said in as jolly a voice as he could, "Let's go to the auditorium and seem like we believe their lies."

Gene chimed in, "Yep, game face on." The two of them walked down the hall and out the door making their way over to building 6 where the auditorium was.

"Wow. Quite the crowd," Gene said, as he eyed the group. Then he spotted Lea. Nudging Enslow in the ribs, "Always like seeing that my friend. Stiffens my resolve to stay here." Lea was quite the eyeful. Twenty five, auburn hair, hourglass figure and a rack that moved independently of the laws of physics.

Snapping momentarily out of hypnosis, Enslow eyed his friend with a suspicious glance. "That's a polite way of saying it."

"You know me," Gene threw up his hands, "always the gentlemen."

"You have never been a gentleman." Enslow scolded, "That's your problem, and you confuse the idea that paying for her meal and expecting sex is somehow noble, like she should service you AND pay for her own food."

"You wound me, deeply." Gene said with a very pained expression, holding his hand to his forehead.

"If you had a soul, that might be possible, but as a soulless drone, you are undoubtedly destined for management," Enslow told Gene.

"Hey! I resent that, and I was going to do you a favor."

"Not gay, I keep telling you."

"Uh- in your dreams. No I was going to add you as a friend on ProNect," said Gene, as he watched Lea literally bounce up the stairs.

"That's the job site? I am going to make it through this, don't need it," remarked Enslow.

"Dunno mang," Gene said making his best Scarface impersonation. "You might need a friend when the day is out".

"Friends I got. It's a career I need, and this place sucks," postulated Enslow as they got to the door, and made their way to the seats.

There was a dull roar of people sharing their perspectives on what was about to happen. Enslow noted the worried expressions on many of their faces. After surviving the last five of these, he was not too worried. Gene had stopped observing Lea when he noticed Kelly, whose movements also seemed to violate natural laws, but was rumored to also demonstrate those supernatural abilities to a select few lucky guys. Scanning the room it seemed odd that some of the regulars were gone. "Bet they already got their papers," Enslow mused. "Best settle in for the same dull speech about sacrifice and how if they just pulled together, then there would be a bright and sunny future for all." Gene had broken his enchantment with Kelly long enough to find the seat next to Enslow and settle in for a round of robotic clapping and feigned enthusiasm.

"Let's make it look good this time, ol' buddy," whispered Gene.

"Sure, you know me, a team player all the way through," Enslow assured him.

A portly executive, the kind who always wore a smile, even as all those around him were in dire straits, walked up to the center and stood before the microphone. Dire straits made Enslow think of the group and then he recounted in his head some of their songs and lyrics. "Skate Away" was always a classic. It was "Money for Nothing", however that emerged to occupy his thoughts. He instantly started rewriting the song in his head, changing the lyrics to suit the situation his company was in, with mindless executives being paid criminal amounts of money, who never seemed to be held accountable for the damage they were doing to people's lives. The executive was named Bob Way, Wrong Way Bob, as he was called. He was famously inept, and in the days of cellophane slides, always put them on upside down or reversed. Of course, his moniker lead to other jokes, most of which weren't allowed in polite company, Kelly excluded.

Bob stepped forward to the center of the stage, his fat fingers gripping the microphone like he was trying to pick up a turd from the clean end. "Hello! As you know, we have a new VP, Paula Roundrock, who has come to us with new vision, new abilities, and new focus on our core competencies. It gives me great pleasure to introduce you to her now. Paula, can you come up and tell us what we can look forward to in the coming months?" Paula Roundrock was a fortyish woman, of no discernable talents, other than plotting and scheming to rise ever higher in an organization. She was not quite heavyset, but not svelte; average for her age. She strode with a determined series of steps and removed the microphone from Bob's beringed fingers. *Honestly, did he think he was Joe Pesci? Who wears pinky rings?*

Paula looked out over the audience, and started off on her prepared remarks. "Hello! It's nice to see you all!" she announced with great warmth. "I have enjoyed getting to know you all, over the last four months, and have made some great new friendships. I'd like to say to all my new friends, I understand how nervous you all are. We have been through some tough times, and we still have some time to go. But I wanted to tell you a story. When I was five years old, I went on a new phase of my life; I went to kindergarten. I was a fat kid, and my parents only had a little money, so my clothes were not as nice or new as the other kids. They made fun of me, and I ran home when the day was over, crying very hard. My grandmother saw me in distress and asked me what was wrong. I told her that the other kids had made fun of me and laughed at me for my clothes and that I was fat." My grandmother told me, "The only difference between a good day and a bad day was my attitude. I thought about that, and I knew she was right. My mother still loved me, my dad still loved me. I still had my grandmother, my dog, my toys and my friends. Quite a lot for a five year old child to assimilate, but while I wanted to be liked, I knew I was still a good person and that the reason they were mean to me wasn't my fault."

"I don't like where this is going," Gene whispered.

"No, sounds like someone is going to take a fall," Enslow agreed.

Paula continued, "So what I want all of you to remember is that someone loves you and your lives aren't over." A dull murmur went up across the auditorium. "Because in order to make this company profitable again, all of you here will be released from work effective immediately. We will give you assistance to find new jobs, and severance packages. Remember, it's your attitude that makes you a winner, and if all of you keep your heads up, and focus on what makes you great workers, you will be able to convey that wherever you go, and you will land on your feet. All of you have made great contributions to us, and we wish we had room for all of you, but we just don't. The economy is struggling, and we are struggling to survive. Your assigned HR reps will be contacting you about the next steps you need to take. While you have been in here, your things have been packed up for you, and will be available in the parking structure. God bless you all," Paula said with some feigned emotion, and she raced off stage trying to look emotional about having been the instrument of slaughter for the two thousand people sitting in stunned disbelief.

"I don't get it. That's it? Eight years of busting my ass and I get my stuff thrown to the curb?" Gene said in stunned tones.

"Looks like," Enslow responded with equal disbelief.

"Did you catch that bullshit? The only difference between a good day and a bad day was my attitude," Gene mocked. "What a crock."

"Seriously, how stupid is that? If I was in a car accident and lost a leg, no matter how positive I felt about it, I'm down a leg. And If I woke up next to my fave actress after a night of animal lust, and she brought me a fresh plate of bacon to start my day out right, you'd have to admit that would be a pretty good start to any day," Enslow spat out with considerable disgust.

Gene and Enslow stood there as the crowded room gradually emptied, most people too shocked to say anything; just file out as sheep do to a slaughter. Some of them were crying. Even the men. "What are we going to do? Unemployment won't cover my bills, and things are hard out here. Where am I going to find a job?" Gene asked.

"You'll be fine, man. Gay is the new black," Enslow quipped.

"Oh, very funny! Asshole," Gene barked back. Then he saw the twinkle in Enslow's eyes. "Thanks man. Let's go get our crap. Then let's go to Bookers and start drinking. Going to be a helluva day when I get home."

Enslow responded, "Roger that, I've got your six. And I'm not leaving my wingman."

Gene said, "Ok Mav, let's go." The two of them walked slowly down the sidewalk to their parking structure to look for their boxes, then drive over to the college bar, Bookers.

"Where you guys going?" Bill Wester asked.

"We are going to go to Bookers and have several beers to regroup and plan our next move. What about you?" Enslow inquired.

Bill Wester was a nice man, well regarded by his coworkers as a competent member of the company. He was not a star player, but could be counted on to always be in good cheer. Right now, however, his face looked strangely pale as if he was having a physical reaction as well as an emotional one.

"Ok, great. I'll see you two there!" Bill replied and he started to spread the word to other members of the crowd.

"Always liked him," Gene said out loud, to no one in particular.

"Me too," Enslow agreed, "but I'm worried for him. All those kids and his wife has never worked, and look at his age. It's going to be tough for him."

"You and me both," Gene instructed Enslow, "My brother has been out for nine months now, and it is not getting better".

"Hate to say it, but you and me got skills. We may take a little longer, but it won't take us nearly that long," Enslow assured Gene. Enslow had been hearing from friends already out in the morass, however that it was getting VERY hard to find a gig at any price. Through all his bravado, there was a rising fear that would make it harder for him to speak so nonchalantly. That day was not here though, and he was going to enjoy a few beers with his friends.

Nigel Day 238

After the events of yesterday the man who liked to name potted plants woke up refreshed and ready to engage. He knew that he was going to find a way to get past that team that was tracking him. Questions lingered in his mind. *Who were they? Why were they tracking him? What was their nationality? Who had intel on them?* He only knew this: they were professionally equipped, they were trained and talented, well-funded, and drove a variety of vehicles. Some were American, some British and some European. They favored powerful large cars and were well dressed. That they were physically in shape, mentally sharp, multilingual (the woman with the short hair appeared to be a cunning linguist), and well armed. Their weapons were American and European, primarily, except for the Israeli Uzi that they used on the M4. The nationalities were primarily Caucasian with one Asian and one darker skinned person who he believed was Pakistani, could be Afghani, could be Bangladesh, but because of the clipped nature with which he spoke at a distance (Nigel was not able to hear his voice), the inclinations of his head seemed to hint of a western influence. He had contacted Kingston overnight to give intel on the team, and they drew a blank. Since they were so well armed and not afraid to a car chase or public confrontation, they were not Interpol. They were capable, trained and brave so they were not French or Italian either. The Swiss do not play games like this, although they might hire mercs, but not bloody likely. Perhaps Spain or Portugal, maybe some undercover operative from South America. He did not suspect any involvement from Germany or Austria; there wasn't a Teutonic face or jaw line amongst the entire crew. *Could it be somebody isn't secure at Kingston?* Nigel just did not know. Interestingly, the internal voice was silent, as if digesting the analysis. Without some one-on-one or hard intel he was in the dark. Operative school taught you to dictate the perception, to lead the deception. The whole thing almost made his head feel as if it were going anti-clockwise. The inner voice spoke up, "American." There was a bestselling book recently, where the central thesis was that your first impression, no matter how irrational, was likely to be correct. The inner voice had spoken. *So if they were American, why chase him? Weren't they working for the same people?* That answer was obvious; "no." *If they were Yanks, then who did they work for? NSA? CIA? FBI? One of the service branch intelligence groups?*

A mind is a terrible thing to waste. His wasn't being wasted but it was racing without the aid of drugs or caffeine. Further questions were getting at him. *What did they want at the end of the day?* He wasn't that big a fish. As a peacock, whose primary function is to go to events and be seen, or fill in labor, he wasn't a big deal. All this attention was out of place. Actually, Nigel wasn't much of a spy all, at least not the cloak and dagger stuff, which made their interest in him even more fascinating. Sure his public profile was impressive. Frankly, a bit scary and just a bit over the edge. When people in the community read his intelligence profile, they always reacted in the same way. They would be sitting there reading Nigel's bio and laugh out loud. He thought it was funny, but here would be a trained operative working for the company, reading the manufactured profile and laughing out loud. There was a point he had once called the "oh shit" moment, where as they started reading it, an idea would gestate in that pink fleshy fruit within their skull. It would start to gel, then it would grow at an exponential rate, once it had taken hold. There was an idea that was buried in plain sight amongst the words and characters that made up the profile. These people, universally, would start to draw the disparate threads together, and the fact that the profile seemed a little over the edge no longer mattered. The embedded, calculated, almost magnificently hard truth would reveal itself like a momma bear who thought you had stolen her favorite cub. This almost imperceptible segment of time, allowed an idea to explode across the reader's brain, just like the brilliance of the sun itself exploded across the morning horizon at sea. It flashed just as you went from darkness to light. It was all brought together, and that is when each and every person, said out loud, "oh shit".

How did this occur? Why did the profile have this effect? The simple truth is that it is so believable. Rather than understate the facts, this manufactured life history seemed to be false. Therefore it must be true, it was too obvious what the intent to communicate was. It allowed the reader to bring into focus the unconscious threads, and then that sold the entire idea. It was much like trying to tell someone how to play a piano, and then they actually did it themselves. The act of telling was different from the act of doing. His cover was that he was a computer services executive. His next level down was this profile that had the amazing dichotomy of seemingly unconnected jobs that actually was very effective at selling his credentials to most people.

Then there was the final level of his resume, planted just deep enough in the shadowy worlds of the intelligence communities. This is the level that made trained people take pause when dealing with Nigel, which was all that was required, that they take pause. Multiple real and projected events were connected together with psychological profiles, along with various weapons certifications that made him out to be a ruthless, get it done at any cost, detached professional, who let nothing get in the way of his objective. There were operational details of events that only a few other intelligence organizations were aware of, and if an event was unknown to other agencies, by taking key pieces of information from the dossier, they found a sort of confirmation that added to the aura of who Nigel was dictated to be. Various stories confirmed his extreme vigilance to professionalism, no school kids or old people, but also no problems with shooting a suspect or their families in the leg to get what he wanted. It was alluded to, without specifics, that he had an extreme prejudice when dealing with enemies of the state, such as terrorists, their command structure and even just the financiers of the actions. In one instance, Nigel had drugged the wife and oldest child of a Middle Eastern money man, and stood there with his pants off and a video camera, claiming he would film their violations and publish them worldwide on the web.

In another, he held two of a target's children up by ropes over an industrial shredder, and threatened to drop the children in unless the guy talked. When his bluff was called, he cut the rope holding the first child and let him drop. What was generally unreported was that the gagged child was unable to scream that it was all fake. The bundles of meat expelled by the shredder, was in fact a partial cow, hidden by the shredder and that when dropped, the child merely fell into a soundproof box. When Nigel had the information that he wanted, he let everyone go. It didn't work out so well though. When the terrorist group thought they had been sold out, they blew up the poor guy and his wife. The children had mysteriously 'vanished'. The story stuck, however, and it enhanced Nigel's credibility.

Another instance was Barcelona. In the Barcelona operation Nigel was performing routine courier operations and inadvertently stumbled on a drug importation at the shipping docks. Not only did Nigel perform his courier operations, he killed three drug dealers and their accomplices with only one 9MM Ruger. He was shot four times, but was still able take out the entire crew and most importantly, made his escape without being discovered by the authorities. No hospital, no police, nothing. It was a clean escape while badly wounded. Although this entire event was a fabrication, the photos and accompanying police documentation was a first class effort.

Many other operations in his profile were similar; despite taking fire, Nigel got the job done. Any time he did execute opponents, it was necessary with a clean and clear dispatch. It was not a question of simply achieving the objective, he was almost completely robotic. He showed the professional detachment just as a video game player was detached when blowing up a UFO in a video game.

Time after time after time in all of these operations Nigel operated in a very distant and cool manner that was noted in different ways in different intelligence archives including Interpol, the Secret Services of France, Belgium, Switzerland; even the Vatican had a profile of him. There was an unfortunate situation where there was a very bad bishop who was visiting Portugal who arranged, as he always did, for young altar boys to be his playthings. The Vatican knew that the heat was about to drop on him and they simply couldn't stand somebody so highly placed in yet another scandal. They approached Nigel's organization and asked that something be done. Nigel was recorded as not only willing to take the assignment, but he volunteered, and refused all hazard pay, all bonuses, took vacation time to do it, and asked that the agency take no money for the job. It was simply a matter of honor that the bishop was quietly dispatched in a roadside accident with a delivery lorry, where his car rolled down the mountainside. The bishop's driver was ejected from a vehicle by the second flip and the unfortunate bishop suffered multiple fractures and a broken neck as his car rolled down five hundred feet along a rocky precipice of the mountain. Enough witnesses were there to see the event, that there was little question as to the innocent nature of the bishop's departure. No questions, no inquiries, and no curious reports. It was suspected deep within that community of molesting priests that it was a hit, but they had no evidence, so they kept quiet, and in fact curtailed their activities. A win–win scenario, especially for the orphans and the altar boys. The only public confirmation of the results was a series of other accidents and a lot of early retirements. These and other events built up an operational profile of someone who was best to be avoided. Nigel of course, relished the 'mojo' of being a badass. It led to fewer confrontations, and made life easier. Borrowing from Clint Eastwood, when someone would challenge Nigel, he would reply, "Ever notice in life you come across one of those guys you shouldn't have fucked with? I'm that guy. Look me up. I'll wait."

Why would other intelligence services believe such stories? It was really quite an easy thing. After sourcing some people in multiple services, and deliberately salting stories in other places, the databases of various agencies were themselves storing this information, so that when one service wanted to corroborate their facts, the other service had most of the same facts and some new ones. It was easier to convince someone that they weren't a traitor if you didn't ask them for information, merely to insert some new facts in. When they looked at the facts, as they were actually expected to do, it didn't seem too different from what they knew that they had on other agents. Sometimes, one of these low level contacts might ask why they were putting it in, and the answer was often a believable story about information sharing, or it was part of an effort to trap a double agent; just really any kind of a story to assuage their concerns. These people were always paid handsomely for the information input, though they did not know what it was.

While those cover stories helped convey the weight that Nigel needed when he needed it he also had to be useful when the heat was off. Nigel always had a natural ability to talk to anybody about virtually anything. It was really a very simple technique. You don't have to know as much about the subject as to just have a good sound understanding of the current state of various things. For cars, aviation, computers, weapons, etc., all you had to know was what was technically feasible. For example, if carbon fiber was suitable, would aluminum also work, and what properties and cost factors could lead to one conclusion or another? What was the trend or direction of the technology and why? By asking good questions, and letting others talk, you could understand a lot about the person and appear to be knowledgeable yourself when you didn't come up with any answers, only good questions. Often restating what someone just said allowed you to agree with the person, and give them reinforcement that their views were correct. People like to be agreed with. They also like people who agree with them. Men in particular like to talk, but so do women. For many women it's about the sharing of information, not the information content. By agreeing with people, and reinforcing your agreement with positive body language and a warm smile, you can quickly build rapport with a wide range of people. As an illustration, if one were at a diplomatic function at the Belgian embassy and the Deputy Minister for National Defense from Senegal is there, you ask him what he sees as the most challenging aspects for maintaining the air defense systems in terms of pilot training, operational costs for fuel, and have they considered perhaps going to less expensive aircraft for training. Have they noticed how the bottom has dropped out of the market for the L29's, making a large amount of spare parts available, as well as surplus aircraft? Because of the widespread use of those aircraft and the economic situation in countries that flew them, you could pick up a lot of skilled people on contract to do the work, or train your own crews. As long as the director for National Defense from Senegal doesn't realize he is giving up any state secrets, you can get people very engaged because they see you as a new source of useful information that they can take back and score points with.

With women, Nigel behaved as politely as he could. Always the gentleman with a door or a chair, but he behaved in an abrupt manner. No topic was exactly safe. If he believed a woman was being a bitch, he had no difficulty saying so. If she could dress less like a prossy, he would say so. Nigel was not anti-woman or dismissive of their abilities, quite the contrary; Nigel was a curious mix of proper behavior and ultimate feminism. There was very little a woman couldn't do that a man could, limited primarily to acts of physical strength. In the realm of equality, he had no problem being as abrupt, rude or straight with the facts. This won him few friends, but garnered him a sort of respect. You might not like what he had to say, but you knew exactly where he stood.

Enslow Unemployed Day 2-7

The alarm squawked its familiar claxon, again and again. Enslow's eyes peeked from underneath their fleshy covers. His hand twitched with desire to shut the damn thing off. Before he could muster the strength or resolve to move, a familiar, soft, supple and still sexy hand after fifteen years of marriage, stretched across his chest and gave the clock radio a whack, whereby the jarring command to wake up was at last, blissfully silent.

Ella Spengler was 36, trim, and quite fit for a mother of two. For a native of Wisconsin, she was strangely olive skinned, but there was no mistaking the peculiar accent from the upper reaches of cheese land, home of the Cheddar, land of the Swiss. Ella rolled back flat again, her eyes closed, and she mumbled, "Honey, you got to get up." Enslow replied, after drawing in a morning yawn, that forced Ella to do the same, "Nope. Today is a day to rest, I've earned it. No job, remember?"

Ella didn't respond for a minute or so, and then she said, "Ok, take today off and get your head right. A little yard work might help. But Christy at work said her husband didn't take it seriously when he got laid off, and he wished he had. So don't you make the mistake and miss out on a good position somewhere. You have to get to it as soon as you think you can. We are almost out of spring, and the jobs people are hiring for will be gone soon. I can't believe how many people we know who have been out of work for six months or more."

Enslow opened his eyes, and stared at the ceiling. "Remember Jimmy, from over on Elm Circle? He just lost his house to foreclosure."

Ella sat up, "Really?"

"Yep. Don't know what he's going to do. He spent almost all of their 401 on Cindy's breast cancer. After he lost his job and she couldn't work, they fell behind."

"I feel so bad for them. Is there anything we can do?"

"Nope. It's a done deal. He didn't say anything to anyone till it was too late. Not sure what we could have done, but now since we are under the gun ourselves, we have got to watch all our spending. Let's make a list tonight to see what we can save on. Ok?"

"I'd like that," Ella said in her oh so sultry breathy voice. She planted a good morning kiss on Enslow's head. "But I better get up, since I'm the bread winner now," and before he could return the kiss, she vanished like an apparition into the bathroom, where Enslow soon heard the sounds of the shower heating up. He could only imagine that her nightshirt would soon fall off those delicious shoulders. *Hmmm. Maybe I should get up after all…*

Mid morning found Enslow at his computer, trying to find his last resume from several years ago, as a starting point. After struggling for thirty minutes to recall what he had really done through all the changes they had at work, he then found his flash drive and pulled up his job appraisals for the last few years. *Should be some nuggets in here. This should be simple, at least not as big a deal as most people think. Address has changed, phone number…. Hmmm. Objective statement… probably drop that, I'm applying for a job, so that is my objective. Kinda like buying a pretty girl a drink, I think we both know what the objective is. That leaves extra space for more achievements. Ok. Current, last company, job title… dates there… responsibilities.*

"I have endeavored to persevere under incredibly moronic superiors who insist on serving me steaming piles from silver trays and expecting me to praise it as the best ice cream I've ever had." Enslow chuckled at his resume revision, but then the grin dropped from his face. "Better take this more seriously," he told himself. He then typed, after some forethought:

Content management application administration specialist; business systems requirements analyst; data analyst; very proficient at metadata structure, database design, junior staff management and process taxonomy development. Additional support work provided to other divisions upon request. This included technical analysis, purchasing research, and vendor relations management.

Stop it, you'll either make them laugh or take you seriously. That's always been your problem, you just go too far. Enslow frowned, and his inner dialogue continued. *Better look that over later. Sounds impressive, but does it actually say anything? Let's add some skills.*

Process Optimization
Account Management
Rational Analyst Suite
Requirements Gathering
Proposal Writing
Project Scheduling
Resource Forecasting
Trend Projection
Technical Writing
Report Design
Project Management
Database design
Database Analyst

Database performance Tuning
Report Query Analyst
Business Analyst
Content Specialist
Process Analyst
Process Engineer

Enslow reviewed what he had written, and felt that while it expressed what he'd done, it said little about accomplishments. What had he really done? He went to work every day, did as he was told, worked extra hours when the boss was looking or a project needed to have the effort expended. Had he actually received any awards or some of those shiny things other people put on their desks though? *How is it possible I spent twelve years there and have no gold or treasure to show for it? Let's see. You did speak on that webcast, so...* "Featured Speaker for national company broadcast." *Yeah, that sounds cool. You ran those team calls, so...* "Productivity Leader/Mentor"...Enslow proceeded to explore his new line of attack, but after several minutes he found himself just staring at the screen. An overcast of doubt started to roll in. If he couldn't articulate why he was a great candidate, how was anyone else going to know it? You have to create the persona, and really sell it. It doesn't sell itself unless it is really good.

Enslow checked his watch, it was almost five o'clock. Ella and the kids would be home soon.

Dee Dee was the most optimistic five year old anyone could ever meet. She never had a bad day. If no one played with her, she was fine by herself. If everyone wanted to play, she was up for that as well. Augie was the more serious child, but not by much. He would sometimes contemplate things before he took action, which was a refreshing change from his sister, who was always smiling and getting into everything. Since he was four, and found out his name was Augustus Ulysses Spengler, he seemed to spend more time trying to understand the world. Exactly as most boys did, he took things apart, and while they didn't always go back together, more often than not they did, and with a minimum of extra parts. Augie learned early that the secret to technology was research, so every time his parents got him a new game or whatever, he would search online for tips on how to play it and what it would take to get an advantage. One game was so new, that there were no English examples to look at, so without waiting or asking anyone, he cut and pasted the Japanese text about the game into an online browser based translator and translated the segment to English. This allowed him to learn some tricks for playing the game. What astonished Enslow was that a seven year old boy understood enough about the web, and did it without asking anyone how to do it. He certainly never told them.

Nigel Day 239

Rather than lie low, Nigel had been to his favorite pub, The Badger and Canary. After a hard day of serving his queen and country, he felt a couple of pints would be the proper way to reset and decompress. A couple of pints turned into half a dozen, however, and he was feeling it now. *Fat, forty and bladdered is no way to go through life laddie.* Rolling out of bed, he staggered to his feet and stumbled like one of the living dead to his shower. Adjusting the water anti-clockwise and waiting till it got hot, he stepped in and turned the spray to hit his face. "Something isn't right. Bloody hell!" he shouted and jumped out of the shower, to stand on the tile floor, soaking wet in his clothes. "Brilliant," he said out loud, as he peeled off his shirt, trousers, and socks. "Where are my..." his voice trailed off. *Oh, I went commando last night.* Stepping back into the warm stream of water he had just gotten his hair wet, when the phone rang.

He popped out of the shower, grabbed his mobile and said "Allo, allo, if you aren't a tasty bird then sod off, I'm busy." The popping on the line and the dulcet computer tones told Nigel this was not a casual call from his pub mates. In fifteen seconds a computerized voice came on that said

"Aardvark. We have an assignment for you. Your encryption key will be the electric city. The message will auto delete in five minutes. Kingston out."

"But," Nigel tried to say, and would have, had the call not terminated, that he had earned some down time. *They said it would be a life of adventure. No one mentioned the dodgy mind games.* His mobile phone beeped, and displayed the new mail icon. Clicking on the message button, he was prompted with a counter, showing 4 minutes and 38 seconds, and a password box. "Bollocks" he shouted. He typed in P-A-R-I-S and hit enter, and the password box reappeared with no characters. "Well you git. That's the city of lights. What is the electric city…New York? No, it never sleeps. Trenton? No, that always stinks. Cleveland? God, not Cleveland. Detroit? That would be the city that rots." Nigel watched the counter descend closer to zero. "Electric city? AHH!! He typed in S-P-A-R-K-S –N-E-V-A-D-A and hit enter. The screen went blank, popped up a counter that started going down from two minutes, and then displayed the following instructions:

Go to Byrd & Thayer Fine Tailors, get tuxedo under name of Gavin Brown.
Pay with 100 pound notes.
When clerk asks if there will be anything else, reply, "No, but I could use new socks."
Clerk will hand you package.

45

Open package.

Plan to attend the event outlined in package at French embassy.

Perform duties according to protocol.

Arrive no later than 7:30, leave no later than 11:00. Speak to, and shake hands with 75 people.

Oh lahteedah, another crotched up poncy frog dinner. Bugger. He hated these French events. Always a lot of wine, cheese and panty waisted French sophisticates looking down their Gallic noses at a proper Brit. *Still, a tanner beats a biscuit, and you are being paid quite grandly.*

The counter on his phone reached zero, and then the screen returned to its default. Nigel tossed it onto the counter where it hit with a thud and skittered across where it bumped into his fruit bowl with a ceramic bell sounding 'ding'. Feeling a bit knackered from his previous night's activities, he plopped down into his chair, dropped his head back, and ran his fingers through his still wet hair. *Let's see, five and a half hours to drive, plus delays at the Chunnel, or 30 minutes to Heathrow, plus one hour via British Airways, but have to get a stupid car,* and Nigel loathed Citroens. So about three hours all told, get to hotel, dress, send for limo or taxi, and need to get some cash at the bank and when it's all done, not a decent boozer in all of Paris. On the plus side, he could stop in Calais. He always preferred the A16 to the A26, not as much traffic, and fewer lorrys.

"It's looking to be another beastly evening. Best not to faff while there's work to be done," Nigel announced to the empty room.

Nigel made his way back to the sink, where he lathered up a bar of soap, and proceeded to shave. Finishing his task he looked into his eyes, and made a pucker with his lips, *what a cheeky bastard you are.* He had one small physical trait that he had only heard of others having. He frequently looked in his mirror to see what color his eyes were. For reasons no doctor was ever able to offer a reasonable explanation for, his eyes changed color of their own accord, and for no apparent reason. For a few hours they might be blue, then shift to grey, and then to the green spectrum of a solid green or even a hazel. The length and duration of the change seemed random, and was unrelated to his mood, state of rest or the color of clothes he was wearing. The change could take as long as and last several months. He once got out of a questioning by Danish authorities, because the embassy attaché insisted his eyes were green, while his eyes at the time were blue. The attaché swore that she knew her object of interest had no contacts, and it was apparent to the Danish authorities that the man in front of them also was not wearing contacts.

They were gob smacked that the man in front of them was not the man they were looking for. Just for good measure, he had been wearing latex fingerprints when he was on assignment so the prints they were looking for did not match his, and he was not currently wearing any prints. His cover of a businessman was obviously a cover, but when they looked deeper, his prints would reveal him as a high level UK official, and that all records of his questioning would have to be purged from their systems. As in previous types of encounters such as this, they would just give up.

He still chuckled at the look on their faces when they looked at the background check they were holding. Moronic prat just stood there and apologized as if he'd detained a bigger bloke who could thrash him and his mum. Nigel always enjoyed the cajones his profile conveyed, and he was always mindful to play the part; it was brilliant. It's not who you are, but who people think you are. For the few people who still had trouble looking at him and seeing him as the man they were told about, the rest of their peers always believed what they were told, and convinced them to believe. Was it art or genius? Where did one stop and the other start? To be fair, however, the profile would be nothing without supporting documents, and he had them all. It was part of the magic of being a spy; it was almost a nonstop theatre part.

Walking over to his wardrobe, he put on his slacks, a shirt, fresh pair of socks and his shoes, and walked back across to the counter where he picked up his wallet, phone, keys and a comb. When he got to the door, he looked around the flat to see if he had missed anything, set his exit code on the keypad by the door and walked out to the street where he walked to his Land Rover. It went unnoticed by him that four pairs of eyes were watching him from the house across the street, the van at the corner, the London taxi driving past, and the Audi parked eight houses to the north. It was in the Audi, that Maria watched. She watched Nigel climb into his Land Rover, and after starting it, proceed south. She said out loud so her earpiece would pick up, "Ok he's left. Team one, check his flat, team two go west to intercept, but stay back. I don't want him to run. We need to track him. Langley wants all the intel on him. Nigel out."

Nigel drove west on Clerkenwell, took a left on Faringtdon Rd, then a right on High Halborn, and drove west all the way to Shaftesbury and into Soho. Perhaps Maria and her team had learned the last time they tried to intercept Nigel or he was just too tired and focused on other things. In either case, he had made it to Byrd & Thayer and parked two cars down from the front door. He got out and locked the door and walked to the tailors. He tripped on a slightly raised piece of concrete and dropped his keys. Nigel reached down and picked them up, then went inside the tailor shop. The clerk greeted him with, "Good day, my name is Rupert

Tavish, may I assist you with something?"

"Yes, my name is Gavin Brown, and I reserved a new tuxedo with some alterations," Nigel responded to the clerk's inquiry.

"Very good sir, I'll just be a moment," the clerk replied, who virtually disapperated like one of those spirits in a ghost story.

Reappearing several minutes later, the clerk informed his customer, "Here we are sir, and would you like to try it on?"

His first inclination was to take it and depart, but his inner voice was telling him to try it on. Much to his displeasure, he gave in and said to the rather stoic, typically British butlery looking clerk, "Yes, I believe I will; last one looked great, but was rubbish in the fit around my privates. Two hours of that and I would be ready to sing in the Vienna Boys Choir. Rupert, where would I be able to squeeze into this?"

"Please follow me Mr.Brown; we have our fitting suites just over here. Might I get you a spot of tea, sir?"

Thinking for a moment, he replied, "Roger that, Earl Grey, two lumps."

The customer followed Rupert to the rear of the store, where there were four doors, marked 1, 2, 3, and 4 in sturdy looking bright brass numbers. Rupert stopped in front of number 3, and said in a gentle, friendly voice, "Please try your garment on in here, and if you need anything, please don't hesitate to call us on the courtesy line," which Rupert indicated with a gesture of his hand to the phone on the table, just inside door number 3.

"Thank you Rupert, I should only be about twenty minutes. Should I need any further adjustments, would I be able to get them done in a short amount of time?" Nigel asked in an earnest tone. He liked to look into people's eyes, to see their reaction to his voice and to judge their level of sincerity, honesty and general level of intelligence. Seeing nothing, but honesty and sincerity in Rupert's eyes, he felt a bit more at ease. The whole drama of a new assignment agitated and bored him at the same time. So much foreplay to the event, and then often it was over before you got a chance to warm up. Oh well, that's how it goes. Nigel never thought of himself as a man of action, but he had always felt better if he and his assignment were in motion, rather than all the prep work.

"Without a doubt sir, we always strive to see that our clients get the absolute best service," Rupert replied and then walked away toward the front of the store, to help a portly fellow badly in need of a suit that fit.

Nigel opened the door, and closed it behind him with a satisfying click. He hung up the tux and noticed his tea was on the table next to the chair. "Ahh, nothing starts an afternoon better than a soothing cup of tea." He sipped it, and found it to be an excellent blend. He opened the jacket and took it off the hanger, pulled the pants off and laid them out on the desk, and then removed the shirt which he immediately put on. *Hmm, nice fitted shirt, must be standard spook issue.* Interesting that he could feel the reinforced seams. That told him to look for extra pockets and little presents in the liners. He grabbed the jacket and started feeling the lining and seams for abnormalities. *BINGO!* In the back of the jacket breast pocket, was a false back that contained ten thousand Euros in one thousand Euro denominations. In the other pocket, he found an opening in the top of the pocket that contained a 16 GB micro SD card. In the left side of the collar, he found a thin wire with a tab, probably for garroting some poor bastard. Not his style. On the other side of the collar, he found small a set of carbon fiber lock picking tools. They would not likely survive more than a couple of uses, but that was ok; he had never used his lock picking skills. A careful examination of the buttons revealed small watch type batteries, and the second button on the jacket was a transponder, that used the small batteries. A careful examination revealed that it

52

also had GPS capabilities when combined with the first button. He surmised that it was a rescue transponder, one use only and a limited time of use. Still, it was reassuring that he had it. Morocco and Cleveland were two times he could have used it. Those money grubbing bureaucrats had shorted him then, and he had really needed it. Especially in Cleveland.

The pants underwent a similar examination, and revealed a synthetic band, likely a derivative of carbon fiber, as a band in the waist, specifically designed to be used like a 'Slim Jim," the device police and car thieves used to break into cars by sliding down the window to unlock the car's doors. *That's neat.* The zipper was removable and was made out of a high grade titanium alloy, capable of sawing through most common materials. *Makes you remember to tuck in your willy. Hope the product liability lawyers know about this one.* He tested it on the bottom of the desk table leg. *Blimey! That bugger operates faster than a back alley surgeon at a 2 pound circumcision clinic. Must remember that when I down a few drinks.*

There were false pockets in the rear and a holster in each pant leg down by the cuff. The front pockets felt like an asbestos type fabric and it was obvious that they were actually tear away mittens, for grabbing something and leaving no prints or grabbing something hot. All in all, a typical service tux, well appointed and in style for the current season. A sudden thought occurred to Nigel, and he unlocked his mobile phone, accessed the solitaire game waiting for a three of spades. When he got one off the deck, he pressed and held it for four seconds, and then double clicked the next card that came after it. A new menu appeared, and he selected "tracker" and held his phone to the pants. Sure enough, it indicated a small radio tracker in the reinforced belt loops. He removed the zipper, cut off the second loop with the tracker, and put it in the pants pocket for now, he would lose it later. Or maybe drop it into some unsuspecting car valet's pocket. Last time he did that, some poor blighter got locked up for 48 hours till they figured out the game.

He tried the pants on after the inspection, and found that they fit perfectly. Not too tight so that he could still have children and loose enough that he could squat and kneel without binding or pulling. These government tailors do great work. *Wonder what these would cost on the outside?* Nigel carefully removed his new threads and put them on the hanger, then got dressed again in his own clothes. He finished his tea and opened the door to see Rupert waiting patiently, with a helpful smile and a question on his lips.

Rupert took the hanger and asked Mr. Gavin to follow him, whereby he walked calmly to the register and put the tuxedo inside a new heavy fabric hanger bag. "Will this be cash or charge sir?"

He responded it would be in cash and after looking at the receipt, paid the total amount in one hundred pound notes. Rupert looked at the money and asked if there was anything else, to which came the reply, "Yes, I could use some socks." Rupert handed him a package of socks from under the counter.

"Would you mind terribly to give my compliments to the tailor; it was an excellent fit."

"He'll be so glad to hear it sir. I bid you a good day," and with a curt, almost military spin to the left, he strode off to help a customer who was looking at a rack of suits.

Nigel walked to the front of the shop and noticed through the window that a woman, who looked quite like the woman from the SUV from yesterday, was sitting in an Audi just across the street. *Don't like the look of that. What to do? They'll likely have the rear exit covered. A plan is called for.* David Farragut, an officer of the United States Navy during the American Civil War, once offered: "Damn the torpedoes, full speed ahead!" *They know I'm here. They are waiting for me to leave. If I let them know that I know that they know I'm here, they'll move on me. Or worse, track me. It's not getting caught that bothers me, it's being taken off my game and forced to abandon or change plans for France.* Sun Tzu once said: "Attack your enemy where he is unprepared, appear where you are not expected." Nigel's favorite game was 'follow the leader', but they always assumed because they were following that he was their quarry. Although he was in front, by leading the chase, he could dictate the speed and direction that they followed which gave him the double advantage of being in charge and letting them think they had him on the run.

Dashing out the door and turning right with his suit bag over his shoulder and blocking their view of his face Nigel made his way quickly north. He timed his departure to the moment when a bus crossed the path between the Audi and himself, and that gave him almost a five second head start. It took the occupants of the Audi another four full seconds to react. That allowed him to get almost to the corner on the cross street, and only one car could move in the direction of traffic to intercept him. As he rounded the corner, the occupants of the Audi jumped out to pursue him and the remaining car, which had been up the street now moved with traffic to take the turn to the left to follow him. Having spotted the parcel van that was now even with him, Nigel grabbed the handle at the rear of the van and stepped onto the large rear bumper. The two men from the Audi stopped chasing him, as they could never hope to catch the parcel van. The Mercedes got blocked for a few seconds by a taxi, which allowed the panel van he had hopped aboard to take the next corner and leave their field of sight. Nigel jumped off immediately and ran between the buildings to the rear door of Byrd & Thayer, grabbed the handle, gave it a yank, and walked into the rear of the tailors. He was quite surprised that they did not in fact have the rear door covered. Sloppy work on their part. Either they underestimated him, which they would not be likely to do again or they were in too big a hurry to properly map out their exercise. Still sporting his new tuxedo in its garment bag, Nigel walked back through to the front of the store, catching the eye of Rupert who said nothing, but nonetheless watched him closely. "Forgot to finish my tea," he offered, and that seemed to satisfy Rupert who continued to refold shirts that customers had pulled out and not put back according to his standards.

Nigel made his way out of the store, this time very conscious of the CCTV cameras and got in the first taxi that appeared, instructing the driver to take him to Heathrow. Knowing that he was most certainly being tracked via CCTV cameras and possibly satellites, Nigel waited patiently in the cab till they got to the airport; he paid the fare and gave the driver a standard tip, grabbed his garment bag and walked into the main terminal. *So how did they find you? Were they somehow tracking you? Not with your phone, it was an ultra secure spook job. You are wearing different clothes, so it wasn't anything you are wearing. Your watch and jewelry are items you picked out, so they were clean.* Rather than waste any more cycles on how he was tracked, the more pressing issue, was to get out of this busy airport and go to an alternate address. With all the extra security, however, exactly how did you do that? There was no way he was going to fly out now. By going to the airport and being seen, he most assuredly had to drive to France. He couldn't go home; it might not be safe. Airports are designed to check the relative safety of anyone entering, not the safety or identity of anyone leaving. There was surveillance to be sure, but it was who got on a plane that mattered. He walked out of the loading zone toward the ticketing area. As he stood in queue, he went back over the details in his mind. He first spotted the team when they ambushed him. Too strong a word? When they intercepted him on the road the other day, he dodged them and delivered his 'pizza,' albeit a bit late, but on target as required. Not much he could do and it was a bit of a bright spot in the day when they chastised him about failing his mission, when he told them to look at the bottom of the potted plant in the reception area.

The queue moved quickly enough, and when it was his turn, he booked his flight to Berlin, and said he had two bags that would be delivered shortly that he needed to have tagged. The agent handed him two tags, and asked if he needed to check his garment bag, to which he said he would just stow it in the bin above. He made sure to book his flight under and pay with his credit card in his name, so that it would be instantly flagged and noted that he had two bags, a carry on, and was going to Berlin. Nigel, took his ticket and tags, and casually walked to the passenger area, and as he did so, he added his tags to the nearest two large bags he could find on a cart, tearing off the tags that were already there. He then walked to the left and out the door, shielding his head from the CCTV cameras with his tuxedo bag, hailed a taxi, and left Heathrow for points north. While on his journey north, he changed cabs six times to make sure he had made a clean escape and when he was certain he got out from the last cab and got on a public bus, and made his way to his alternate address. This place was quite a dump compared to his palatial accommodations. It was off the grid as far as anyone knew, however, even Kingston was unaware of it. He converted some monies from one account to another and back again. Then manufactured some receipts to satisfy the accounting staff. Although he paid very little, it was still a vast amount more than the place was worth. It was a mundane basement apartment in a Paki neighborhood. As a precaution that he could be tracked, he always removed the battery from his phone and wrapped it in several layers of foil he would get at a local Paki restaurant. He was beginning to like the food, which indicated that he had had too much of it. His digestive tract, specifically disagreed with it.

One advantage to a lower rent neighborhood is that you were surrounded by a lot of people who didn't ask questions and cash was an easy way of motivating them. As an example, the guy across the street had somewhere between four and thirty kids and seemed to be constantly overrun with the little blighters. Suresh was a first class mechanic though, only his meager upbringing and lack of education kept him from pursuing an engineering career. He was able to fix the most decrepit Mercedes, BMWs, Audis and all manner of German cars that were years past the time of scrapping. He had only acknowledged the man with a casual greeting, but Nigel was very impressed with his skills.

It was starting to bother him that the same team had found him twice in the last couple of days. The first time was no big deal, he could always forgive himself that he was found and after all, he did spot them before they could snatch him. *But why would they want to snatch you? Where would they put you, and who were they?* The second time was the one that nagged at him. *Had you been sloppy? How had they found you at the tailors? They must have followed you, you should have been more careful, but why not just grab you and interrogate you?* They knew he was going somewhere, so they followed him to Byrd & Thayer and then they wanted to grab him. The mission details in the package would be the target of their attentions. His little trip to the airport would keep them busy, rather than give them a chance to reacquire him. He got his 'Go' bag from the closet and left after locking the door. He always thought it should be called a 'run bag'. You never took it when you were going to go, but when you needed to run. His was based on a standard list of items: passports, IDs, credit cards, debit cards, change of clothes, several unaffiliated mobile phones, a netbook and money. He had found that by including some joints in a vacuum packed container, that he could often get results when he was in less than civilized surroundings. They were vacuum packed to hide them from any dogs that might be used to search his stuff and then inserted into those little packets of condiments you get at restaurants. Since the 'Go' bag was used when you needed to flee, he also had special items in there, though he was afraid of when he might actually need it. When Nigel was in training, he struck up a loose friendship with the instructor, who told him stories of his father when he was in the SAS. One of those stories involved running from the local police who had dogs. It was common issue to have little packets of dried blood mixed with cocaine, to get the dogs to sniff it and then they either couldn't track you or didn't care to. Nigel had gone one step further, and secured the blood from dogs at an animal testing facility, when they came into season. In additional to being dried blood, it also came with the pheromones that were sure to attract a dog's attention when they were working the ground looking for a scent. While being chased by dogs seemed very unlikely on his assignments, it was a small piece of preparation that could have great dividends if ever needed.

Laying out his new tux, Nigel also remembered to open the socks. In the package was a simple note, with a series of digits on it. The last digit multiplied by the third gave him the digit that he would need to access the rest of the coded message. He would need to access the orders via a web connection, but he would not do it from anywhere traceable, so he decided to go to a coffee place he knew about on the other side of town and use the wireless access portion of his phone to hit that website. He would need to spend several hours preparing for his assignment by looking over the guest list and a brief bio of some key contacts he would need to make sure and talk to. *Sod it. I'm completely cashed.* He got up, walked over to the bed and set his watch alarm for four hours later. As he closed his eyes he drifted off quite quickly, into what would be one of his last restful sleeps for weeks to come.

Enslow Unemployed Day 8-20

Enslow had called Bill Wester to see how he was doing. That's when it finally got drilled into his head, something was different in the economy, and that finding a job would be much harder than he had anticipated. Due in large part to the number of unemployed folk out there and the rise of social media, it would be of great help to build a 'profile' and start networking on one of those professional media sites. Bill had said that he liked the one for professional connections, ProNect. Enslow browsed the website and began to create his profile. Being new to the concept, he struggled at first, just filling out the basics. Then to look for ideas, he started browsing other people's profiles to see how much and what kind of data they reflected. It was apparent that many people only did the basics, and that wasn't going to get them anywhere. *If I were looking to hire someone, I'd never look at these clowns.* He found that the more details there were about people's lives, the more interesting he found them, but also the more it told him about their skills. While that might not be the right HR perspective, it just felt right. Many people had obviously cut and pasted their resumes with a little additional information, but those who expounded on it, he thought, were much more likely to be found with keyword searches, which is what most of the job hunting blogs were saying, and complaining about. While he enjoyed reading the more complex profiles, unless you had the right keywords, no one who could hire you would ever see it. Kind of like a resume. Traditional dogma was that you could somehow have a 'perfect' resume, and it would get you a job. The sad truth was that when you applied online, no one would likely ever read your resume, unless it passed some magic count of unknown keywords, such as "Analyst" and "Oracle".

That got Enslow to thinking. If he were going to truly exploit his career experience, he might need to create several resumes, one for each type of job, like Quality Assurance, Business Analyst, Project Manager, etc. As much as that task seemed rather daunting, Enslow remembered that his father told him that things worth having were worth working for. So while the task before him was hard or the road long, every journey started with a first step. You had to keep going, and keep taking steps, however, so if the secret to getting a job and providing for his family and oh so lovely wife was to keep taking steps, then maybe making multiple resumes and writing many cover letters might be the key to his journey's end. So what has he done? Step one, make a list. Then do a search of jobs with those titles to see where the most jobs offered were, so that he could strike at the biggest pool of jobs. While it might make sense to go for the fringe jobs,

Enslow had yet to become desperate. He wanted a job that got him back to where he was and got him back to his salary. He had eaten too many steaming piles off of trays served to him by management to go to the back of the line now. Why did he eat those piles that they told him were ice cream when he knew they weren't? It was an attempt to be a 'team' player, in the vain hope that if you ate enough and didn't complain; that the powerful class would reward you with a promotion, but somehow it never came.

It was in thinking about it that he had an epiphany. It was precisely that he ate those piles, and kept producing, that the executive class never promoted him. After all, someone had to do the work. Who better than the naïve little piss ant with actual skills, rather than the credit stealing blame shifting douche bags who usually led the modern corporation. It was really that simple. Every time they talked about 'teamwork', what they meant was that you would have to sacrifice for the good of the team or share credit. It was a one way street. Every time you needed something, you got Jack Squat, and Jack left town. As he thought about every time he had his credit stolen or the blame shifted, it was always about the 'team,' which meant it was about your executives, not you. Unless they screwed up phenomenally, the blame always went elsewhere. Shit rolls downhill.

As Enslow sat there thinking about all the times he never got a raise for his contributions, he began to both get angry and feel ashamed that he was so gullible to fall for the same type of speech every time. It's like when they passed out the CharityOne cards so you could contribute; you were left with the impression that if you signed up and contributed, you would somehow earn the leadership's favor. Enslow saw through that scam early, but not the others. Dwelling on it would not bring back the empty promises or get him back the years he wasted in service to others. This was a new day, however, and Enslow was not going to play by their rules anymore. He would play the game, but now EVERYTHING was about him. He would always look for the advantage for him so that he could bring these benefits home to his family. No more drinking the Koolaid. No more wearing the catcher's mask to catch every turd tossed your way.

Enslow was pretty confident that with all of his experience, experience and work ethics would allow him to function in most environments. He knew he would be able to get the job done at least as well as anybody else. His plan to rewrite his resumes into several types seemed to be paying dividends, although he spent three days researching the right keywords for each resume, he now had six resumes for six types of jobs that he would be suited for, and where he had only been able to apply for four jobs the first day he had sat down, his new idea for the multiple types was allowing him to apply to about fifteen jobs a day that his job search agents had located and automatically emailed back to him. Enslow calculated where that would get him: If he found suitable jobs, then he could apply to about seventy-five jobs a week (5 days X 15 jobs a day).

So that would be about three hundred jobs a month. "WOW!" thought Enslow, "that would get this thing over in a month, surely." He was really quite a catch he thought, even with the amount of talent out there. So for days eight and nine, he furiously searched and applied for jobs. He actually got about twenty a day done, but after day ten, he was seeing some flaws in his plan. While he had applied to almost sixty jobs, he found himself doing a lot of repetitive action. Further annoying him were the jobs that scanned his resume and auto replied, so that before he even had a chance to apply for a second job, he would receive an email like:

Dear Enslow,

We wanted to thank you for your time in applying for the

HR43112 Business Analyst position

After carefully reviewing your impressive qualifications, we find that we can best help you by encouraging someone with such an impressive list of credentials to look elsewhere for a job that matches their career goals and would reward their needs more closely than our organization. We sincerely wish you the best of luck in your search, and should we have anything that even remotely matches your impressive credentials, we will contact you. In the meantime, so that your search continues unimpeded, please consider any other opportunities that may arise, both here and elsewhere.

Best of luck,
The HR team

If you were so impressive, that they had to use the word twice, why was this very nice kiss off letter arriving in your email only two minutes after sending it? Clearly, no human had read your resume, so your clever use of language and keywords had failed. Enslow noted that he received about 20 percent of his rejections within fifteen minutes, and the rest within twenty four hours, so far, about 40 percent had said nothing. *Was that a good sign? Or were they just too busy or arrogant to reply at all? Perhaps a systems approach might make this process more successful. If you are going to receive a low number of responses, then the requirement for success would be to increase that number. If your rather brilliant resume was only going to garner a few meager responses, then what you will need will be an even more brilliant resume (or series of resumes), or, you will have to vastly increase the number of applications you make. OK then, think about this. You are going to need to record and distribute information needed to apply to jobs. Let's make a list: first name, last name, middle initial, street address, street name, phone number, previous job information, college information, recommendations (and their contact information), achievements, and awards. Let's break everything down into two elements, the list name for the elements, and the element itself. Then you can use those elements as text items so that we can simply cut and paste and fill out the online applications faster.*

Not all companies run the job boards the same way, the order is always different, and sometimes they want more information, sometimes they want less. Creating an automated response system could take a lot longer than finding a job. While the companies pay lots of money to get their job requests on one of the job boards it might be able to command more consideration if you can find the company by applying on their website rather than the job board. One of the tricks might be to isolate elements of the job description and do a search on the Internet to see if you can locate the actual job then go to their company website and apply. Depending on how they are organized, you can usually put your core information in and then put in specifics as to the requirements for a job. Since there are thousands of companies you going to need to optimize your time. It was at that moment that Enslow had a sudden piece of inspiration. It was the kind of inspiration some might have called genius, but Enslow never liked that title. Genius, he thought, was for the wheel and penicillin, not just his knack for adapting technology and stuff to new uses. It was this knack that allowed him to succeed so well in the IT field because he looked at a problem and would have a sudden inspiration for how to solve it, that either grabbed victory from the jaws of defeat or just saved immense amounts of labor by finding a way to automate a process. The solution wasn't necessarily original, as almost everything has been done before, but Enslow was often able to have that leap of inspiration to advance the work he was on. Enslow opened up the document that had his notes on the speech application interface he had made while researching how to use the built-in speech recognition engine in his laptop. Looking over the notes he found the instructions where he could set up a command mode to run on top of the OS. It was the same command mode that allowed the speech recognition and to execute things like a speech to text narration for dictating notes, operating applications via the microphone, etc.

Enslow grabbed his mouse and clicked on his user interface for his development environment, and started a new project and added the library for speech recognition. He dimensioned an array for speech commands, and added a command button to the screen. He would use that to start the program. As life is a circle, he therefore needed a shutdown button; the speech engine could be a bit finicky. Merely closing the program could leave the speech engine running, taking up memory and processor cycles.

Step one at startup was to initialize the speech engine and wait for start. When started, then you need to open the database of keywords and the speech catalog of stored words. *Dang. Haven't trained it yet.* Okay, so he opened a new catalogue, grabbed his microphone and started speaking the speech commands he would need, and speak all the words like, "First, Last," etc. After ten minutes, Enslow was satisfied that he had a list of each command word. Then he realized that he was making this too hard again. No catalogue was needed. By using the reverse algorithm, he only needed the speech engine to correctly realize that the spoken word "FIRST" was comprised of the letters F,I,R,S and T, so that it could then do a speech to text and use it as a keyword search of the database, so no stored speech segments were needed. It made the whole thing substantially easier, but it required another two hours of reprogramming and database changes. Now when he added the code for a command phrase he would also run a reverse algorithm and convert his speech back to text. A SQL lookup on the database would now return the text value for that command. When he would say "First," it would translate that into F-I-R-S-T and return the data value "Enslow." Each spoken word worked the same way, for "Last," Phone," etc.

It was for this reason the very smug smile crossing Enslow's face was exactly why he thought he was smarter than the other job seekers out there. After he finished coding his application, Enslow went back to the code and ran it in debug mode. To step through it he checked each word. Now he opened notepad, as it was the easiest piece of software to test against. He said "FIRST" and promptly his first name appeared in notepad. "LAST," and his last name appeared. *That works!* Trying the other commands he said "DELETE" and his last name promptly deleted from the page. "Tab" barely passed through his lips, and the cursor on the page moved roughly five spaces to the right. *Excellent, this is going pretty well.* Adjusting his microphone because it looked uncool the way it stuck out in front of his nostril, Enslow continued by saying "RESUME." He was expecting the drive and folder specification of his general resume to appear, but nothing happened. Frowning, he realized that this is what happens when you code, and you haven't coded for awhile. Enslow clicked the stop button on his programming language environment, and clicked the little disk icon, for "SAVE." Sorta stupid; who saves to floppies anymore? The active program stopped execution.

Looking at the code for ten minutes, he could not find the problem. So he looked at the data. "Hmmmm," he said out loud, and then bingo! There it was, he had two 'R's in "RRESUME." No matter how bright you are, your fat fingers always seem to fail you. So he fixed it and tried it again. This time, when he said "RESUME," his complete drive specification and file name now appeared on the screen. He now recorded and created the corresponding records for "RESUME-B-A" for his Business Analyst resume, "RESUME-Q-A" for his Quality Assurance resume, and so forth till he had a database entry for each type of resume. He then recorded his college information and his references. As a final thought he realized that some sites would want a password to return for other postings, so he created a password. He recorded "PASSWORD," and set its entry in the database to the password he had created with a suitable transposition of letters to numbers, like E to 3, etc.

"Nothing like a real world test to see what you hath wrought," said Enslow to no one in particular. He scanned his email inbox to look for a likely candidate. Seeing a typical posting for a QA role, he clicked on the "Apply Now" button and that brought him to a new page where it asked for a login ID, and since he had been there before, he said "EMAIL" and his email address filled the box, and then he said "TAB" and the focus shifted to the next box. He said "PASSWORD" and his password appeared, or at least he thought it did, as the characters were masked by very large dots, one for each character of his password. Then he said "ENTER" and the program sent an enter keystroke to the webpage, and although it was the activity he hoped for, Enslow was nonetheless a bit giddy when the page logged in and he was ready to enter his information using his new program.

Wanting to see how well it worked, he knew approximately how long it took to apply for a position by typing and cutting and pasting. He looked at his watch and waited till the sweep second hand on his Seiko chronograph passed the 12 position, and then calmly and methodically spoke each of the key words that he needed to use to fill out the application including his proper resume, work history and references. With his right hand, Enslow clicked the 'Submit' button and then he looked down at his watch to see how long the process had taken. The amount of time was astonishing! He had filled out and submitted his application and uploaded his resume for the position in less than two minutes! Stopping the application environment, he again pressed save, and then compiled the program, rather than run it in interpreted mode. If he could apply to a job in two minutes, with searching for and analyzing which job to apply for, he reasoned that he could likely apply to ten to fifteen jobs an hour, or in an eight hour day, upwards of a hundred jobs. That would be at least five hundred jobs a week, making roughly two thousand a month.

It took a couple of minutes for that to sink in. A stunned silence descended over Enslow, realizing the enormity of what he had done. If he could find two thousand jobs a month locally or nationally, he could apply to them all. And if he couldn't, he could also apply to the smaller companies where he might be more likely to get someone other than a machine to look at his application. And there were many jobs that, in a more traditional market, he might be able to get, that now, he could apply for because the level of effort was now reduced. Perhaps he could also sell it to other people and raise more cash. But by selling it, he was giving away his advantage, hard won with his creativity. Maybe after he got a job, he might sell it. For now, the mission had not changed and he needed to use every tool at his disposal to get back to work. But, maybe the brilliant story of how he applied to jobs and used his god given talents might impress someone in an interview. How ironic that a tool to apply to thousands of jobs might be the thing that makes him look better than the rest of the people who apply.

Feeling like he had had a good day, and noting that it was now 3:30 in the afternoon, Enslow saved his work, closed his browsers, and logged off. Ella would be home soon, and he wanted to cook a nice meal, since she was the big breadwinner. When he got a job in the near future, he would not likely have time to spoil her, and she was worth spoiling.

The phone rang and it was Gene. "How you doing? Any bites yet?" Gene asked.

Enslow replied, "No but I think I have something figured out. If your luck is like mine…"

"All bad?"

"Yep. I am getting almost no replies to my applications, so what I think we need to do is to pound the crap out of every job opportunity. This seems like it is a game of numbers."

Gene acknowledges, "Well duh. I have applied to over fifty jobs and got one no thank you response. So far no one other than that has even sent me a letter saying word one about being interested, not interested, or go jump in a lake."

Enslow confided, "I may have an answer for that, at least as far as applying for more jobs. If we can't hit them with quality, then we can hit them with quantity."

"How?"

"Remember all my bag of tricks? Like the voice tools?"

"Yeah…"

Enslow went on, "I have been playing with the voice tools, so that you can drive the web pages, the application process, and the resume selection by voice. It translates what you say and uses stored responses to essentially cut and paste faster than you thought possible"

Gene replied, "Really? That sounds cool. But what do you mean, resume selection? How many do you have?"

"Enslow replied, "Well so far, it seems to me that you need one for each kind of job you are applying to. That way you can stack it with the keywords you need to get past the screening programs."

"Screening programs?"

Enslow lectured Gene, "Yes. They electronically scan your resume and cover letter for keywords, and give you a score. If you are above some threshold they set, they you get forwarded on to a real human."

"Crap."

"Crap what?"

Gene sounded dejected. "You are so much smarter than me. That makes so much sense I was laboring over creating a perfect resume and wondering why my wonderful paper was getting no bites. I guess I need to figure out what I've done and create three or four resumes to target what I want to do or can do. I can only seem to apply to six or eight jobs a day and I'm beat. How many do you pop a day?"

"If I can find the jobs, I can tag about one hundred a day," Enslow answered.

"For real?"

"I wouldn't shit you my friend, you are my favorite turd," Enslow quipped.

"I appreciate that. I feel like a turd. I've been shit out by the corporate world and apparently I am the biggest brown trout in the pond. No one wants me."

Enslow reassured his friend, "You are no turd. You are a hard working dedicated IT professional, and companies just don't know how lucky they would be to have you. It is just a game of supply and demand, and supply exceeds demand. If you can up your numbers, and I'll send you a copy of my program and some instructions, then I think your chances will improve."

Gene said, "You are the first person to give me any hope lately. I think we should take a small break, and get a beer. Wanna go to Bookers?"

"Sounds like a fine idea Gene. Say maybe in an hour?"

"Cool. See you there. Later."

"I'll be there.. see you", and Enslow hung up the phone. *I'm going to need pants.*

Enslow dashed upstairs and put on pants. Then he fried up some hamburger and boiled some spaghetti. In less than thirty minutes he had a hot meal for Ella and the kids. Then he wrote her a note, saying he was over at Bookers strategizing with Gene on job searching. He knew she would see through it, but at least he had a hot meal ready. Enslow got in his car and was driving down the street as Ella and the kids approached. Their little smiling faces were pressed against the glass and they were waving. Enslow smiled and waved back. Ella waived as well, knowing he was off to somewhere. Because he usually left her a note, she didn't slow down or roll open her window. She just drove past and pulled up to their house. Enslow drove on to the bar, and met up with Gene.

The next day, Enslow was eager to try his new program, so he logged on and went to his email to see how many jobs his search agents had found. There were 43 new jobs since yesterday. That would only take three or four hours. Perhaps he could do additional searches. So Enslow started in on his task and whittled it down further to twenty seven jobs that he was either suited for or would otherwise want. Each day would be different, so he started in and much to his surprise he impressed himself again, and applied to all twenty seven jobs in two hours. *Gotta be a record.* Not wanting to let any advantage slip, he decided to reexamine some of the jobs he had passed over. The first two were clearly just something he would not want to do, wrong industry, wrong part of town. The third and fourth jobs looked like he was about 80% there, as far as the requirements, which cheered him up a little bit. If he was 80% the way there, surely his winning personality would get the rest of the way. If he had this down at least 80%, then he felt he might be a solid candidate.

He clicked on the first job requisition number, and he filled in all of his information. He was then presented with a couple of blocks that he had never seen before. One was a space for cover letter. So he opened his cover letter for generic situations, changed the dates, job title and company name, then copied and pasted it in. He clicked submit, and then proceeded to the next job on his list, and dispatched it with equal robotic efficiency. After completing another eight jobs from his reject list, the digital warrior (as he was called by his peers), closed down his applications and logged off. Applying to thirty seven jobs before lunch was sure tiring. Excessive thinking was strangely fatiguing. He went upstairs and switched on the television. Settling on the news after scanning some of the channels, he watched with mockery as the blonde news reader mentioned current unemployment figures, which led to two stories on the economy. Following that was the latest sports scandal for some overpaid spoiled brat. Then there was a story about arms smuggling to some Chechen terrorist group. Finally, the human interest story about gay penguins and could they ever find true love. *And why shouldn't they? He was getting roundly rogered by the world; why should penguins miss out on the* fun?

Over the next several days, Enslow made several important changes. First, rather than waste the time going to disk and doing the I/O, he preloaded the entire array of keys and data elements into an array in memory, and parsed that rather than perform a read to the database when he needed to retrieve an address or such. While it wasn't a lot faster, saving maybe 20 seconds per job application, it just seemed like the sort of improvement that made sense. Enslow had the time to spend on it.

The next morning, Enslow got up after his wife had showered and made her way out the door. He was living the life of luxury. He logged onto his email account and found 35 emails from the jobs he had applied for. All rejections. How is it that he could have been rejected so quickly for most of the jobs he applied for? He had a good resume, he had filled it up with the right keywords and he had added a cover letter describing his brilliance. Was it an indication of just how hard this was going to be? *You will just have to keep at it. One day does not end it all.* The rest of the next two days, Enslow applied himself to his task even harder. By expanding his search to additional keywords, and expanding the distance he was willing to drive, he was able to come up with 128 jobs to apply to. *Wow. Better keep them all, and what you can't get today, you may need for other days.*

He clicked on the first e-mail message which took him to the response from Industrial Metal Fabricators which read:

Dear Mr. Spangler,

Thank you very much for applying to position 19346, Quality Team Lead Manager. After carefully reviewing your qualifications and resume we find that we are unfortunately not able to offer you a position at this time. Please continue to think of Industrial Metal Fabricators as you pursue your career. We seek only the best people for the best company and very much want to encourage you to keep this in mind as you pursue your goals. Again thank you very much from all the staff at Industrial Metal Fabricators.

Once again, Enslow was trying to understand how he could be so right for a job, and be rejected so quickly. He could hardly believe that anyone out there had "carefully reviewed his resume and qualifications" and be rejected as quickly as he was. How careful could they be if they thought his name was 'Spangler' instead of 'Spengler'? He was solid on 80% of the job requirements. He really did know all the things they're asking for very well. After recovering from the pang of such a quick rejection, Enslow was perplexed. Either he was a good candidate or not, but without being able to talk to a human, he would never know. So, he was left with his original idea, which was to make this a game of numbers. Large numbers.

Enslow postulated that his efforts at keyword selection were at fault. He could fill in resumes faster than anyone on the planet. His search agents could scour the job boards and the company websites and hunt down the opportunities. *Enslow old buddy, if you are that clever, someone else is. You should concentrate your efforts on keywords, and maybe finding the jobs not posted. That is going to require 'human' research. Dig through your old business cards, and let's see who we know and where they are. Let's keep on with the automated stuff, but maybe start researching how to conduct your campaign 'on the ground', instead of on the net. What was it Bill Wester had said? He mentioned that social networking site, ProNect.*

Enslow started a clean browser, and opened a copy of his resume and his job information like recommendations, etc, and went to the website, where he had to create a password and a login ID. Selecting EnslowCareerSearch as his ID, he created a password based on his usual scheme of password generation, and began the task of creating his online profile. By cutting and pasting bits and chunks from his resume, he was able to flesh out who he wanted to tell people he was. Then he filled in his educational history and achievements, and his recent employment history. *That took what? Fifteen minutes? Let's see what others are saying and how hard they work at it.*

He did a search for people he knew from work, and some people he remembered from college. Some had extensive profiles, some had meager profiles, and some just had placeholder accounts, if they had anything at all. Being unsure as to the right amount of information, Enslow considered the different amounts of time people had obviously put in. The more you say about yourself, he reasoned, the more likely it was for someone to find you with a keyword search. It might say you are more serious about your career because you invested much more time in filling things in and expounding on your work history and achievements.

As he surfed through the pages, he discovered that there were forums which were organized along defined ideals. One forum might be a political forum; one forum would be an alumni forum for a school. Others were organized along industries. Looking through the lists was taking too long, so Enslow utilized the search function, and was quickly able to locate his college, his high school, and others for his industry experience and his interests, such as algorithmic trading. The next two full days were spent searching for and joining forums, and then looking through them to see if there were any networking opportunities. He did not really know many people from his college *(it was a long time ago),* but it looked like a promising hunting ground for leads. Realizing that it would be best if he spoke simply and from the heart, he composed the following letter to send out to prospective 'targets'.

Dear ABCDEFG,

My name is Enslow Spengler, and we are both alumni of Mack Island University. Recently I have been considering some career choices and was wondering if I could arrange a twenty minute meeting with you to get a better idea of what the key issues are for your industry and perhaps some specifics on how you think your company performs better than its rivals. I'm not looking for inside information or a job, but finding out what makes your company able to perform so well in this difficult economic time. Your insights on your industry will help me to understand what elements of my experience and abilities might be applicable. I appreciate your help with my quest.

> Sincerely,
> Enslow Spengler
> (555) -567-0012
> Enslow.Spengler@PublicMail.com

Within 72 hours, Enslow had succeeded well beyond his expectations. He had received 22 positive responses (and two "Who the hell are you?" emails), but there were five separate Vice Presidents at the local bank chain who were eager to meet with him and share their knowledge. He also found that by searching forums of interest, he could narrow down who was working within a certain number of miles from his zip code. This gave him an additional group of people to scout for networking. Pursuing this track took him another three days. He was able to send out another two hundred approach letters. Unfortunately, without the somewhat tenuous bond of being alumni he had a far worse success rate trying to network with total strangers. Viewing any positive response was the correct way to ascertain whether he had spent his time wisely. Rather than look at the percentage of positive responses versus the total number of inquiries, he had to be content with the 25 people who said they would meet with him for a coffee or quick office chat. A win is a win anyway you can get it. It only takes one good connection to get back in the game he kept reminding himself. It was a feeling of dread he was getting from the state of things that made him feel like it might be some time before he was going to get that one lucky connection. *You idiot, if you are going to rely on luck, you are going to lose your house and maybe even your wife. You need to make your own luck, and by working every angle of every system and outlet for networking you can find, that is how you are going to get a job.*

Jackson Dupree Day 181

Jackson Dupree stood in the darkened room, sweating profusely. Nothing in his military career had prepared him for what he was about to face. For a decorated combat veteran, his task before him was bound to change his life forever. After all the times he took fire, had been wounded and survived, the enormity of what he was going to do WILLINGLY made him shake his head. How had he come to this? It was one thing to follow orders, but quite another to just jump and pray that someone caught you. After serving two combat tours, he had earned the right to take no more risks and rotate home. He just couldn't see himself doing anything else. His whole life had led him here and he was determined to see it through. In a few moments, all it would take would be a signal and he would take those definitive steps toward which there was no turning back.

"Dude, you ok?" asked Ramón Santiago. Ramón was one of those guys you loved to have around you in the good times, like that club in Boston where they drank all night and clear into the next day, but he was definitely one of those guys whom you wanted with you when things got tight. Ramón was from Nicaragua and had signed up to serve in the Marine Corps. His service to his adopted land would hasten his path to citizenship and allow him to bring his wife Maria and their daughter Concepcion to the U.S. and live a life of freedom and opportunity that his parents had been denied. Ramón was a bit shorter than Jackson, but he had the heart of a lion. Once, on their first tour, Ramón had taken three hits from an insurgent's AK-47 and while standing there bleeding, charged the position, grabbed the startled Jihadi, and proceeded to bitch slap him till the sound of laughter from his platoon, who had chased after him, caused him to let go and realize he was bleeding. In the brief amount of time his hands were off the insurgent, the terrorist had pulled the pin from a grenade and screamed some loud scream of triumph, no doubt that he was about to get his 72 virgins for killing these infidels. Faster than he thought someone could move, and faster than someone who was wounded should move, Jackson watched as Ramón grabbed the startled attacker and threw him through the closest window, giving them two full seconds to duck as the wall protected them from the worst of the blast. Ramón was absolutely one of the guys you wanted with you.

Ramón had noticed an almost complete lack of color in his friend. He had never seen such a case of nerves affect him. It was understandable of course, and he knew when he was younger, he had probably looked the same when he was faced with the inevitable. Still, he had been asked to come, a volunteer, and he was honored to stand with his friend. If by his being here, he gave Jackson the courage to step forward and face the journey in front of him, he could rest, knowing that he had given support to a friend and a brother when he needed it most. That's what the Corps was about. Duty, Honor, Brotherhood. He had grown up seeing dubbed movies of John Wayne, Gary Cooper, Henry Fonda and Clint Eastwood, and it had inspired him to be tough and to try to become an American like those men on the screen.

Reggie Smith was an improbable hero as well. The only son of a drug addicted single mother, he ran loose and free in the wilder areas of Chicago. Getting into trouble at a young age was just what you did; it wasn't out of a desire to go down a dark path of personal destruction, it was just what you did because you were bored. Running without parental direction, he was bored a lot. Somewhere, somehow, he never made the critical step to becoming a true criminal though. He was fourteen when he heard the girl scream as she was dragged down the alley. Reggie knew what was going to happen to the stupid bitch. She probably deserved it. What was she doing in this part of town anyhow? Who did she think she was? As her screams turned to cries, however, Reggie knew what was happening to her, and he hated it. Her pain seemed to reach deep into him and awaken feelings of shame, anger and disgust. Before he knew it, he had grabbed a pipe in the front of the alley, ran into the group who was holding the girl down, and bashed two of them in the heads so hard they were taken off their feet, and then before they could mount a defense against this lone young crazy man, the girl had gotten up and gotten behind her young hero. Seeing the look of anger in his eyes, they quickly backed off, and ran the other way. She collapsed against him crying and thanking him. All he could do was to hold her and try to comfort her. When the police arrived, having been alerted by one of the older neighbors, Reggie could only describe the perps as a group of thugs he didn't recognize. The girl was unable to offer anything more than a general description of her attackers and after a series of congratulatory praises, the girl left with the police, and Reggie was soon on his own, walking home. His mind could scarcely grasp it, but he had turned a point in his life, where he instinctively put himself at risk to save others. In the next few years, he spent his spare time lifting weights and avoiding the activities that his attackers had obviously followed. He did not go down that dark and rocky road that they did, but instead, he had chosen a righteous path. When he graduated high school, (that his mother failed to attend), he knew what he wanted to do. He wanted to be a warrior for just causes, and he joined the United States Marine Corps. It wasn't for him to determine what causes were just, his job was to fight those battles. As a bonus, he got to travel the world. He always knew the guys he had to go up against were, in their own way, these same cowards who dragged that girl down the alley. Where the vermin wanted to satisfy their lust and exert their will on a world where they would not have opportunity to do either, usually the enemies of America wanted to do the same. Some were misguided, some were just evil. And some, he was sure, were the exact same kind of scum who just wanted to kill. Reggie was here to make sure that they had no chance to do any of it.

So these three men stood patiently in the darkened room, waiting for the call. The call would be for them to step out, and once again come face to face with that that awaits all men. Jackson remarked, "I wish I was wearing our regular jackets, these things are too restrictive. I know we have to match our surroundings, but who can function in these things for any amount of time?" Ramón nodded his head in agreement, and Reggie reached out his clenched fist and held it there. In the dim light, Jackson saw it, clenched his fist, and bumped knuckles with Reggie's. It was at that moment, there was a slight knock on the door, and a voice from outside said, "it's time." Jackson said, "You two have followed me into every tight corner one man can follow another, risking your lives to stand by my side. You have been loyal and true."

He turned his head slightly and murmured to his friends, "Thanks for standing with me, now, in this place, at this time." Reggie whispered through his lips, without moving them, "It has been an honor."

As the three warriors stepped out, their eyes squinted at the sudden amount of light. A hundred pairs of eyes were instantly upon them. There was nothing they could do except to walk forward, so they did. They marched forward in single file to the center of the room and stood there, silently, dignified, heads held high, resolute. They eyed the crowd and the crowd eyed them. Then a door opened at the far end of the room, and an organ +
.began to play "the wedding march." Jackson's fiancée, Nancy, entered room, the bridal train flowing behind her. Jackson's heart beat even faster. After all he had been through; he could at least have this normal moment. When the priest would ask him if he would love, honor and cherish her till death do they part, he was going to mean those words as much as he had ever meant anything he had ever or would ever, say.

Nigel Day 240

Nigel opened the package of socks, and inside one of them was a slip of paper with a code, as before. Nigel used his mobile phone to access the public website indicated (by the hosiery company who the socks were from) and entered the computational result that the code indicated. It brought up a fictitious customer order, with the following comments:

Plan to attend the event in four days at the British embassy in France.

Perform duties according to protocol.

Arrive no later than 7:30, leave no later than 11:00. Your directive is to speak to, and shake hands with at least 75 people.

Typical stuff. The only thing that was more boring than a protocol dinner was thinking about how you needed to keep a smile on. It was the prep work that made for a successful assignment, but that wasn't his role to play. Nigel was what was colorfully called a "peacock"; he was to attend various functions and public events as well as go to specific places and be seen. That was about it. He was on a huge retainer; mostly unregulated expense accounts, great cars, first class clothing and watches, and all his needs like maid service, food, medical and dental were met. He spent nothing, and was able to amass a substantial kitty. It was time to spend that kitty. That car chase could have gone the other way and he wasn't going to be caught in a situation where it could go against him.

Nigel noticed through the filthy window of his hideaway flat that Suresh was home for his customary lunch, and this might be the perfect opportunity to solve a problem. So he got up, walked briskly to the door, and went through it to the street and shouted "OY! Suresh! Can I have a word?" Suresh looked startled that his until now quite aloof neighbor wanted to talk to him. He wondered if he was going to get complaints about his kids and their commotion, just as all the other white neighbors made. So he was quite surprised by the conversation he got.

"Listen, Suresh, I notice you are quite the artist with a spanner, and I need to get a car for me mum. She lives in Birmingham, and you know it's rather rough there. She doesn't live in as nice as surroundings as these. Would you be able to get a nice car for her and make a few modifications? I'll pay cash up front."

Rather stunned, he considered the man before him, and knowing he needed the money, whatever it was, decided to accept the opportunity thrust upon him. Looking him in the eye, he forced a polite smile to his face (white people like it when you smile), and said "Ok, what would you like me to get for her?"

"I'd like a 2003 Mercedes W211, but I want a 5.5 litre engine from the 2006 model fitted to it."

Being a bit confused by the request, Suresh responded in guarded tones, "Perhaps I am not the right man to find your mother a car, you seem to have a specific idea in mind of what you want. I just fix up old beaters and make them run for a while longer. Nothing fancy."

"I know how good you are. I've seen your work. I want the best for me mum. I expect what I want will cost, and I'm willing to pay for it." Reaching into his pockets, he took out twenty-five thousand pounds in crisp new notes and put them into the now mesmerized Pakistani's hands. "This should cover it, and I need it in three days. Give me what I want, no junk, and keep the rest. But I want it in three days."

Without raising his eyes to meet Nigel's, he slowly shook his head up and down and stammered "Yesssss."

"Oh, and I took the liberty of making a list of

further modifications I need for peace of mind. See to it and let me know what additional payment will be required." Nigel placed an envelope into the still stupefied man's hands and walked away.

After 30 seconds, Suresh put the money in his pocket, and then proceeded to open the envelope. He pulled out the piece paper inside, unfolded it and read it:

Roll Cage – hidden as best you can, car will need to provide maximum rollover and collision protection.

Reinforced Bumpers – I don't want a bloody taxi pushing her around.

Fuel cell – In the event she spins out or flips, I don't want any problems with the tank leaking, something in the 30 gallon range.

Supercharger - I'll feel better knowing she can get out of traffic fast.

Nitrous Oxide system - A fifty shot should be sufficient.

Run flat speed rated tires - Mum will need tires that can run flat for up to fifty miles, and up to 85 M.P.H. while doing so.

Radiator will need to be split into two parts and relocated to the inside of the front wheel wells, with suitable mesh protection from road debris. She was hit once in the front, and when the antifreeze boiled out, she was stuck wherever she stopped.

Seats need to be modified to have storage compartments in the seatbacks, but look to be factory stock.

A cable operated winch with a grappling hook needs to be installed under the car, operated by a switch on the dash for leading out and recoiling.

From the rear of the car, I need a long metal spike to be able to be deployed while the boot is open. It should deploy hydraulically to a length of two feet from the last edge of the bumper. It needs to be at least two inches thick and cut and polished to a fine pointy end. Same from the front, but built into the left front frame member.

Replace side mirrors internally with four inch monitors, and mount camera feed in the front grille and the rear fascia so that the side mirrors with the monitors now function as mirrors normally wood, but the cameras front and rear need to be able to zoom digitally by at least 50x.

I'd like a switch to turn off all rear lights, signals, brakes, etc.

I also want an anti theft system, and voice recognition for starting and vital functions.

Modify or remove whatever you have to without altering the car's appearance, to compensate for the weight added by these modifications.

Additional modifications as requested.

Suresh realized that this was not for the man's mother, and it was quite likely that more money would be needed to meet these changes. This was an opportunity surely handed to him by providence itself. He could make the money he needed for his children, including the one now on the way. This opportunity would give him a chance to create and build, not merely restore nearly dead cars to again driving condition. He put his thumbnail into the space between his teeth and slowly turned left to walk to his waiting wife for a quick lunch, and then back to work. The ideas were starting to flow into his brain and as he walked past the last window just before his door, he saw that he was smiling from ear to ear.

Enslow Unemployed Day 22-45

It was getting harder to look Ella in the eyes.
Barely three weeks had gone by, but doubt was
starting to sink in. It had been a little over a month,
but after applying to over two thousand jobs;
Enslow had only had two phone interviews, and
maybe one hundred or so rejection letters. Nothing
much came out of it. Bill Wester had called earlier
in the day and they had talked about the relative
lack of interest they were finding. Though it had
been only four weeks, they both had a bad feeling.
Every day they saw new unemployment numbers
and got more calls from other friends and
colleagues about their own job losses and hunting
futilities. Bill Wester had told Enslow that there
were job transition groups that met at some of the
big churches, where you could get help on
interviewing, resumes, etc. The big score, however,
was that you could network with other people, so
that if you found a job open at Company A, you
might find someone who had a friend, relative, or
neighbor there, and maybe they could help you get
your resume in front of someone to get the
interview. Bill and Enslow had agreed to meet at
his church, a nice Catholic complex with a chapel, a
school, and several meeting rooms as part of their

community center. Enslow called Gene and told him about the transition groups, but Gene was not open to the idea. In the recent weeks, he noticed how his work buddy from the last several years, was growing distant. Enslow reflected how people who you saw everyday for years, often drifted away quickly when you no longer worked together. He knew Gene was in trouble, but even with Enslow's voice response program, he knew Gene was getting a bit depressed. Enslow had decided to check up on him less frequently, but not cut him off. He hoped he would come around, but until then, he had to keep at it and see if there was some way he had not explored. This gathering of the jobless might yield some fruit, it might not. Enslow told himself he was going to explore all options. If this one didn't work, he was going to try others. As he pulled into the parking lot, he noticed Bill had just arrived. They opened their car doors at the same time and after shaking hands, went into the church to see what all the hoopla was about. They walked in on a Thursday morning, at 7:30 a.m., and sat down in a row of seats.

The speaker for the day had a series of points he wanted to make about cover letters and sending letters when you didn't get the job, and follow up letters in forty five days after you didn't get the job. Writing a good cover letter to reiterate your qualifications. Always sending a thank you letter would impress people with your professionalism, and might spark them to think of you when they had another opening. The gem of the discussion was that by sending a follow up letter after you didn't get the job, was that the chosen person may not have worked out, and they can short circuit the replacement search by using you, who they had already vetted when you applied or interviewed. Since you had sent these series of communications, you should have impressed them enough to look at you again, possibly letting them see the error of their ways when they selected the candidate who didn't work out before. Quite a sneaky way to work the system actually.

After the forty five minute talk on the subject for the day, the group broke up into smaller groups where introductions were made and business cards exchanged. A short pockmarked man Enslow more or less remembered, walked up and stuck out his hand, "Enslow, right? I remember that tool you wrote for us last year. Saved our ass on that database consolidation project. Damn clever of you to use a virtual server to run the old OS and the new one on the same system." Feeling rather proud and humbled that someone remembered his work in a positive light, Enslow vigorously shook his outstretched hand, and said "Jake was it? No Jack, I'm sorry. How are you? How long have you been out?"

The broad grin on Jack's face was infectious,

and soon Enslow was smiling too. "It's been thirteen months now, since they let me go."

Furrowing his brow, Enslow replied "Really? That long?"

"'Fraid so, I have applied to almost nine hundred jobs in that period, and got two interviews. One job required fifteen years experience, a Masters degree, and guess what they wanted to pay me to be their senior software engineer?"

"Sixty?" postulated Enslow.

"Thirty five thousand a year." Jack said, still clearly insulted by the offer.

Dropping his jaw slightly, Enslow uttered incredulously, "Thirty five thousand a year? That's what I made my first year out of college! Are they crazy?"

"Seems like they are" came the reply from Jack. "Could hardly believe it myself. Lots of companies are taking advantage of the situation and think they can use and abuse the available talent pool, and sadly, I think they are right."

"But don't they realize that if and when things improve, all the people they are screwing will leave and they will have to start over and hire new people and train them all over again?"

Jack reached out and lightly slapped the shoulder before him and said "They know that, and they don't care. I have never seen it like this. I never thought I would be out this long; but here I am, thirteen months and counting. I can probably keep going for another six months, but then I'm tapped out."

"What will you do then?" Enslow asked with genuine concern, realizing that this man was the same as him. If it could be that long for this guy, Enslow might be in real trouble. He couldn't last that long, he had already calculated his money. It would last roughly another four months.

"I'm looking at taking three part time jobs at the grocer, the home improvement store, and teaching a class or two at the junior college. All three together, seventy five hours a week, will just make the mortgage and utilities. The world has changed, Enslow. The media, the politicians, are lying to us. This economy is worse than anyone is letting on. I know that sounds like a conspiracy, but look around you. You know many of these people. Good people. Solid professionals who are good at their craft. And every one of them is here because they cost more than some kid. Years of loyal service, pissed away in seconds by some pasty finance weasel who is still pulling in two hundred large, and banging his secretary."

"Bastards one and all I agree. Can't say I met many executives I ever trusted" Enslow offered with a look of complete honesty.

"A few are probably good men, or maybe not corrupted yet," Jack opined.

"Are you saying there is no place for honesty and integrity?" Enslow asked.

"There is, it just doesn't pay well," Jack said while holding in a sarcastic laugh.

"I'd like to think if I was ever in a position of power, I would behave differently."

"You would, till the power caught up with you. Absolute power corrupts absolutely" Jack reminded.

"You might think I'm talking outta my ass, but I wouldn't behave unethically, unless something big was at stake."

"Like your bonus?" Jack smirked.

"No, that's only money. I don't mean world peace either. I'll never have to make that decision.

But I believe there is still a place for hard work and honesty in our world," Enslow stated with just a hint of moral superiority.

"You are a real Boy Scout. I admire that. But where did all your hard work get you? It got you here, with the rest of us."

Seeing that the conversation had run its course, Enslow agreed with him, "You are right my friend," and he stuck out his hand. "Best of luck. Let's connect on ProNect. Look me up."

"Will do cowboy," Jack promised. Then he turned and walked over to another group of people trying to network and uncover some kernel of helpful information. Enslow went over the conversation in his head. Thirteen months? Even with his auto applier he wrote, he might have to prepare for it. Jack might be a bit jaded, but he was certainly right about the world changing. The man who adapted to the changing conditions was the one who would survive. Enslow by God, was going to learn to adapt and survive. Ella deserved it, he deserved it and he was going to honor his commitment to her as partner and provider. How would be the trick.

For the next thirty minutes, Enslow shook hands, and traded cards with people in the group, listened to their stories, swapped useful strategies and just talked like people used to talk at work. He realized that coming here would be a useful experience, just to socialize and get out of the house. But it could also become a dependency thing, a crutch. If you wanted tips on scoring with chicks, you didn't want to hang out with virgins. Or to phrase it more succinctly, if you wanted a job, hanging out with the unemployed was only going to get you so far. You do your best business on Main Street, and if you wanted to work, go where you would meet people who had jobs.

A woman Enslow vaguely remembered from a conference last year, walked by and he said excitedly, "Donna? How are you?"

The woman, with her bottle colored hair, spun on her heels, and walked twenty feet towards Enslow, when her face lit up in a broad toothy smile, "Spengy! How are you? I thought for sure they'd hang on to you; you were always so bright and creative. I just loved your stories. Have you been out long?"

"Just a few weeks really, but I am finding this quite hard."

Donna gave a look of sympathy, "Don't worry about it. It is hard, but it isn't personal. Many people know you and know how good you are. You'll land before these other folks."

Enslow judged that she was either trying to be kind or was clueless, because after seeing the caliber of people who were unemployed, and running into an absolute void of interest for the number of jobs he had applied for, he was convinced that either or both of his postulations were correct.

"What kind of work are you wanting?" she inquired, still with a look of sympathy that he was having a problem judging.

"You know," Enslow said with as much honest sincerity as he could muster, "I'd like to be a BA, SE or EA, but I would consider anything that kept a roof over my head."

"Forgive me hon, but even though my brother is one of you, I don't understand those crazy letters"

Apologetically, Enslow explained. "That they were Business Analyst, Software Engineer, and Enterprise Architect."

She let a look of warmth and concern cross her face, and said, "Let me ask my neighbor. She serves on about every committee at church. If anyone knows someone who could help, she would be it. Give me a couple of your cards, and I'll see that she gets them."

Enslow reached into his pocket and after a brief amount of fumbling, fished out several cards and handed them to her. "Donna, I really appreciate this. Even if she can't help me, I appreciate the help. It is just so tough out there, so any help is wonderful."

"Glad to help. You keep your chin up! A guy like you, something will turn up. I gotta run now. Bye-bye." She turned and walked to the end of the meeting room and out the door. Possibly out of his life forever. Who knows if she will be of any help, but inside, Enslow was grateful for the lifeline she had thrown.

The crowd was dwindling, so Enslow made one more circuit of the room and after a couple of friendly conversations and commiserating, walked out the door that Donna had left through a few minutes earlier, and he walked across the slightly uneven asphalt surface to his car, where he opened the door and climbed in. Just as he was about to put the keys in and start, his cell phone rang. He didn't recognize the number, but answered it anyway. "Hello?"

A male voice, a bit gravely, said "Enslow?"

"Yes."

"My name is Major Hurst. I work for MilaDyne Corporation. I was looking over the resumes that we received for a Systems Analyst, and I noticed that you had a great deal of the requirements we were looking for. Are you still looking for a job?"

Trying not to tremble like a school girl being asked out for prom, Enslow cleared his throat and said, "Yes I am still looking. Can you refresh me as to some of the details?"

"Yes, but I would rather see you in person. It makes it easier to explain what we do and what we are looking for. Can you come in next Thursday at 9:30?"

Enslow had failed at trying not to tremble. His hands were slightly shaking. This was his first bite that sounded promising. Usually they wanted to do a phone screening, but this one wanted to start out with an in-person interview. Enslow replied (and tried to not let his voice rise in excitement), "That would be fine. Where do I need to go?"

"Oh, it is a bit complicated; I will send you the details and a letter that will let you get onto the base. We are quartered at Fort Prairie. I look forward to seeing you then. Good day." Before Enslow could say thank you or ask another question, the line was dead.

Nigel Day 244

Nigel heard some damn pounding again and again. Rubbing his eyes, he was able to bring the ceiling of the grotty flat into focus. A quick panic subsided when he knew that no one could have tracked him here, and that the pounding was more of a polite knocking; it was merely his hangover that made it a pounding. Staggering, his weight shifting uncertainly from foot to foot, he made it to the door. Shouting at the door in the most gruff voice he could, "Sod off, you noisy bastard!" He threw the door open to reveal a quite surprised Suresh, holding a set of keys in his hands. "Sorry to awaken you at this late hour, I assumed you would be awake by now, but I wanted to inform you that your, uh, mother's car was ready."

A confused look crossed Nigel's face as he listened to what the man in front of him was saying, but it wasn't registering. He said, "Sorry, I don't speak Pakistani, what are you saying?"

Seemingly taking no offense, Suresh, decided that this drunken Englishman might understand him if he spoke more slowly, so he said as slowly as he could, and with as much precise diction as he could muster, "Forgive me, sir, but I have

111

completed the car for your mother as you requested."

Standing there will a dull look on his face, it took Nigel almost ten more seconds to absorb what he was being told. When comprehension at last dawned on him, his eyebrows raised and he smiled and said "Oh, where is it?"

Rather than answering, Suresh gestured with his right hand, seemingly drawing a still craggy Nigel out to the street. When Nigel at last saw the red Mercedes sitting at the curb, his face noticeably brightened and his step quickened. Gone was the still drunken hold that last night's pub time had imparted to him.

As they got to the street, without saying a word, Suresh held out the keys to Nigel, who scooped them up as a child would his favorite candy. He walked around the car without saying a word and then crawled under the front of the car, noting the addition of a skid plate that he had not specified. Clearly, Suresh understood what he was being asked to do and was concentrating on the details. Nigel stood up and brushed the grit off of his knees and walked to back of the car, carefully examining the bumper reinforcements. With these not only having met his directives to Suresh, but exceeding his expectations, he then opened the bonnet and whistled low and slow, sounding exactly like a New Jersey construction worker would who had seen a pretty secretary at the hot dog cart during lunch.

"You sir, have outdone yourself. That is not only functional it looks like it's a factory installation. Well done lad. Just brilliant."

Suresh struggled to contain his pleasure at making the client happy, but he was also swelling with pride that his work has been seen and understood for what it was.

"Is that the 5.5 I asked for?" Nigel inquired.

"No sir, it's not, I was able to modify the bore and stroke and actually give you a 6.2 litre engine, and that allowed me to use a slightly larger displacement supercharger, giving you a total projected horsepower rating of 700 horses using the nitrous, and about 625 horsepower without."

"All that from the NOs and the blower?"

"No sir, I was able to polish and port the intake, the exhaust ports, as well as call in a favor and extrude hone the intake manifold, and added a set of headers and almost doubled the size of the stock exhaust."

"Spectacular" said Nigel, with a touch of

amazement to his voice. "I notice I now have louvered vents on the fenders."

"Yes, they allow cool air induction to facilitate cooling for the radiators I embedded in there. I was not able to cut the radiator as you suggested, but I instead used heater cores from municipal buses that would warm the passengers during cooler weather. They fit more precisely in the space that I had, and were faster to adapt than rebuilding your radiator in two parts. I also used the cage fans from the same enclosure; they allowed me to fit up more nicely."

"May I show you the vehicle?" Suresh asked but it was really more of a directive than a query.

Without saying a word, Nigel followed him to the rear of the vehicle. Suresh pressed a blue button on the second remote, and the car started. Pressing a key on the second remote, the boot lid raised up in a motorized fashion, rather than popping up slightly with the spring pressure one might suspect. In the boot was the hydraulic arm from one of those small skiff bulldozers, and when the remote for the boot was pushed three times, the hydraulic arm then extend itself backward, with a two foot piece of sharpened metal now protruding almost two feet beyond the bumper.

Nigel took his finger and gently touched the

point to see how sharp it was, and promptly drew back with a small drop of blood welling up on his fingertip. As he inspected the rest of the installation to see how well it was attached, his attention was drawn to the rear of the back seat and the strange lining on the inside of the raised boot lid.

"Sorry, don't understand this." He pointed to the somewhat puffy layers of fabric.

"Oh, I reasoned that your mother might come to some harm in Birmingham, what with all the groups there that they have trouble with, so I lined the rear of the back seat and the boot lid with Kevlar. When the lid is raised, it combined with the rear seat should prevent any projectile intrusion to interfere with your mother's trip to the store," Suresh said calmly and matter-of-factly, without a hint of sarcasm, but Nigel was unsure if he actually saw a glint of it in his eyes.

Acting more like a kid at a science fair who was trying to impress his teacher, Suresh now took Nigel to the car's interior. Grabbing the tops of the back of the front seats, Suresh pulled and a Velcro ripping sound accompanied the seat backs pulling away to reveal snug compartments with internal Velcro holding straps. That could easily accommodate guns and extra clips. Actually, upon inspection, it was hard to imagine that they had been designed for anything else. Clearly, Suresh understood what he had been asked to do.

"Please sit in the driver's seat," Suresh asked politely, again sounding like a person who was both quite pleased with his skills, and desiring to get recognition for it. "Use the mirror control to center the mirror behind you, and try to focus on the yellow lorry at the end of the block."

Somewhat confused, Nigel did as he was instructed, but said that the lorry was too far away to focus. Suresh said, "Oh, twist the stalk anti-clockwise to zoom in."

So, Nigel pressed the button, and a genuinely amazing thing happened. The image in the mirror of the yellow lorry began to increase in size, until it not only filled the entire contents of the mirror, but it was able to focus on and easily read the license plate. It was then that Nigel realized that the mirror was not a mirror, but a four inch monitor fitted to the mirror housing.

"Neat trick, how'd you do that?"

Beaming now with pride, Suresh told him that he had parted a couple of camcorders and put the displays in the mirror housings, the imaging sensors into the rear fenders just above the taillights, and added the zoom into the passenger rear window button. Down meant zoom in, up meant zoom out. Suresh told the now quite pleased Nigel that using the rear driver's side control will shift the control to the front, where he had added the bits from a second unit. Additional mirror servos had been added to the camera assemblies to allow them some range of movement so that they did not just zoom in on a fixed point in space.

"I also added a second set of controls on the passenger side. Should your mother have a passenger, they can observe things in front of or behind them the same way."

Nigel asked "How did you get a second set of controls to look so factory on the passenger side?"

Suresh smiled, as he was proud of his efforts, "I was able to locate an American version of the door panel, and as it would be the driver's side in that country, it looks like a factory installation. I only had to dye the vinyl to match the rest of your mother's interior."

After exiting the Mercedes, Nigel did have a complaint to address. "I do have a small complaint. I would wager that a red car would draw a lot of attention to an old lady. Could we paint it a different color?" Nigel inquired with a look of concern on his face.

Suresh just stood there grinning.

"Did you understand me? I think the car will attract too much attention," Nigel now said in a sterner tone.

Suresh at last responded, "Actually sir, it is a silver car which should blend in nicely with most other cars in traffic and not stand out."

Not accustomed to having his facts questioned, and feeling at a bit of a loss that something so obvious was not getting through to the man in front of him, Nigel placed his hand on Suresh's shoulder and turned the Asian man's body to face the car, pointed at it, and in a fatherly tone, said "I think you are talking rubbish. Look my friend. I appreciate how well you have completed my task I assigned you. I'm sure you worked very hard and long, and perhaps you are more exhausted than you think. Do you see that Jaguar over there?

"Yes."

"What color is it?'

"White."

"Do you see that Citroen by the lamp post?"

"Yes."

"What color is it?"

"It is blue," came the reply.

"What color is my mum's Mercedes?"

"It is silver."

Nigel dropped his hand from the man's shoulder, and said, hanging his head, "No. I see a red car."

"Perhaps sir," said Suresh with a puckish grin, "what you see is a car that appears red."

Squinting, Nigel said, "And how is that different?"

Suresh explained, "Are you aware of those advertising cars for products and such? The ones that advertise beer and the logo and slogan are all over the car, from front to back?"

Furrowing his brow, Nigel tried to follow the line of query, not sure how it applied. Then a sudden spark of understanding fired through his synapses, and it came to him in a sudden flash. "It is a silver car but it is covered by a red false skin! Like a bloody snake. Brilliant!"

"You are correct," came the satisfied reply of Suresh, sounding much like a teacher whose student at university had finally gotten the correct answer.

"That's fantastic. I will need three more colours, all different. Make one yellow like a taxi. Also make a removable lighted taxi sign, probably magnetic? How big an effort is it to change its colour?" Nigel asked.

"Well, with some forewarning, I can create a new skin in a couple of days. It only takes about two hours to apply the vinyl skin," Suresh informed his client.

Nigel held his gaze on Suresh, and understood that this man had created for him exactly what he needed and he was no fool and would not treat him as such. "I wanted to thank you for your efforts. You could have bodged up something close to what I asked for, but instead you applied your skill and creativity to craft for me a solution that met and exceeded my needs. Do I owe you anything else?"

"No sir, it was a delight to do the work. I enjoy the money, and I have slept little, but as you know, I have a large family, so I am grateful for the opportunity to serve you. I only ask one thing."

"And what would that be?"

120

"If any of your friends would like cars for their elderly mothers, I would be most happy to build them vehicles as well."

Nigel understood that Suresh likely knew this car was not for his mother; the extra bits and the second skin indicated that. Things unsaid, however, can be as powerful as things that are said. Nigel none the less said "Suresh, I promise you that I will, and I will send all of my work to you."

"Please understand I mean no disrespect, but I will not work on any car unless I know it is connected to you. I have my family to worry about and I would never put them at risk. When I first heard we had a new white neighbor that came and went at odd hours, and was often gone too long to make sense, I was suspicious of you. But I heard how you chased away the boys who were bullying my oldest son, and how you stopped the car who was not giving proper consideration to my wife as she crossed the street. I knew then that I had misjudged you, and that you were a good man in a bad neighborhood. Why you are here is something I do not understand, and do not wish to understand. Many torrents surround you. I hope that your path is clear. Besides the fact that you paid me quite well for my efforts, I felt that as one man to another, I owed it to you that for whatever you are doing, I could give you every advantage I could in the limited time I had. May Allah favor you in your journeys."

Reaching out silently and shaking Suresh's hand Nigel bowed his head slightly, and then released his grip, turned on his heel, and walked over to his door. He twisted the handle, stepped through into his grotty flat, and closed the door. *Looks like you have made a friend. Troubling though, that he sees in you something you weren't trying to project. If you are going to be able to pull off your next assignment, you will need to become the man the records say you are.*

Enslow Unemployed Day 46-70

Enslow was growing tired of the ups and downs. One moment you were up because you found a job that was perfect for you, then you were down because you got another rejection letter or you got nothing at all. You were up because you met some new people you might be able to network with and find out about a company or a position and then you were down when they didn't return your call. You were up for every victory; you were down for every failure. The problem was the ups didn't balance the downs. The growing weight of failure was causing Enslow to get short tempered and snippy. Friends were not as eager to take his calls and he realized he was becoming bitter, but who wouldn't be? This was stupid, unfair and tiresome. He knew he was good at what he did. He knew he was harder working and more tenacious than other people. He would often hit a stride of productivity at the end of the day, when the interruptions diminished, and his peers were finding excuses to go home. None of that mattered however, he was one of hundreds or perhaps thousands applying for each position, and without someone on the inside to put his resume in the stack, he was destined to be eternally rejected.

So far the kids seemed to take no notice of what was going on. Kids are resilient that way. Enslow knew from his own childhood, that while kids may not understand everything going on, to never assume they were stupid. They knew daddy was at home and not working. And they knew that he had to work to pay for things. Like the house and food. They really didn't understand how much things cost, but Enslow knew that he would have to explain it to them in the near future, that they might have to move out of their house. Things weren't that bad yet, and wouldn't be for a while. Enslow and Ella needed to make sure the kids understood when or if the time came, what was going on. Dee Dee might be fooled, she was young. Augie wouldn't buy a lie. He would for a while. It was just as likely that he already knew what was going on in the world based on what his school friends told him, and what he was reading online. Augie was smart and web savvy.

Enslow reviewed his ProNect profile every day, as well as searching for additional forums to join. Then he would search the forums for suitable networking opportunities, and hit them up with an approach letter. This was an opportunity to fatten up his accomplishments and job descriptions, that on a resume you had to cut out for the interests of space. In this environment, you could extol your virtues and thereby make more words and terms that someone could search for and find you by. He decided to fatten up his associations and looked for forums to join for additional areas of specialty he possessed. Some were for Database Analysts, others for Call Center professionals, etc. Enslow had his specific political views, advertising them might just get someone to not select you based on that. He saw little problem with personal interests like golfing, but that also meant very little as to your ability to perform your job. Might be a plus if they were looking for an executive, but there was really a rich body of things to select from that added interest to your persona and created a fuller picture of who you were.

Enslow found that by searching for events in the neighboring cities in the event section, he could come up with a list of potential networking opportunities. He found that prospect a little depressing, but you couldn't make any sales if you didn't make any calls. So he was going to need to keep going at it. On the next Tuesday, Enslow went to another job transition group to keep up the human side of networking. As the inquiring and comradic talk went on, many of the people found what Enslow had to say about using ProNect fascinating. They had not joined any groups, or searched for events to attend, or approached anyone from one of the forums to do cold call networking. The facilitator of the group asked him if he could prepare a presentation to share his understanding with the group.

"Wouldn't that be giving away an advantage that I have worked up?" he asked somewhat guardedly.

Gary Hurst, the group facilitator, said "There is always the possibility, but in reality you will get a lot of satisfaction from helping the rest of the group. They are all looking for help, and if you seem like the helpful guy, that may be just the extra help you need."

Enslow frowned, "Not following".

Gary instructed "When some of the people land, they will likely hold a high opinion of you for being helpful and smart. When they find openings at their new companies, you may get the first call."

Recognition dawned on Enslow's face, "I see. I get a boost from being up in front, a boost for being Mr. Helpful, and I get moved to the front of the line for people they consider or refer opportunities to. You are correct. It is a win-win."

"Now you are tracking with me. The real benefit is helping your fellow jobless friends, but there are the other benefits you mentioned. Could you put something together by next week?"

Without thinking, Enslow said, "Absolutely.

I'll cover the basics and then go into some discussion of the advanced topics. Do you have a projector and a laptop?"

Gary raised his eyebrows and said with a smile, "I do, and I'll bring a laptop with me. Just bring your presentation on a stick. I'll send out a notice to the distribution list that there will be a working session on ProNect and how to use it. I appreciate your help. This will mean a lot to a great many people. Thank you."

Feeling somewhat embarrassed and feeling like that speech was a bit over the top, Enslow replied, "Glad I can help." Gary shook Enslow's hand and was quickly engaged in other conversations around him. Maybe getting in front of people as an expert was just the thing he needed to gain back a little of the confidence so shaken by the constant stream of bad employment news in the media, and the constant unrelenting idea that he was a career failure because he couldn't get a job or even an interview. Enslow's wife Ella had been and continued to be very supportive, but the strain was beginning to show that he was under a great deal of pressure. If he could do this, it might really be a confidence builder.

Enslow walked out of the meeting hall and went to his car, started it and drove home. When he got there, he went inside to his office and started to

127

make some notes on what would be needed to fully instruct people from a zero level to a high level on ProNect.

Step 1: Gather your resume (s), cover letters and previous business cards to draw information from.

Step 2: If you have not created a ProNect account, go to the ProNect website and create one. One job hunting tip is to get an email account just for job hunting. Sometimes scammers find you, and why have your primary email address filled up with junk or filled up long after your job search is over. (Fat chance)

Step 3: Discuss and show how to fill out the basics of your profile, making sure to put in all the personal information you want to share, and then to fill out the other section, at least in outline form. Education, work history, honors and awards, etc.

Step 4: Create "Associations" of business contacts, co-workers, and friends, whatever. This increases the size of your network and might give you a way to find someone who can help get your resume in front of the hiring manager or just let you know about a job opening.

Step 5: Job searching, how to research a company and look for networking connections.

Step 6: Basics of Search Engine Optimization and how it applies.

Step 7: Join the forums. How to search to your advantage.

Step 8: Search for events, how to exploit, to be in front of people.

Enslow reviewed his outline and found that he not only liked it, it immediately satisfied what he would have done to include all the basics at a higher level. Now he just needed to expand it. As he began to fill it in step by step, he constantly went back to the ProNect website, to make sure he used EXACTLY the language they used. *That should be a good start.* Creating a step by step program to present took substantially more time than Enslow had figured. What was killing him time wise was the painful step by step, where he had to list the exact verbiage used by the website. The reason he was going to so much trouble, was that so many of the job seekers were older folks, and many had no experience with social networking. Well, he can just not tell them how much time he spent on this.

The next Friday, he went to the church a bit early to ensure that all the equipment was set up. Most of it was, but when he tried to turn on the projector, it wouldn't come on. Remembering to always look for the simple solution, he found that the power plug was loose at the back of the projector. A snug push and the green LED came on indicating that the projector now had power. A quick flick of the on button, and a familiar warm rectangle appeared on the wall, displaying the contents of the laptop's desktop and icons. Enslow put the data stick he had into a USB port and used the mouse to navigate to his presentation file. It was at this moment that Gary walked in, and seeing Enslow, came over with his usual warm smile.

"Good morning! You ready for this?"

Feeling confident, but not knowing what to really expect, Enslow said, "Yep, as ready as I can be."

With a playful grin, Gary lowered his voice a bit when he spoke next. "That's good, I sent out a notice to the list of attendees for the last year, and asked that people indicate that they are coming. My mailbox got full, so I really have no idea of how many people are coming."

Being a bit shocked, Enslow asked "How many do you think will be here?"

"Don't know, but I am guessing over a hundred. It's a testament to how well you are perceived by everyone. It sure isn't your looks,"

Gary said, again with a wicked smile across his face. A quick slap and a grip on Enslow's shoulder told him Gary was kidding, but Endow knew that.

The crowd began to filter in, and when the chairs seemed to be almost all full, the crowd looked around like lost children. The church staff brought in a floor roller stacked with another twenty five chairs. This was an action they would have to repeat two more times. Before Enslow even began his presentation, the crowd had swelled to almost one hundred sixty people. He was not really used to speaking in front of that many people and it made him nervous. The kind of a pit in the stomach, sweating, nearly shaking kind of nervous. This was why a lot of people just didn't like to speak in front of large groups. He reminded himself that they were looking for information, not a floor show.

Seeing that the room had more or less settled down to watch whatever he was going to do, Enslow approached the lectern, grabbed the microphone and began to speak. "Good morning, and thanks for coming. I hope this morning will be of some use to you. I want to apologize in advance, as some of this will be old information, but with a group of this size, I just will have to make a one size fits all presentation. The format will be a general presentation and then drilling down to more advanced topics, and questions and answers at the end. Firstly, I want to say that everything you will see here is my opinion, and is not to be considered gold. Shall we begin?" After a brief pause, Enslow clicked up the first slide, and resumed speaking.

Step 1: Gather your resume (s), cover letters and previous business cards to draw information from.

"So from a zero state, what you need to do is to gather up all of your information. If you are like me, it takes time to remember all of your previous jobs, duties, titles and work addresses, so this is why I suggest you start here. It will form the basis of how you populate your profile. In this economy, what you did for your last job may not be what you can get hired doing. Typically, you diminish over time in the mid of a hiring manager. Due to budgets being slashed that hiring manager or HR manager may be in their early twenties. These people only remember two or three presidents and maybe one pope. Their ability to judge you is extremely limited due to their lack of experience. The roles and responsibilities of who you say you are; are only regarded as being as good as your last five years. In the world now, which I am sorry to tell you has changed, you need to find something you have done, that is still marketable or gives you more appeal than someone who is just focusing on their last five years. Think about it. Do you want to hire a project manager or do you want to hire a project manager for a software development project that used to be a developer on the platform you are using?" With just that brief explanation, Enslow saw a few faces light up with understanding. *Perhaps people will get something out of this after all.*

He went on from there. "In ProNect, and some of the other social media platforms, you are no longer constrained as you were on a traditional resume. You can put down ALL of your relevant experience, and give yourself the weight of value that it adds. Also, it will open you up to being easier to find. This is because the more you can put down about yourself the more often you will turn up in searches. In a traditional recruiter's world, they relied on a network of people and a rolodex of names to call for certain types of skills. Over the last several years, recruiting firms have utilized databases of their contacts so that they could more quickly find the talent that they wanted to put up for a job. Human Resource departments often did not have the time, money or expertise to do this, and so still relied on recruiters. But in today's world, employers can pay a small fee, though that is a relative term, and search ProNect themselves. And not just locally; they can find the talent they want nationally, and if it is the right candidate, work to recruit them. That's the dirty secret here. You aren't just competing against each other, and the younger, 'more affordable' worker. You are competing regionally, nationally, and even globally for that position. You need to be even more competitive than before and one of the easiest ways to compete is to be seen before someone else. The easiest way to be seen is to exploit the number of terms that someone can find you with." Enslow clicked through to the second slide.

Step2: Create a ProNect Account using a new email address.

Enslow now took a breath, and was just a bit surprised to not see anyone with a bored look on their face. After taking a drink from the water bottle he had placed on the lectern, he proceeded to start a deeper dive. "Now that you have your career information together, if you haven't already, go to one of the websites that offers free email accounts and register for a free account to use solely for job searching. In this day and age, there are lots of scammers and ID thieves that will target you, so by using this new address for job searching, you will be able to avoid some of these threats. But primarily, when you land your new job, and I know you all will, you can walk away from this email address, and not have your regular/home address filled up from now on. I myself receive as many as five hundred emails a week, and that would just overwhelm my personal email box. So once you have done that, if you choose to, you now need to log on to ProNect dot com, and register for a

ProNect account. Then you will need to start using your resumes, etc. to flesh out the account. Only put down the information you are comfortable with, and for me, I won't put down my home address or phone number. That just hands information to the scammers. Start with your basic information and then add in your education."

Now he took a pause and asked if anyone had a question, and a few hands went up. He selected the one closest to him.

"Do you have to use a new email address?" asked a large mid-fifties gentleman.

Internally shaking his head, but straining to not do so physically, Enslow replied, "No, I just think it is a good idea for the reasons I stated, but you don't have to."

Remembering that the woman in the middle with the red sweater had had her hand up, Enslow pointed at her and inquired, "You had a question?"

To which, she replied "I don't want to use any of my previous resumes; is it possible to just start fresh?"

Enslow said "Yes. I'm just trying to give the best general starting point. The surest way to fail is to use this in the same way you would a regular resume. What you want to do is go to the next level, but having substantially MORE content than a resume has. This is really a different sort of environment than a resume. This is an interactive, searchable history of you and your value to an employer, both in what you say, how you say it, and showing much more content than you normally could."

Without waiting to be called on, a surly, slightly fat, pompous executive that Enslow remembered he didn't like, barked out "How do you do that? That's why I came here, to get more insight into what I can say on my profile."

"Well, we will get to that, but a lot of these people need to hear how to start, and that's where I am trying to go. If you have specific questions about the topic as we cover it, please raise your hand, but everything has an order to it, and so does using ProNect."

Enslow, grabbed his pen, and wrote 'douche bag' on his notes. "Ok, let me get back to where we were."

Step 3: Fill out the sections: Education, work history, honors and awards.

"Put down any education you have, such as area of study, degrees received extracurricular activities, college clubs, etc. I would suggest NOT putting down when you received your education as that may open you up to some age discrimination, and worries that you will be too expensive to hire. I don't know that those fears are justified, but I can't say they are or aren't. I would not have thought those fears were valid a few years ago, but living it now, I am not so sure. Just select your school and major from the drop down boxes but you may notice that sometimes a school will change its name, or for any reason, your school, major and activities may not be available. See what happens when you select 'Other'? A text box appears next to it where you can enter information if it doesn't otherwise exist. So if you went to Berlin Polytechnic prior to World War II and now it is called the National Technical University of Germany. You can put it down. The reason is that when you apply for a job, you need to be extremely accurate, so as to not give them a reason to disqualify you. I know it seems silly, but even though that school changed its name, your degree will have the old name, so it's my opinion to be accurate with school names, etc." Not pausing for questions, Enslow continued, "Now for work history. Using your resume, go ahead and fill out all of your employer information and job titles, where you can, for the moment, cut and paste your job duties from any soft copies you have, or type it in fresh. But I want to stress that this is the start of this process, not the end. Because for each job you can now add about one thousand characters to describe what you did. You can make it more conversational and less fragmented. Ever notice how when you have always done a resume, you employ substantial fragments rather than complete sentences? That's because a resume is both content and a visual document, and to make it look balanced or to make it fit on a page neatly, you would drop words. Now you don't have to. Once you have done this in outline form, I beg you, please, go back and fatten it up with additional words, but try to use action words like led, managed, and particularly content words and terms, like 'Project Manager', 'Analyst', and platform words of the vendors you used. For instance, even if you are not an IT person, what kind of machine was it or what environment? If it was a UNIX or Linux system, use that word. If it was Oracle, or PeopleSoft based system, use that. Things like 'Accounts Receivable', 'Inventory', and 'Lifecycle' are all words people search by. This is your chance to communicate, and one of the key things is to demonstrate that you know how to communicate. By writing tight descriptions of what your roles and responsibilities were, you can make yourself stand out. As you all know, in today's world with so much work occurring nationally and internationally, the ability to communicate clearly is a required job skill." Enslow clicked the next slide.

Step 4: Create association of business contacts, co-workers, and friends, whatever. This increases the size of your network.

Enslow again took a drink of water from the water bottle, and started to speak again. "Now is where we start to get into the part that helps. Everything up to now has been infrastructure. Like where we build the foundation and the frame, we now need to add the interior walls and plumbing and carpet, etc. How you will be able to use ProNect, is to expand the number of people you are tied to. These are called associates. Start with your friends, family and co-workers. These will give them access to your associates, and you can get access to theirs. To get an association, you need to invite that person to 'Associate' with you. Just click on the top menu item, 'Associations,' and when the menu pulls down, click 'Invite.' Then type in their name, their email address or do a more complex search. They have to be in the ProNect system to associate with them, but every day more and more people are."

A round faced curly haired woman raised her hand, and when Enslow pointed at her, she asked, "What if I can't find the person I want to connect with?"

Enslow shook his head in recognition, and instructed the room, "Try searching for them by different ways, like if you are looking for John Smith, try adding a company you know he worked with or what school he went to, use some piece of information in the Advanced Search panel to try to locate them. In fact, I would really strongly suggest that whatever you are looking for, whether it is a person or a company or an event, to use the advanced search panel. It allows you to add discriminators like city, state, relative distance, or other qualifiers. This will speed up your search time and allow you more time to concentrate on the thing you are looking for and what to do with it, rather than finding the person, place or thing. Now another thing you can do is that if you can't find that person on ProNect, call them or email them, and ask if they are on ProNect. Inviting them to join that way might allow you an opportunity to reestablish a previous friendship, and just reaching out allows you the opportunity to mention you are in transition. Never say you are looking for a job. In ANY communication or reaching, never say you are looking for a job. It puts people on the defensive, and they sometimes shut down. You need to keep them at ease. When someone calls you and says they need a job, the first reaction is to think you don't know of a job, and you can't help this person, so you sort of shutdown. Everyone wants to help, and when they can't or think they can't they feel embarrassed that they can't help. But the secret is that they can, they just don't know it. What they can do for you is to give you the names of people they know, who may work at a company you want to work for or someone who can give you a perspective on a new industry. And that conversation can turn into others."

The 'douche bag' spoke up, "That all sounds warm and fluffy, but I don't have the time for all of that, I need to get back to work."

Enslow looked straight into his eyes and told him, "That's true, but the world has changed. More and more good people are out of work for no other reason than times are hard. To compete in the new reality, you need to marshal skills you may not possess or haven't had to use. We are in the inverse side of the supply curve right now. As good as think you are or as good as you may be, there are hundreds if not thousands of people as good or better than you are, and you need a new set of tools to compete."

Porky spoke up, "Well, that may be good for everyone else, but I have the experience and credentials and I don't have time to play these games. I shouldn't have to waste my time with a lot of silly phone calls about the weather or whatever."

"I'm sorry you feel that way. As I said before, I'm just trying to give my perspectives and share with you what I know," Enslow said, trying to sound sympathetic, but it was having no effect on the complainer, who quietly gathered up his belongings and left the room. After the door closed, Enslow was tempted to make a smart ass comment, like "The 9:30 show is completely different from the 7:30 show, enjoy the veal, and remember to tip your waitress." Sensing that he had the high ground, however, he proceeded to step 5.

Step5: Job searching, how to research a company, and looking for networking connections.

"Ok, we have entered all of our information, and we have filled out a brilliantly conceived thesis on our contributions to the world; now what? Let's go to actual job hunting. Suppose we want to work at Direct Distributors. You have always heard what great benefits they have. Let's open up the advanced search panel, (remember?) and put in the company title, 'Direct Distributers', and let's say we only want to look for associates who live within twenty five miles of our home, and (after filling all of that in) we press Search, and voila! We have a list of twelve people I know who work there. But if you look closer, I only know one directly and the rest are one or more degree away. Remember how every actor is within six degrees of separation from Kevin Bacon? That's what is going on here. The lists of people are ranked by the number of degrees away from me. So if I wanted to talk to the third one, who appears to be a director, I click on his name, and it present a list of the people in the chain from me to him, so I can contact this person or that person, and see if they can set up an introduction for me. Now, if you don't know the name of a company you want to work for, but you want to do the same kind of work you did at your last job or as I said early on, something you did several jobs ago, go to the advanced search and type in that job title, and search for people who do that kind of work. You will discover some companies you never knew about that might be able to use your skills, and you may discover that someone there is an alumnus of your college or lists himself as a windsurfer or Boy Scout or some other kind of an opportunity to approach them for networking. It's really up to you how you search and how you approach, but this should give you some ideas how to start searching."

Other than the one arrogant attendee, Enslow was somewhat startled that the entire crowd was still here, and appeared to be finding his presentation useful. He was also somewhat surprised that he was enjoying it. Probably due to the crowd being gracious and not throwing fruit. (Who brings fruit to public events?) Aside from the one jerk, they all seemed to be learning from his experience, which made him feel good and useful again. After being out only this long, he was starting to lose a little faith in whether he really had

143

anything to offer anyone.

Step 6: Basics of Search Engine optimization and how it applies.

"This brings us to some of the real meat. Search Engine Optimization. I've mentioned searching and how important it is, but what happens is that you need to have more than just the right word. You need the right words, and lots of them. For instance, what happens is that in addition to your profile turning up based on a search term, it is ranked by the number of times it turned up, and its relevance. If an employer is looking to hire a Business Analyst, if you did that twelve years ago, you can see why they want someone who is more current on the terms and technology for that. So to increase your ranking and get to the top of the list for those people who match, you use the term as often as you can and couple it with your most recent employment, so even if you are not currently a Business Analyst, if you performed that kind of work in addition to other tasks, talk about it in your work experience. One of the things I like to do is, if you go to the top of your profile," and Enslow clicked to the top, "you can see that you can enter up to three websites for information about you or your company. So I like to insert my profile URL, that complete address thing at the top, and enter it as a website in my profile, like this." Enslow then highlighted the entire URL at the top when his profile was displayed, then edited the first website address, and entered "Business Analyst," and for the 'at business name,' he then pasted this complete URL. "Now let's say I also want to be considered a project manager. I'll do that in the same way. "And he edited the second company website, and entered "Project Manager," and pasted his profile URL there as you would a real company website.

"Ok, what happens is that when someone is searching for a 'Business Analyst', your name may come up because in addition to having it listed as a company name, the link attached to it also uses the words 'Business Analyst'. When the search engine crawler is looking for that term it ranks you higher because in addition that term, it is repeated throughout your profile. That link was on your page, so it is the referencing page. See? It's a little more complicated than that, but in essence you are forcing your page rank to be more elevated than someone else who has no links about being a Business Analyst. Sneaky, huh? Therefore, in summary, I would suggest you search on the web for the basics of how to optimize search results, and try to apply those discussions to your job history and employment details. I'd like to go on further, but it probably a bit too technical for the time we have left. I will go on to the next subject," and he clicked through to the seventh slide.

Step 7: Join the forums, how to search to your advantage.

"I've mentioned the forums before, and what they are is a collection of people grouped by a similar interest or participation in something. These could be a school, a college, a sports team, a professional association, or in some cases by being an inventor, whatever. Join the groups that you are legitimately able to claim the right to belong to. For instance, if you never attended Harvard, then don't join them. Even if they let you in you will have trouble networking to anyone on there because it will become apparent that you never went there and don't belong. Here are some examples I found: Congress of Business Analysts, Boy Scouts of America, Harvard University alumni (I know, I had to throw that in). It is really whatever you can find, and the two ways are to search for an organization or look and see what your associates have joined. I belong to the Innovations Society, a group I had never heard of, because a friend of mine belongs to them, and I saw it while looking at his profile and joined."

Step 8: Search for events, how to exploit to be in front of people.

Enslow looked at his watch and saw that he was almost 15 minutes over the scheduled time, but that no one else had left. *Never thought I was an expert, but I guess it's what they think you are.* "I apologize for this taking the so long, but I have just one more topic to cover, then I'll open the floor for questions. If you are looking for an opportunity to pass out your business cards and meet new people, to try to find opportunities, then I suggest you search for events on the Event menu. If you know of an event you can enter it and that allows other people to find that event. But let's do that real quick. So I will go to the Event menu, then click on Advanced, then enter our city, and a range of twenty five miles, because I don't want to drive very far, and click 'Search', and....ta-da! It has now posted a list of upcoming events, like various Chamber of Commerce events, trade shows, and such. Some of these events are closed, but usually they will say that. If they appear here, it is because someone entered them and they are open to the public. The chamber events are great places to search, because the people there are either working or own businesses, and you might be able to strike up the opportunity to do some part time work for them. I know we are all looking for a real job or one that pays what we were making, but look at part time jobs as a 'paid' networking opportunities. Temporary things have a way, sometimes, of going on and on, like fixing your car with duct tape. You can make some money, some new contacts and who knows, someone there may have a friend or brother or sister who works at a company where you would like to work. Every opportunity you can expose yourself to is one potential door to a new start for you. And that concludes my presentation. Any questions?"

But before anyone could ask a question, Gary stood up and said "Thank you Enslow" and started clapping. A generous and sincere round of applause filled the meeting hall taking Enslow quite by surprise. Certainly a round of applause was courteous, but he found this rather humbling. All he did was take the time he had, and get up to share. Gary then said, "Unfortunately, the church needs this hall to be clear for an event in an hour, so if you have any questions, please take them up with Enslow by email. I hope he will forward those to me, and I can post them to our job search blog, and maybe we all can benefit. Enslow, thanks again, just a marvelous job" and then more clapping ensued. A few people came up nonetheless and started asking questions, and he responded as well as he could, but was mindful that the church had let them use the hall and had the scheduled an event, so for the most part he gave them his card and said to email him. After several more compliments and a few harsh words for the arrogant early leaver, Enslow was able to make his way back to his car, trying not to smile the whole time. *You did a good thing. I think you really helped people. You got so far into that, you never realized you don't like crowds. It's like you were playing a part. They didn't know you, didn't know you were scared. Show no fear, and they would follow you anywhere*!

That Thursday, Enslow showed up right on time at the appointed place. He sat for some time waiting to speak to Major Hurst. After thirty additional minutes (which Enslow thought might be a test of some sort), Enslow was ushered into a small room with a desk, two chairs and some seriously beyond their prime plastic plants. A pock marked man in a suit with a rugged air about him stood up and said "Hello. I'm Major Hurst, how are you?"

Enslow stuck his hand out, gave a firm handshake, and said "Good sir."

"Please sit down," Major Hurst said as he gestured with his left hand to the chair opposite his desk. "I'm glad you came. I am sorry about the delay, the last candidate seemed like a really good match, but after some further checking I have decided to move on and look at you."

"So quickly? Isn't there a series of interviews for this?" Enslow asked, a bit confused by the accelerated nature the previous statement indicated.

"Well, I like to make my best decision and move on. We have too much at risk to waste time on candidates who fail my questions or a

149

background check."

"Well. I came here to see if the job is right for me, or if I am right for it." Enslow stated, while being sure to look the major straight in the eye.

"Excellent. Is your resume and employment history up to date?"

"Yes."

"Have you ever been arrested or charged with any crime outside of minor traffic infractions?"

"No."

"Have you ever had a security clearance before?"

"No."

"Is there any reason you could not get one?"

"No reason I am aware of."

"Is your credit history good? No late payments, no bankruptcies?"

"Yes, no, and no." answered Enslow, rather proud of his ability to detect that there were three questions requiring separate answers.

"Mr. Spengler, here is what we are looking for. We are looking for a systems analyst who has the stability to follow precise directions for the setup and configuration of the BDS, secure comm sat links and the ability to diagnose problems related to that setup. Primarily this position will involved supervising those teams, but the ability to understand the work will greatly enhance your ability to achieve a successful outcome. Any questions?"

"I think I understood all of that, but what is a BDS?"

"Battlefield Data System. It is essentially a hardened computer system a lot like an industrial PC, but able to withstand more dirt and vibration. They are systems installed at off base sites, used by operations personnel to do everything from ordering supplies to access battlefield intel for troop deployment."

Enslow spoke to that statement, saying "I've read the material regarding the position, and I understand it will be out of the country, can you tell me where?"

"Typically, it would be in a service area, and this particular position we are hiring for would be in Afghanistan," replied Major Hurst, watching

Enslow to see if he flinched or in any way reacted negatively.

Enslow had guessed that his full, positive attention was required, and any look of fear, disdain or doubt might cost him the chance. Not that it really sounded like it was something he wanted, but it was easier to find a job when you were working, and perhaps having this hanging over his head might spur him to work even harder at getting a job. Worst case, he could do this for a while, because at that level, he could work three months, and save up enough to live for nine. "Well," Enslow said slowly, "I wouldn't be sitting here if I hadn't had the skills you were looking for, and while I don't know everything involved in the day to day activities, I do know that I am an excellent problem solver. So let's cut to the chase. If I am a candidate you are interested in, what would be the next step?"

"Direct. I like that. Should we accept you and offer you the position, we would conduct a background check on you, and you would have to be able to obtain and maintain, a Secret Clearance all the while you work for us. In order to advance or hold certain other positions, you will have to obtain and maintain a Top Secret Clearance. Of course responsibilities and pay go accordingly. But whatever role you are selected for, if any, the work will be challenging and occupy most of your day.

There is nothing to do other than sleep, eat and work. Precious little time to lounge around. Am I clear?"

Enslow considered what Major Hurst just said, and replied, "Yes sir, crystal clear. I understand this will be a hard assignment, but one that would be rewarded as well. How much down time is there?"

Major Hurst, sensing perhaps a fish on the line, said "There is one day or R&R granted for every twenty four days of work, but you can only take it seven days at a time, and no more than fifteen days at a stretch. Travel is your problem, and it can take you up to three days to get stateside. So if you want to take a seven day break, you will really only have one to three days at your destination, the rest is travelling. But with what we are paying you, the travel costs will be no big deal."

Curious, as he knew they were considered to pay well, Enslow popped the inevitable question, "What would that be?"

Major Hurst recited the amount and the qualifiers, "Standard pay for this position is eighty five thousand dollars per year, but we cover transportation costs to the job theatre, housing, food costs, medical, dental and vision costs while there, as well as clothing and your satellite time for personal use, but the amount of time is limited. We suggest you bring your own laptop, and an IP phone for calls back home."

"Eighty five thousand? In this economy that is a generous offer, but I was under the impression that the pay was better than that."

"Well, then there are the incentives. If you are outside of the United States for more than 180 days, all pay earned out of the country is only taxed above eighty eight thousand, and the rest is taxed at standard rates. If you are working for us and your assignment is out of the US, then your pay is multiplied by twenty percent. Then if you are working at a military base, the pay is also increased by ten percent. If you are stationed at a base in a designated 'hot' country, then your pay is multiplied by forty percent. If your assignment is in a combat country, your pay is multiplied by twenty five percent and if you work at a forward area, your pay is increased by twenty five percent."

Thinking for a moment and trying to do the math in his head, Enslow said after fifteen seconds, "That would bring the pay up to two hundred and thirty five thousand a year, less the eighty eight thousand at full rate, and allowing for forty percent taxes, gets you somewhere in the neighborhood of one hundred sixty thousand dollars cash, real pay. With no expenses for living I should be able to bank most of that. Is there a signing bonus?"

Major Hurst could see that Enslow was every bit as sharp as he had believed him to be. He had to walk most people through the cash calculations. While his numbers were a tad low, they were quite close, which was more than many of the applicants could do or could understand up to this point in the process. "No," he answered, "there is no signing bonus. But there is a retention pay program that equals fifty percent or your base pay AFTER you serve a second contract."

"So another forty grand-ish after a second year?"

"At the start of a second year contract."

"Oh," said Enslow surprised, "That is better I was thinking it was at the end of a second year. What would you like to know?"

Major Hurst opened a file folder to his right, on the top of the desk, and took out a stack of papers. "What I have here," he said as he handed the stack to Enslow, "is a personality test and some of the specific questions we have regarding your responses to specific work situations. I'd like you to go through the door there," he gestured with his right hand, pointing, "and I'd like you fill out as many answers as you can. After thirty minutes, I will open the door and collect your papers. When we have reviewed your answers and if you are selected, we will call you with a job offer along the lines of what we have discussed. If selected, you will have three days to agree to our employment terms. Good luck." Major Hurts stood up and waved his hand at the door, indicating that Enslow needed to step through and begin.

Enslow got up, and said "Thank you." He walked through the door, to a rather drab office with a small table, and a chair, and a desk holder full of pens. As the door closed, he looked at his watch, and sat down to begin the test. The questions were fairly standard personality and situational questions that Enslow felt the best way to go was to answer them quickly and honestly. These tests often had ways of tripping you up if you thought too much about the answers. Working quickly and as methodically as he could, he read each question, briefly reflected on his answer, put it down, and went to the next one. In all too short a time, Major Hurst entered, collected his papers, and escorted him back to the front desk where he collected his pass, and thanked him for his time saying that he would be notified one way or the other.

Enslow walked out, thinking he had done well, but more worried that he got the job. His wife would definitely NOT like to have him going into harm's way in a foreign theater of war. Not that he would see any combat, he would likely be safely tucked away on some base, but just that he was not at home, and in a hostile environment, would likely worry her. He would explain to her that he was doing it FOR her, however, not because he wanted to be there. That was the cold hard fact of the current world. If you were over forty, you were out of work, or likely to be the next one to be out of work; take what you can get, he thought. He hoped she would understand, that as a man, a husband and a father he had no choice, but to do whatever was required to fulfill that obligation. He need not have worried. Ella knew her husband too well, and knew that he was not prone to bad judgment. He was correct, she didn't like it, but he also knew that in this economy there was not likely going to be anything that paid more than half of what he used to make. Deep in her heart though, she was going to worry.

Nigel Day 245

Unable to sleep well, Nigel got up a bit earlier than his alarm was set for. He stood up from his bed, stretched and heard his joints pop. He then cocked his head sideways and popped his neck bones. Feeling a bit looser, he made his way into the kitchen, if you could call it that, and made a cup of coffee. He hated the taste of it. Nasty bitter stuff, but it usually did the trick and woke him up, a natural benefit of the caffeine, and the fact he still hated the taste of it. Opening the bread, he put two slices in the toaster, and pressed the lever down, and could hear the current flowing through the old and cheap appliance. When it finally performed its task and the warm toast popped up, he spread a bit of jam on it. While chewing it, he noticed the mouse he was aware of that was sharing his flat, had scurried across the floor and was hiding just beyond the light near the bin. Nigel tore off a bit of crust and tossed it to his roommate, who dodged the missile only to return to it and sit up on his haunches and start chewing. When he was finished he looked at Nigel with his black eyes, and acted as if they were old friends, and could he have some more?

"Not today my friend, make your own bloody

breakfast," he said quietly.

When his morning meal and coffee were consumed, Nigel made his way to the decrepit and crumbling shower, turned on the hot water, which was never really hot and had a distinct rusty smell to it, and took a quick shower, making sure to wash his hair and do a proper job of hygiene. When his shower was finished, and you could always tell it was because the water would turn cold, he went over to the sink, which, like the shower and mirror, had all seen better days. He carefully shaved and took extra time to make sure that he did not cut himself. He grabbed the bottle of mouthwash when he was finished and gargled loudly, spitting out the minty waste with equal aplomb.

Walking out to his desk, he logged on to his computer, and punched up the previous map route he calculated, and sent the map to his phone. In twenty seconds, his phone buzzed to indicate that it had received the mail. Seemed easy enough, and better than the headaches of getting on a plane. Besides, he had the new car to shake down. *Let's see, get to the A201, then the A2, the A20, the M20, Exit 11a at the Chunnel, then A16, then E15, and straight on to Paris, then follow the voice prompts to the hotel. Dinner is at 7:30, reception follows, so figure five hours, maybe five and a half, plus hotel check in, additional traffic, parking, arrive thirty minutes early, get dressed, he would need about eight hours to make it safe, damn,*

its already ten o'clock, better get popping, you laggard.
In less than fifteen minutes, Nigel had packed his
new tuxedo, added a full day's extras, socks, etc.,
and grabbed his laptop, phone, charger, and his
mission details. He was about to gather up all of
his things and go to his Mercedes, when he took the
plate he hadn't finished and dumped its remaining
contents on the floor. "Sorry," he said, "didn't
mean to forget about you. My luck you'll be more
loyal than Greyfriar's Bobby." Then he grabbed all
the gear and went through the door, placing his
things on the pockmarked and crumbling concrete,
locked the door, stooped down to repurchase his
laid goods, and after looking around to see who
might be watching, went to his red Mercedes and
placed everything in the back seat. Shutting the
door quietly, he then opened the front and hauled
himself into the driver's seat and gently shut the
door, mindful to not make too much noise.

Nigel twisted the key in the ignition, and the
car sprang to life, idling smoothly. He pulled his
mobile from his pocket, and spoke to it "Trip1." In
a few seconds, the mobile started speaking, and
said "Turn left in 100 meters," which would put
Nigel on the A201, and then to the A2, into the A20,
becoming the M20 and on to the Channel Tunnel.
Then just a leisurely drive down the E15. He'd have
to watch for those bloody awful speed cameras
though. Somewhere around Feuillères, and another
near Ressons-sur-Matz, and yet another just before

Romainville. He didn't want to attract any undue attention, with his plates being bodged up from his printer. So he settled in for a dull four hundredish kilometer drive. *It will be nice to get the car on the road and shake it down.* As he got on the A2, he started to play with the cameras and monitors. Except for the times when there was direct sunlight on them, they worked rather well. He needed to ask Suresh to put in a dimmer for night time driving. Until he chanced to twist the mirror attenuating stalk, and discovered that it did just that. *I'll need to see that he gets more compensation. Just brilliant.* Deciding that he wanted to hear some music and feeling the need for something just a little less pop, he selected Bond, that astonishingly gorgeous quartet who played strings in a way that no one else did.

The drive to the Chunnel was uneventful. His red car blended well enough, except that he only saw a few red cars. If the need arose to change to silver, that would make it very hard for others to find him. He got there in time for the car transport and after loading his car; he relaxed for the thirty five minute or so trip across the channel. To be exact, the trip under the Chunnel. After unloading he was once again the master of his own ship. The rest of the drive was also completely boring. The speed traps were uneventful also. Always helped knowing where they were.

Nigel arrived at his hotel around 5:15 and pulled up to the front where the typically efficient if not contemptuously disdainful French hotel staff swarmed over his car, extracting his luggage and taking his keys to park the car almost in one fluid motion. Nigel tipped the staff a bit over standard, but portrayed a look of near indifference on his face that communicated "Leave me alone, keep my stuff safe." A twenty-something young man, probably of Moroccan descent, drove the red Mercedes away to an underground parking spot, and brought the keys back to the front desk. The front desk clerk was friendly and professional, but Nigel suspected that he didn't quite like the middle-aged Brit in front of him, just on general principals. No matter. Nigel signed in, presented his ID and payment card, and directed the hotel lackey to take his luggage to his room. Nigel made his way to the bar and ordered a drink; might as well start the night off properly.

While sipping his drink, Nigel watched the bar to see who was coming or going, but where he didn't want to be obvious, he practiced watching reflections in his glass or took quick note when he raised and lowered his glass. Forty three people in the room, seventeen women and twenty six men. The man at the second table hadn't turned the page he was reading for ten minutes, which suggested to Nigel he might be someone else who was doing what he was doing. He had no wedding ring, but had a mark where it had been. Just then, a younger man came in and sat next to the reader. From Nigel's vantage point, he could see the older man shift his weight, and saw the younger man touch his thigh under the table. Rather discreet, but perhaps not enough. He had no idea who the man was or what line of work he was in, but guessed he was a gardener. Nigel finished his surveillance and left the bar to go outside to the balcony, overlooking the busy streets of Paris. He turned his micro blue tooth ear comm on and in a few seconds it paired with his phone. Using his hand in his pocket, he pressed the autodial and soon he heard a familiar voice on his comm. "Kingston here. Stat rep Aardvark."

"I will be leaving for the party in forty five minutes. Any further orders?"

"Make sure and speak to a tall Russian, Vladimir Konstantinov. He is tall, mid to late thirties, missing the tip of his right hand little finger. Believed to be involved in arms smuggling in Chechnya. His date will be a tall blonde Ukrainian model, Svetlana Olesky. She has clearly defined attributes. You will likely see her first."

Fancy that, some honesty for once.

Kingston continued, "Stay till approximately 11:00, any later may look suspicious. Use your best judgment. If the crowd is not thinning, then stay. Remember your cover as a computer services executive. We have a service answering calls from your business card number."

Nigel assumed that all calls were going to be traced, and anything notable, would be kept from him. "Roger that. Anything else?"

"That is all. We suggest you stay the night in your hotel and check out at a normal morning hour, then return to your flat."

"Is that advisable? Any idea who was there?" It took an obvious three extra seconds for Kingston to respond, and that was unsettling.

"It was a raid by the local constabulary. They had the wrong apartment. The target of their raid was the apartment above you."

"Confirmed Kingston, Aardvark out," but Nigel knew better. It was just too easy to have it be a mistaken raid. Nigel suspected it was the team that had followed him a few days before, but he never got a satisfactory answer for why they were following him. Nigel thought it was part of his ongoing training at first, but now he was having doubts. If he could get a lead on any of them, he might be able to discover who they were. All he really had that was useful was the picture he took with his mobile phone camera. He thought about asking Kingston for an identity search, but if they were in on it, that would serve no purpose. *File it away. You will get another crack at them.*

All that Kingston used to convey their conversation departure was a beep and a click on the call. Hardly polite, but coldly professional. Nigel had to remind himself that he was a bit player in this vignette of deceit. He didn't know what the true objective was or even if there was one. All of this may have just been a test. Take this Vladimir and his plonk. They may work for the company and are there to test Nigel. It was always a game of one up or a test, or a complete circle jerk waste of time. He was getting paid to do just as he was told, and he was going to see that he matched their orders and expectations.

Nigel walked back through the tables, now starting to fill up, and walked across the polished marble floor of the lobby, noticing how the marble looked like it was from Italy, but possibly Greece. He took the elevator to his room, where he put on his service tuxedo in less than ten minutes and left his room, locking the door. A delightful older couple held the door for him on the elevator and he responded by holding the door for them when it reached the main floor, she apparently had some mobility problems. When he made it to the big lobby door, he walked outside and shouted to the valets "OY! Lads, red Mercedes." The ever eager university student scampered away to fetch his car. Only moments passed before he heard the now familiar sound of the exhaust of his car and the just perceptible whine of the supercharger, come around the corner and pull up to the curb where a dashing and dapper Nigel stood in his tuxedo. Smiling in a friendly way, he passed a couple of ten Euro notes to the young man who handed him his keys and held his door for him. Slamming the door gently shut, Nigel pressed the accelerator and moved into traffic, headed toward the Belgian Embassy. He pulled up to the gate, and a polite but crisp young woman asked him in French if she could see his invitation. *Here goes my first test.* She looked at the invitation and asked him again in French if she could see his identification.

"Just a minute, love, ah, here it is."

"Pardon me, monsieur, I presumed you were French." She added a metallic sticker to his invitation, and told him to pull up to the curb, and a valet would park his car. Smiling in a friendly way, but at the same time conveying the annoyance of someone of his stature, he gently moved the car to the curb as asked and for the second time today turned his motor over to a complete stranger. Not wishing to appear too concerned, he turned his head away as his car drove off and walked up a short run of stairs to the front door, where a very well built and polite man asked for his invitation. Without looking at it, and using his peripheral vision, Nigel noted the CCTV camera watching him, but gave it no notice. The man holding his invitation looked at the metallic tag on the ticket, and eyed Nigel for a few seconds, checked his list, and told him, "Thank you, please step inside."

Nigel could hardly contain himself, he had done it. His invitation and ID had passed and he was in. *Maybe tonight will go off without a hitch.* His comm chattered to life, and Kingston said, "Well done. We were monitoring you from across the street, and we have tapped into the embassy CCTV feeds. We hope to be able to help you tonight."

"I don't need a bloody babysitter," Nigel hissed.

"Perform your assignment and go home. We'll alert you when we see Konstantinov. Stick to the meme we've created."

"Again with the nagging," a terser Nigel said.

Nigel made his way to the ballroom through the grand hallway. Originally, the mansion had been the home of a French plantation owner whose Indochina plantations had made him wealthy. On one trip he had contracted cholera, however, and died shortly thereafter. He had inherited his father's holdings after the Franco-Siamese War of 1893, where his father had been assassinated by his Vietnamese courtesan. She, in turn, was shot by his bodyguard. Rather a lurid tale that had all the papers in Paris serializing the affair. The story was filled with errors however, as the press never let a good story get in the way of the facts.

Entering the ballroom, Nigel walked over to the first person who in his estimation might be a good starting point, stuck out his hand, and said "Allo, I'm Nigel Jones. It's a pleasure to meet you."

The rather startled gentleman, looked down at Nigel's outstretched hand, looked back at Nigel, took the offered hand and said "Hello. I am Bertrand Molyneux. It is a pleasure to meet you Nigel. You are British, no?"

"I am British yes; Scottish on me mum's side. I'm in Computer Services. We made a nice donation to some charity, and my boss couldn't make it at the last minute, so the obligation passed to me."

"Even in this economy, there is always room for outsourcing and such. Are you staying busy?"

Nigel responded, "There are ups and down of course, but on the whole, we seem to be making our numbers."

Bertrand looked impressed, "Perhaps we could do some business. I know of some government contracts coming up."

"That would be fabulous! Here is my card; call me anytime and we can discuss." Nigel handed a crisp new card to Bertrand, who took it and passed one back.

"Excellent, I look forward to speaking with you in the future," Bertrand said, to which Nigel bowed his head ever so slightly, and said "Merci beaucoup".

One down, seventy four to go, and before he could even finish his thoughts his comm said into his ear, "Aardvark, nicely done." Nigel said nothing, but checked his watch and walked straight ahead to an Asian gentleman and repeated his approach and a bit of small talk. Again, the exchanging of cards took place. Kingston did not comment after every approach or disengagement, but only made comments that seemed to reinforce Nigel's technique. If they felt he could have done something better, they seldom said so. On a few occasions, they were able to identify pending approaches and informed Nigel who he was about to talk to, with their name, company, or even key events from their towns, such as construction projects, sports scores, etc. When confronted with someone who seems to know you, most people will suddenly act glad to see you, lest they seem embarrassed to not know who you are when you seem to know them. So most of those encounters seemed to be quite warm and genuine, but you never know, sometimes it can also bring unwarranted attention, making Nigel place his trust in Kingston, to make sure that they knew what they were doing and who they were selecting for this specific treatment.

Nigel said to his comm, "I'm getting hungry and thirsty. I am going to grab a quick bite and a glass. Confirm."

The familiar, dispassionate computerized voice he knew as Kingston responded with, "Confirmed. We are going off air for twenty minutes. We will be shifting to another satellite. Kingston out."

Nigel made his way over to the bar where he asked for "Scotch, neat," and as he waited for the bartender to complete his request, a voice behind him said "Hello, Nigel?"

Turning around, he saw a smiling face he did not recognize, "Sorry, have we met?"

"No," came the reply. "I'm Lester Wyndham. I'm a security consultant for business executives. I was speaking with Bertrand Molyneux and he seemed to think you might be able to use our services." Lester handed Nigel a card and Nigel reciprocated with his own.

"Hadn't thought about it much. 'Spose it might be worth looking into. What precisely do you do?"

Lester informed Nigel, "We do physical threat assessment, background checks, and armed escort for those people like diamond merchants, all manner of physical security audits. Is there a time we could talk? Perhaps next week at your office?"

Nigel looked up and to the left, a sign to people who were used to reading body language that Nigel was being truthful, and said "Now that you mention it, it is a much more dangerous world. Next week, actually the next whole month is rather difficult, but I would be interested in discussing it further."

"That would be great. We may not be the least expensive providers, but we pride ourselves on offering the best value proposition for what we provide, which is confidence and peace of mind. In a dangerous world, it is just smart to be safe and sure," Lester pitched.

"You know, what would work for me is someone who could help me do a background check on potential players before meetings. Could you do background checks with as little information as a picture?"

"Well," Lester said, with just enough pause to give himself some wiggle room in his promises, "We often can."

Nigel leaned forward, to simulate interest and excitement, and said, "The other day, I saw one of those new Porsches, you know, the GTR? And when I looked at my camera phone, I completely missed the car, and snapped some bloke who was looking at it too. Could you do a check on his identity to test how well your services work? If you are as good as you say you are, I could see us engaging your services for all of our executives."

"Fabulous!" Lester said with the excitement that only came with the promise of a big score, "Do you want to send it to me?"

"Tell you what, I can send it right now, Is this your mobile number on the card?"

Lester responded "Yes, go ahead and send it."

After navigating the menu on his mobile, Nigel said "Done. Send me as much information as you can get and I'll check it out with our internal folk, and if it matches, we can likely do a deal."

"I'll get back to you as soon as I can. It will be a

pleasure doing business with you."

Nigel smiled and stuck out his hand, to make a firm shake. "I look forward to it as well." *Now I may find out who those bastards were that were chasing me.* Because the Porsche story was made up. The picture he sent Lester was the face he snapped of one of his pursuers. If Lester was as good as he said he was then he might get an answer. He could have asked Kingston to look for the person, but they had acted so uninterested in the whole thing that he had been reluctant to tell them he had a picture of one of them.

The next hour was spent shaking more hands. Kingston came back online and made a few inputs, but mostly Nigel was doing one of the things he did best, being Nigel. It was almost nine o'clock, and he still had not seen Konstantinov. When he had a chance to raise his glass to take a drink and speak into it, to mask his talking to Kingston, he said quietly, "Any sight of Konstantinov yet?"

Kingston responded, "Negative."

Nigel was standing to the side, much like a schoolboy at a dance, who had no partner. Kingston piped in, "Don't stand there. Keep moving."

Nigel countered with, "Konstantinov is close."

He also pulled out his phone as if he were making a call, he sensed that he was about to get into a bit of an argument, and would not be able to have a conversation without attracting attention.

"We have no track on him, where is he?"

"Dunno."

Now Kingston was getting impatient, "Then how do you know he is close?"

God I've still got it. "I can see Svetlana Olesky; Konstantinov has got to be close."

Kingston seemed confused, "We don't have a track on her. She isn't in the direction you are looking, and we have a cam pointed in that direction."

Nigel was disappointed in his handlers; were they blind? He retorted "I'm not looking at her. She is to my left, and I can see her with my peripheral vision."

Kingston said, "Aardvark, you are good, but no one can make a positive ID without direct viewing."

"Well, lads, unless I am mistaken, her dairy cannons entered my field of vision whole moments

174

before she did. Blimey, you sure did understate her attributes."

Back in their control center, Kingston was able to pan left and saw that in fact, Nigel was correct; he had picked up Svetlana Olesky from the side. Konstantinov was almost thirty seconds behind her, and he appeared at her side, grinning like a Cheshire cat.

"Think she is pretty?" Kingston inquired.

"Posh bird, but other than the eye candy, does she have a purpose?"

"Aardvark, that is either her purpose or she has another one. You make the call." Kingston intimated that her other skills might be less than professional. Or on further reflection, extremely professional.

Nigel considered for a moment, his quarry. The flashy skirt with the jiggling mountains told Nigel that Konstantinov was a vain man, determined to flaunt either his wealth, power or to compensate for an internal lack of confidence, so he needed to parade around with this trophy on his arm. Nigel wanted confirmation as to the contact with Konstantinov. "What precisely do you want, just to observe or to make contact and speak to him?"

Kingston explained, "The parameters have changed. You are to observe if you can, who he interacts with. Watch his body language. What things does he notice? What does he drink? We want you to work up a profile. Submit a report and we will compare it to our standard workup. He is a field test for you. Pass this, and we will consider moving you from peacock to operative level 1."

Nigel asked, "And what level would that be, pay wise?"

The response came back "GS16, with an operative's level one field account, and additional expense considerations."

Nigel said nothing, considering for a moment what would be involved. Konstantinov took Svetlana off to the side, made his way to the table where he wanted to sit, and signaled for a waiter to bring him his drinks. *Ok, he's in control and saying so.* Nigel continued observing, noting that Konstantinov did not tip the waiter and seemed dismissive of the serving staff. He also did not speak to Svetlana, at least not conversationally. She appeared to be at the night's events for her own reasons, which might be at odds with Konstantinov's true motives. Suddenly Svetlana got up and left the room, not too slowly, and Konstantinov seemed a bit agitated and followed her. Without realizing why, he followed them. When they got to a side hallway, an argument started, with Konstantinov becoming more irritated. Although he was speaking in Russian, there was no mistaking his hand on her arm, twisting it, and the angry glare from his eyes. Ever the observer, Nigel also noticed the heavily furrowed brow, and lips turned down. Not a happy man. Her eyes told a story as well. She did not like him and regretted being here. When he pressed his point, whatever it was, with an additional twist of her arm, she grimaced and let out a bit of a small whimpering scream. When his grip relaxed, she swung her palm at him, slapping him square in the cheek. He bellowed and swung at her with his palm, intending to land a blow she would not be able to duck, and one that would teach her a lesson. His palm arced through the air, accelerating and aiming at her and would have connected with that delicate Ukrainian cheek, but for a third hand that stopped his arm by grabbing the wrist and arresting it inches from her face.

"Vat the hell are you doing?" Vladimir Konstantinov bellowed, "Just who the hell are you? This is none of your concern."

Nigel let go of his wrist, removed his other hand from her arm, and inserted himself between her and Konstantinov. "The lady doesn't deserve this treatment. A man with your stature doesn't need to treat her this way. I'd like you to apologize to her, NOW," Nigel said, his voice delivered sternly, but low key, his quantum blue eyes never blinking, and he leaned even closer to Konstantinov than straight men are usually comfortable with.

"I asked you a question. Who are you? This is none of your concern" Konstantinov hissed.

"I am Nigel Sinclair Jones. I know you are commed. I'll wait for your team to tell you who I am and then if you want, you can swing at me, but know two things, you will not hit this woman again, and be sure you want to swing at me. It won't end well for you." Nigel's eyes had not blinked still, and his nostrils were flared.

Konstantinov glared back at him and was obviously listening to an ear comm and was getting, figuratively, an ear full. His facial expression broke after a few seconds, and his body became less rigid. Then his eyebrows quivered slightly in what can best be described as raising them. Nigel had no idea what was being said, but he could guess. Konstantinov became almost apologetic.

"You are correct, Mr. Jones, I overreacted. I behaved poorly, and in a manner not becoming a gentleman. Thank you for pointing out my error."

"That's all very nice, but it's not me you need to apologize to," with a nod of his head, he gestured at Svetlana, who seemed to understand nothing of what was being said, but when Vladimir spoke to her in Russian, she smiled and responded in a polite tone. She then turned on her oh so shapely legs, and walked back into the main ballroom.

"Watch yourself. I shall not forgive or forget your impertinence," Konstantinov spat.

Nigel again closed the distance between himself and the Russian, and said, "Sometimes, in life, the only winning move is not to play. I'm not your enemy. If you want to see what he looks like, look in the mirror. Know this: I will not be watched, followed, catalogued, traced or in any way fucked with. Bigger men than you have tried."

"I shall have to ask them what they could improve upon," Konstantinov snarled.

"Then you will likely need a Ouija board," Nigel responded.

"And vy is dat?" the now rattled Russian barked.

"Dead men tell no tales."

"You westerners. Always the cowboys. You

179

confuse bravado with righteousness. What makes you so sure you will see the bullet coming?"

Nigel considered the absurdity of the situation, and responded "I have neither the time nor interest in measuring our dicks. But I won't need a bullet. I'll use whatever I find at my feet. Don't incur my wrath. It's terrible and unrelenting. When I am properly pissed off, only God himself can stop me. Now if you'll excuse me, I need another drink." Nigel turned in a casual manner and sauntered back to the ballroom, trying hard not to swagger, but also trying to not appear too casual. Nonchalant was what he was striving for. He was such a bad ass he didn't need to care. Except for the fact that Konstantinov was now likely to want him dead. The key point was that the Russian bought every word of his speech. Konstantinov considered him based on his performance and the intelligence still coming in over his comm, to be a thoroughly dangerous man. Konstantinov was not a man to back down from a challenge which is what he considered Nigel's existence to be.

Kingston said "Aardvark. We only wanted observation, not confrontation. But we must tell you your performance was well executed. We used the sudden change in plans to add tracking devices to Konstantinov's room. But don't ever do that again. Your orders are to be followed to the letter."

Nigel spoke defensively, "Then why didn't you stop me?"

Kingston answered, "You moved too quickly. Had we tried to talk you out of it, you might have become distracted, or worse, let on that you were commed. A good spy always adapts to the current situation; not everything can be planned for."

"In that case, I still have some additional contacts to make to complete my mission parameters, and if Konstantinov comes back, I need to be there to own the space. Anything less would not be in character, correct?" Nigel inquired of a somewhat startled Kingston.

After thirty seconds of dead air, Kingston confirmed "Correct."

Nigel considered several items to be of note. *First there are other assets here, so that bugs could be planted. Second, Konstantinov was not a test, but a mark. Third, he was being watched and he was being tested. The whole evening was a legitimate op. Things are always on a need to know basis, and he didn't need to know. As all plans should be adapted to changing conditions, you seem to have figured out that there is a larger game here.*

Feeling a bit keyed up from the adrenaline in his system, Nigel needed to find a way to burn some energy. As he made his way back to the ballroom, he heard another woman's desperate voice. Although he couldn't understand her, he thought a second white knight routine would be a sporting bit of fun. He walked in through the kitchen entrance, where he saw half of the orchestra, surrounding another man whose hand was wrapped in a towel, soaked in blood. "Oy! What's going on?" he shouted.

The petite singer, in the best English she could speak, said, "It is nothing monsieur; a member of the orchestra had slipped and cut his hand. Do not trouble yourself."

"Oh, sorry to intrude. Will it interfere with your playing tonight? I thought you were brilliant."

Her face seemed to drop a little in a sad sort of way, "Yes, it will. Miguel is our only piano player, and the other members consider it unlucky to play when a member has been hurt."

Sensing a way to burn off the adrenaline he had built up over the last ten minutes, Nigel said excitedly, "I can play."

Seeing her eyes start to sparkle, then fade, he was ready for her excuse. Before she could offer one, he said to her, "I am really quite good, love. Give me a chance. On my family honor, I shall not let you down."

"Very well and thank you monsieur," she said her eyes again sparkling, "We shall start to play again in ten. Be back in ten minutes."

Giving a slight bow, Nigel said "I will go and warm up." He dashed out so quickly that no one was able to stop him. Nigel walked to the end of the room where all the instruments lay, sat on the bench, and began to play. Instead of Bach, Mozart or Brahms, however, the music he chose was what he liked. When he alone went to the piano, some people watched to see what a single man in a tuxedo was doing at the piano, but most took no notice of him. At first. Because the music he played was like nothing that had ever been played before at such an event. Classical was fine, and the backbone of civilized society. In his youth however, Nigel had chanced upon some old 78s. That was the music that spoke to him. When he was old enough to play, he searched for every example of it that he could find. He then branched out to its variants. As the first few notes began to play some of the crowd turned their heads. By the time the second measure was played, almost all eyes were on him. Before half the song was finished, half of the people were smiling. Nigel was quite adept at the American styles of Ragtime, Boogie Woogie, Stride and Swing. The music that burst forth was from the brilliant minds of composers most of the audience had never heard of. Composers like Jelly Roll Morton, Fats Waller, Scott Joplin, Duke Ellington, Cab Calloway and the Boswell Sisters. Nigel played for over seventy five minutes before he looked up to discover that the diplomatic crowd had been dancing and having one of the best times that anyone could remember at these functions. Only some of the musicians had joined him, but they had indulged in a good old fashioned jam session. They didn't know what he was playing but they liked it, and added their own talents and creativity to the music. Sweating thoroughly, Nigel stood up and bowed to the people gathered in the ballroom and then he bowed to the musicians who had joined him. In a most undiplomatic manner, the gathered captains of industry, diplomats and minor heads of state, broke out in a strong and thunderous round of applause.

"Well, that went rather well," Nigel said without realizing he had said it. "I'm sorry about the music. I felt I needed to own the night," Nigel said, trying to justify his ragtime recital.

Kingston briskly confirmed, "You did. Kingston out."

Nigel waved to the various people and took their congratulations, acting as humbly as he knew how. That was also a first for him. He couldn't remember ever being humble.

Agent Logan Day 248

Agent Logan thought long and hard about the old axiom, "Be careful what you wish for, you might get it." He had found Maria to be abrasive, rude, dictatorial and perhaps even cruel. What her agenda was he never quite knew but he wished he was working back with her. Eight days ago he had made what he thought was an innocent comment of disappointment when their operation failed in isolating and interrogating a person of interest to the intelligence community. Their target on the M4 proved to be more than they thought. They were expecting a simple 'placeholder' agent, and instead he had training in surveillance, detection, pursuit driving as well as tactics and avoidance. Clearly a higher level operative than they were told he would be. He had just wanted a different assignment, any assignment, other than working with her.

Now he was deep in shit however, and it was at neck height. He was hiding behind the front wheel and engine block of his disabled Chevrolet Suburban, trapped now in a firefight that came out of a routine intercept that had gone bad. Lying at his feet was a man he never really knew, Agent Stefan Widmer. Widmer had seemed like a decent guy, but he never got the chance to know him and he never would. Agent Widmer was lying at his feet in a pool of his own blood with at least ten bullet wounds, two in the head. Two hundred feet away were three Albanian drug smugglers, and four other bad guys he could not identify. He was outnumbered seven to one and he was running out of ammunition. Before the radio in his Suburban was disabled he put out an agent in distress call. He hoped help was on the way, but it didn't look like they would arrive in time. If you've ever heard of the mean streets, they didn't get meaner than this.

It was an industrial area more or less abandoned and people here minded their own business. Gunshots were not uncommon although one would think the volumes of shots going on this time, something big was occurring and that alone might elicit a call to the authorities. Not that the British police were equipped to handle a situation like this. It probably didn't really matter. The fact was that his ammunition was running out. It didn't matter anymore to Agent Widmer. He had taken two shots, one in the thigh, and one in the abdomen. He had used his belt as a tourniquet to stave off the blood loss to his leg but the one in the abdomen was slowly letting his life slip away. As he resigned himself to his fate he wished he could tell is parents that he loved them. He knew they were proud of him even though they were not quite sure what he did. All they knew was that he was a

Marine who had moved on to another government career and he had enrolled in some kind of government service and there were things he couldn't talk about. He had told his father that he was now doing stuff to keep this country safe, to keep them safe.

He was starting to weaken and knew the end was close. He fired his last shot, and knew the seven assailants would soon charge his position, but something wasn't right. Something he could hear was out of place. It just didn't make any sense, except, oh yeah, or in an industrial district what he heard was the sound of a large industrial diesel engine installed on some kind of a truck accelerating very hard. He had now slumped down by the wheel. The group of seven seeing that his rate of fire was weakening or over assumed he was running out of ammunition or he had been hit. They were starting to break cover and advance on his position and take him out for good. The sound of the diesel engine became louder. All of a sudden, the east wall of the warehouse opposite his attackers burst open like one of those popcorn things covered in foil you cook on your. As the popcorn heated up, the foil expanded and would stretch and eventually burst, and popcorn flew out. That was exactly how the wall of the warehouse looked as the wall of steel burst open and a medium sized mobile crane powered through it at ludicrous speed.

He stared at it incredulously, wondering what happened. Had the brakes slipped? Had the driver had a seizure? Who was this madman who would drive through a building? His attackers were equally amazed and also unable to move, much to their detriment and with unfortunate results. Because this crane weighed forty thousand pounds and was traveling at fifty miles an hour as it burst through the wall of the warehouse, and it was pointed straight at them. They scarcely had time to react. One of them almost got away but went directly under the front quad tire. This was one of those cranes that had multiple wheels up front and in the rear and could steer in almost any direction. If this guy was worried about his waist and fitting into his jeans, it was no longer going to be a problem. He not only could fit into these jeans, but quite likely he could fit under the door of any building he had ever been to.

The remaining six raised their weapons and poured round after round into the crane. Due to the sudden nature of the crane's appearance, their aim was off. In the excitement and haste they should've been running for their lives. It is this very thought that crossed their feeble little minds as they realized all was lost and they tried to duck for cover. The game was over and it was too late. The forty thousand pound crane traveling at fifty miles an hour continued to accelerate and was dragging about half of the warehouse wall with it, scraping on the ground in a stupendous shower of sparks. It plowed into, then over their vehicles with most of them gruesomely sandwiched between all the bits of crane, wall, and their now crushed transportation. Two of the vehicles were now compressed into a weird sculpture.

One would hardly want to paint a critically graphic picture of the event; however, it was an interesting item to note that in this collision at least two of the men between the vehicles extruded their organs through their mouths much as one would squeeze a tube of toothpaste. It was easy to see they would never sing again. The rear door of the crane opened and a forty something gentleman got out and stepped down from the structure. He surveyed his handiwork and saw no need for further action as the gunmen were all quite dead. He calmly walked over to the mess of the vehicles with one vehicle having vomited its occupants from the back out onto the chipped and stained concrete.

The crane operator walked over to where an undamaged Suburban was and found the agents. One was quite dead. His color was looking pale and his eyes glazing over with no discernable pulse. The other was also quite pale and had a very bad wound to the right thigh that was tied off with a belt. It was the wound to the stomach area that was of concern though. It had only bled a bit which indicated that it was bleeding internally. Agent Logan was barely conscious. As his eyes were able to focus, he suddenly recognized who was helping him into the only undamaged ride around them. "YOU!" he said, "Why are you helping me?"

"Shhh, we are on the same side" Nigel assured gently, "I am going to get you to a hospital."

"We aren't on the same side. I'm CIA. You are someone's asset we've been tracking. Who do you work for? GCHQ?"

"I'm a birdwatcher."

"We suspected you might be Box 850. What kind of work do you do?"

"I do C4I. Command, Control, Communications, Computers, and Intelligence."

"Not buying it" Logan said slowly, his vision was starting to fade and his arms were so heavy. "You handled the Evade and Escape as well as any field agent. I pegged you as a wheel artist. Fact is we lost you clean. I heard you slipped out of our floating box in London a few days later. I got curious so I pulled your file. Man that is some of the best window dressing I have ever seen. They are still not sure what your game is or what level you are."

"Bloody hell, I have a file? What next, teenage girls throwing their knickers at me?" Nigel smirked, and then a bit more seriously, "What do you believe?"

Logan drew a breath and did not respond. After thirty seconds he said, "Not sure, but am convinced you are living in a wilderness of mirrors." Desperately trying to focus on Nigel's face, he asked "Why are you helping me? It would have been easier to leave me."

"A friend of mine, a Marine named Ramón , once told me dying is easy. It's living that's hard. Call me stubborn, I just didn't want to see one more Marine die," Nigel said calmly to Logan.

Logan looked into that quantum blue eyes "How'd you know I was a Marine?"

"Once a Marine, always a Marine. Semper Fi," was Nigel's response.

Logan hesitated at the door of the car, and looked Nigel straight in the eye. "I never would have figured you for one of us. But I see it now." He drew in a breath, and said "Nigel, the world is not what it seems. If you think you know what you are doing, you don't. The only people telling you the truth are the people who are lying to you. If someone is your friend, he isn't. The only people you can trust are the ones you can't."

Nigel responded with a grin, "Tell me what I don't know. I covered all of this back at Spy-U. Elemental stuff. I did so well my instructors wanted my papers to be required reading for the course. Would have let them have them too, if I hadn't burned them during Espionage for Beginners."

"A spy with a sense of humor. I need a favor from you. I only ask because I don't think I am going to make it. I can feel myself slipping."

"Listen up Gladys; you do not have permission to leave on my watch. I won't allow it," Nigel commanded.

"In my wallet, under a leather flap, is my parent's real address. Tell them how I died, at least what you can. Tell them I love them," Agent Logan said, his voice now quite weak, coming in short bursts. Nigel removed the wallet and took out the phone number then returned the wallet to Logan's pocket.

"You will tell them yourself. You don't get off that easy. I thought you were a Marine, not some fluffy nancy boy."

The smashed bits of SUVs, cars, wall and crane

had started to smolder. All that mechanical mayhem had undoubtedly caused a fuel leak or some short from the batteries was causing a fire. They had made it to the SUV and Nigel helped Logan into the rear seat and used Logan's jacket to support his head. As he bundled it up, he could feel the mobile phone in the breast pocket. He slipped it out and then put it in his pocket. *Might get something useful from that, perhaps some good numbers in there.* Perhaps it was his training, perhaps it was his computer experiences or perhaps, he was just a clever bastard, but Nigel never missed an opportunity to grab some intel. He leaned over to Logan, whose breathing was slowing. "Logan," he said softly, "I'm taking you to the hospital now. I need to shut down your mobile's security; and it will interfere with the equipment. What is your code?"

Logan kept his eyes closed but whispered "Seven-Seven-One-Two-Five-pound-pound-star. It's L5." Nigel knew that L5 security was 4096 bit encryption and he would never decode the SIMM card without the code. He hoped whatever was left of Logan was telling him the truth.

"Logan, if I need to contact you, I'll go by the name Calico. Got that?"

Logan whispered so low that Nigel had to put his ear next to Logan's lips, where he heard him repeat, "Calico." He walked over to the now smoldering mass of vehicles, crane, and squashed antagonists, took out Logan's mobile phone, and calmly took pictures of the vehicles plates, and the faces or what was left of the faces. Where there was some question as to the original configuration of the face, Nigel was able to get a close up picture of the fingerprints. Near the now quite disabled vehicle, were three large duffle bags, bulging with their contents. Reaching down and picking up the three bags, Nigel briskly brought them back to the only remaining operational vehicle without looking at their contents.

Realizing he had missed something, Nigel ran back to the agent's disabled SUV and using one of the flares he found in its road kit, started a fire in its back seat and grabbed Agent Widmer in a fireman's carry. Walking back to his waiting ride, Nigel placed Agent Widmer into the passenger seat and hooked up his safety belt. Not that his passenger would ever need the security the belt offered, but Nigel needed to move the body and couldn't have it flopping about. He decided to leave that agent's phone alone. One missing phone could be possible; two phones were a dead giveaway. He popped off the battery to Logan's phone, so it couldn't be traced. Nigel started the SUV and grabbed his own mobile, and selected voice commands. "Find Hospital," and his mobile device plotted the path. Jamming his foot down on the accelerator he propelled the five thousand pound vehicle down the decaying industrial road toward the exit where Nigel followed the driving directions now being spoken out loud by his mobile phone. As they pulled away, flames finally erupted and began to consume the wrecks behind them making identification of the bodies much harder. Driving at speeds sometimes in excess of one hundred miles per hour and usually fifty percent above the posted limits, Nigel piloted the SUV to the nearest hospital in less than 18 minutes. He had called ahead and had a trauma team waiting, and as he pulled up, they were, in fact there. Sliding to a stop, he jumped out and yelled "Front and back. Two men have been shot and have lost a lot of blood!" The trauma teams rushed to the SUV, flung the doors open and gently if not quickly, extracted both agents from the vehicle, secured then in gurneys and rushed the men inside.

The security official who always attended a shooting, asked "Who are you and how did they get shot?"

Nigel looked at him with a steely stare, and barked at him, "Sorry. Crown's business." Before he could be detained or questioned further he got back in the idling SUV and sped off down the road, heading north back toward where he had stashed his car and taken a taxi closer to the docks to watch the goings on. He stopped at a bridge overpass, got out, and retrieved one of the three large bags he had rescued. Opening it, he saw a sight that caused him to suck in air loudly and let it out slowly. While you might have expected it to be full of weapons or even severed human heads, it was something altogether different. It was full of cash. Each bag held just over eight million dollars in crisp $100 US bills. *Daddy likes.* Seeing that his Mercedes was sitting there undisturbed, he clicked his boot open with the remote and transferred the bags to his car. He went back to the SUV, started it and put it into gear and sent it down the lightly traveled road. The SUV gathered speed and eventually hit a small stone wall and flipped over. Before this little vehicular dance had completed, Nigel's red Mercedes had turned around under the bridge and drove the other way down the street. Hopefully there was no SAT surveillance, and if there was they might not notice him. If they did, he would pull a color change. *Time to go Taxi. Bloody hell, I can afford another entirely different car. I should get back to my roots.* As he ran his fingers through his hair, he said out loud, "Yeah baby, its shagariffic!" The idea occurred to get two cars, a Jaguar and a Mini. "You cheeky bastard. I guess laying low isn't your style. Wait till Kingston finds out," *No, check that, stupid gits don't deserve to know.*

Nigel drove just over six miles before he saw what he wanted, a self wash car wash. He pulled in, closed the bay doors and took out his car keys.

By sawing gently just under the fender, he was able to get up the edge of his chameleon red color. Gently pulling the adhered vinyl wrap off, he was able to change his car from red back to its original silver in less than ten minutes. Then, clicking his remote, popped opened the boot and stuffed the wadded up fake skin inside. He put several coins into the machine, and proceeded to give his car a proper wash, removing most of the adhesive that had remained. When the high pressure sprayer ran out of time, he put the wand back in its holder, turned to face his car, and exclaimed "Brilliant!" *That worked exceedingly well.*

Nigel opened the door and slid in behind the wheel of the once again completely mundane silver Mercedes. Before starting the car, he turned and reached behind him for his go bag, and fished around looking for a mobile phone. When his fingers felt it, he grasped it and removed it quickly. He reached into his jacket pocket and removed a phone number. Checking his mirror to see that no one wanted the car wash, he dialed the number that was handwritten on the paper. After several rings and clicks, common to an international call, a woman answered, "Hello?"

"Hello Mrs. Logan. My name is Thomas Wicker. I need you to go and get a piece of paper and a pen, I'll wait."

"No I've got one here. What is this about?" she asked.

"I need you to listen very closely. I am a friend of your son Keith. I am calling to tell you that he has been badly injured and is at this moment at Royal Mercy Hospital in London, likely in surgery at this minute. He has been working for the government, so they will likely play games with you, but don't let them push you around. I would suggest you leave immediately to see him."

Stunned silence on the other end lasted for fifteen seconds, and a faltering voice asked "Are you serious? Keith has been hurt?"

"He was wounded in service to his country, taking several hits. He was alive when he got to the hospital. Before he passed out, his last thought was of you and his father. He wanted you to know he loved you."

An obviously stunned woman asked again, "Can you tell me the information again?"

"Yes ma'am. I am Thomas Wicker; I am a friend of your son. He is in surgery at Royal Mercy Hospital in London. I suggest you leave immediately. I'm sorry but I can't stay on this line any longer. Call the hospital and ask if a man was brought in, injured on Crown's business. Don't give up on him. I know he'll make it. A lesser man would not have survived it. You should be proud of him."

"Thank you Thomas. Do I have you to thank for getting him to the hospital?"

Nigel said, "Yes ma'am. Good luck." As he drove away, he removed the battery from the phone. Then he pulled out of the car wash, and tossed the phone into the rubbish bin as he passed.

Enslow Unemployed Day 71-90

Enslow started his day like every day. He got up, helped his wife get ready and go out the door. He read his emails looking for that positive one where they wanted to talk to him, but they never appeared. Any emails he received as part of his job search were always "Thank you but…" type emails. Through all of this he was building a good network of people to support him, at least emotionally. It was the financial side that was getting to worry him. If he could get a part time job, he could extend the savings he had. He could calculate exactly how long his money would hold out, unless he suddenly needed a furnace or tires or a root canal. Then the amount of time he could survive was less.

Feelings of being a failure kept creeping over Enslow. It wasn't he who had failed though, it was his executive leadership, his politicians, and the economy in general, but he had not failed. The constant reinforcement he got from Ella was beginning to be the only feeling he had that he could make it. He knew she loved him, but to the degree that she never complained, and always said she believed in him gave him the only reinforcement he got. Dee Dee and Augie brought in there piggy banks and all their Christmas money and offered it to their Dad. They understood what was going on, (it seems they had been spying on their parents), and they hatched a plan to help. Two hundred forty seven dollars was a lot for two small children, but they offered it freely to him. He told them that their generosity was the most wonderful thing he had ever heard of kids doing, and thanked them. He did not take their money but he hugged them very hard. When they walked out happy, Enslow closed the door and started to cry. He struggled not to. The tears were not flowing freely, and he was not sobbing but he did feel hot wet tears sliding down his cheeks. He was proud of his children for wanting to help and he felt ashamed. Ashamed that he was making his family worry. Ashamed that he couldn't provide for his family. Ashamed that he felt like a failure. And ashamed that for one brief instant, he thought about letting his kids give him their money. He realized that whether he was going to admit it or not he was in trouble. He was going to have to find something to do and soon. Enslow realized he was heading into a dark and dangerous area and he needed to avoid it.

It was his eightieth day of looking for work. He had applied to almost three thousand jobs and had nine interviews face to face and a dozen or so phone interviews. His favorite was the one where they wanted fifteen years of industry experience and a master's degree and they were offering thirty five thousand dollars a year. He politely told the nice lady that he appreciated her calling him, but that he could make another ten thousand dollars a year and get free soda being an assistant manager at the local Gas and Chips.

Each day was like the rest, Enslow filled up his time with looking for jobs, going to networking functions, going to support groups, and teaching others how to use ProNect. In fact, he had actually been paid to present lessons on how to use ProNect. Money is money, and while not any real amount of money, it filled his gas tank for another week.

On his eighty fourth day Enslow found himself bored. So to entertain himself, he began to 'flesh out', his training character. *Let's make him appear to be one thing and he is actually another. He needed a cool name.* Enslow logged into his training character on ProNect. He edited his name, changing it to Igor Stanislov Gregor for no reason he could think of. *Let's have him graduate from Berlin Polytechnika and make him an electrical engineer. Ok. Employment. 1st Job out of college, he works for the TravelGroup, managing their Hotel in Baghdad. Then he sells agricultural equipment for AgriTrack in Pakistan. That would give him the ability to travel with a purpose while allowing him to look around. Hmmm. What next? Food Service? Ok, he made Igor the Regional Division Manager for PizzaKing in Moscow Russia. After all, who would look twice at a pizza delivery vehicle? Now a direct allusion.* There was a not so secret radio intercept analyst at Darriman, Victoria Australia, so he got Igor a job there as a signal intercept analyst. *How about a more subtle approach? Ok, make him a sales representative for Universal Exports. See if any Bond fans can figure that one out. HAH!*

The weird part was that the details, both large and small, just flowed. It wasn't a supernatural event but it was just a bit odd. The entire story of a man's life, his work history his education, his associates, just emerged from Enslow's mind. Perhaps it was something from within his subconscious, but more likely, it was the result of his creativity, which for these many months was stifled and suppressed. All good programmers can take a logical concept and after years of development experience, were able to fill in details and steps in a process almost automatically. This was likely an example of that. If after some level of job history or joining a forum, another detail suddenly appeared in his mind, he could go up or down the page, or move up or down to the best section to put it in. What school would look impressive? What association to join would jive with the meme he was constructing? In a few cases, Enslow employed a free form thinking technique, where he went to the web and just started searching for matches to terms he would type in. After looking at several pages, new links from those pages would take him somewhere else, and whole new ideas would then occur to him. For example, if you were looking up information on the B-25 Mitchell, you might discover information on Billy Mitchell, who the plane was named for. Then in reading the history of Billy you might see the name of the lead prosecutor at his court martial. The name of the lead prosecutor might be similar to a city you grew up in, and that city had as a statue in its main park where as a kid you spent a lot of time, the statue being of a long lost naval hero. That naval hero's name might sound like a company you know about that does global security work, so you gave Igor a work history there. Rather convoluted, but that's how you might come up with new information in a way that no one could follow. The randomness of it really simulated real life. Life is a series of random events through which we are defined. The undercurrent of those events is our work ethic. Our honesty and our character are almost always apparent to anyone who looks closely. It was this undercurrent that Enslow was trying to build for Igor. He wanted it to appear to be legitimate but not obvious. If you were to read the entire story of Igor's life, it would seem odd that an engineer in signal theory would work at a Pizza King.

In roughly two hours Enslow had created a much more fleshed out Igor. He added a believable if not fantastic work history, education, and forum memberships that defined in a spectacular fashion, who Igor really was. To say Enslow was unaware of what he was writing would be ridiculously wrong; he was aware of every word. He smirked and laughed out loud at segments as he was writing them and gave himself a mental pat on the back when he was able to tie things together in a substantially clever way. When he had finished, he reread the profile from top to bottom and bottom to top. As weird as it was that this only took two hours. It was equally odd that other than spelling mistakes, Enslow only made three small changes that he deemed were too perfect and seemed even more contrived than the whole package.

Enslow pushed himself away from the keyboard and desk and went to the kitchen to get a drink, and then plopped himself onto the couch. Fingering the remote he started to watch the news. More drivel from the newsreaders, more bad economic news, and more international concerns. Would those merchants of death ever see justice? Enslow doubted it. The good die young, and the rich get richer. Bored with the news he clicked over to the classic movie station, and caught one of his favorite Cary Grant movies. It had just started. Not that he hadn't watched it many times before, but he had been a good boy today and he reasoned he deserved a guilty pleasure of wasting a couple of hours. He had applied to almost fifty jobs though he expected it not to matter. It was at a crucial moment in the movie when the phone rang. He picked it up and only heard hysterical laughter on the other end. Enslow looked at the caller ID, and saw that it was Bill Wester's number and sure enough it sounded like Bill Wester, but there were no words coming out, just hard gut laughter and a little bit of crying. Enslow asked, "Bill, are you ok?"

The laughter died down for a second and Bill's voice said with some pain "Ohhh god. That hurts."

"What hurts, man?"

"I haven't laughed like that in years. My wife came in to see if I was ok and all I could do was pound the desk. I never would have been able to call you if I hadn't had your number in speed dial."

"Glad you are happy, but why call me?" Enslow asked, now genuinely perplexed as to what he had to do with his friend's fit of fun.

"Igor, man, that's just too funny."

"Why did you read Igor?"

"I saw an update come across that he was one of your associates and that he had new employment history. So, I clicked in. And what I read was the seemingly most disjointed block of work history anyone on the earth could ever have. Then after the third job I got it. It just stands up and cold cocks you in the back of the head. Man that is brilliant!"

Grinning to himself, and forgetting that he had not intended to make the profile public, Enslow said "Well, I am glad you enjoyed it."

"Where do you come up with this stuff? I swear that was fuhh-nee."

Enslow assured his friend, "It wasn't really intentional. I was bored so I sat down to juice him up. Just bored and looking to entertain myself a bit. What you read was the result of that. No grand plan, it sorta flowed."

Bill responded with great acclaim, "You should be in show business! You missed your calling. That was great!"

"Since I have you on the phone, Bill, any change in your status?"

Bill said, "No, but something will come along, it just has to. Your money is tight and getting tighter, just like mine"

Although on the phone and Bill could not see, Enslow nodded in the affirmative and replied, "Don't I know it. I think I will be taking that defense job I told you about."

"They made you an offer?" Bill exclaimed.

"No, but I am hoping that I get the interview and that they do. While neither Ella nor I are crazy about me going over there, I feel like I haven't got a choice. The money is very good."

"There is no way my wife would let me go, and frankly, I am not sure I want to go. I am both jealous and sorry for you. But what are you going to do? I got a gig the other day at SlushieWorld, as assistant manager. Imagine someone with an MBA from Colgate going to be an assistant manager at SlushieWorld?"

"Hard ass times my friend," was the only thing Enslow could say.

"Hey I got to go, but I just had to tell you, you made my week man. That was just beyond funny. I'll catch you later," and after Enslow also bade farewell, Bill hung up the phone. *Well, if I can make a man laugh who has nothing to laugh at; I have done my good deed. Perhaps providence will smile upon me.*

Agent Logan Day 251

Keith Logan did not wake up for three days. He was aware of medical staff working on him, changing his bandages and his IV drips. He was also aware of a gentle and reassuring presence in the room, but he was in such a fog from the drugs, blood loss and surgery, that he was unable to identify it. As he opened his eyes, he was aware that it was dimly lit in the room. He could hear the beeps from the medical equipment monitoring his vital signs. A nurse noticed his eyes open, came over and said, "Good morning. How are you feeling?"

He blinked his eyes hard a couple of times and responded, "I feel terrible, and I can hardly move my arms. I'm so foggy."

She told him in an, oh so sweet voice, "That's to be expected. You lost enough blood to kill most men. I'll get your mum, she's here." Before he could really register what she had said, she left and just as quickly, returned with an older woman, whom he recognized but couldn't yet lock onto.

"Keith," she said in a strong voice that somewhat hid some faltering.

"Mom?" Keith Logan let out with a small whimper. "How did you get here?"

"Thomas Wicker called me. He said you made a last request. Had it not been for him, you might not have made it to the hospital. He called and told me you were badly hurt and I came immediately. None of these bureaucrats would let me see you, so I pushed them aside and sat here every hour waiting for you. No matter what they said, I stayed here."

The head nurse, a rather stern looking woman with a grand smile spoke up, "She wouldn't leave your side. In fact, she talked to you most of the time or even sang to you. We decided that being your mother, she might be able to reach you in ways we couldn't. We also couldn't get her to be quiet. Your mother is a very stubborn woman but it likely had a role in waking you."

Keith smiled, "I spent the first ten years of my life wanting to be stronger than her and then the next ten realizing I would never win that contest of wills. I learned when I was fifteen; you don't poke mama bear with a stick."

The head nurse nodded a very learned smile to him, demonstrating she completely understood. Having been on the end of this woman's stubbornness for only three days, she could imagine butting heads with her your whole life. Before she could contemplate her good fortune in not growing up under this badger in pearls, the door opened and three men entered. They gestured for everyone to leave the room, but Mrs. Logan wouldn't budge.

"Ma'am, we need to have a private talk with Agent Logan. Unless you have a top secret clearance, you'll need to clear the room."

After thirty seconds of no one moving, Keith spoke up, "Go ahead mom, I'll be fine. Stay just outside the door if you need to."

Glaring at the three men, Betty Logan spoke sternly "Don't push my son any harder. He's weak and needs his rest."

The first agent met her gaze with a smile, and said as warmly as he could "We just need to debrief him. We'll be gentle."

"You'll answer to me if there are any further problems," Betty Logan proclaimed, her eyes holding firm on the lead agent.

"Of that I have no doubt, ma'am."

For another fifteen seconds the two sized each

other up, and then Betty Logan turned and walked smartly out of the room. When the door had firmly closed, the first two agents moved to it, one taking up station inside the room and the other going through the door to take up station just outside it.

"Agent Logan, my name is Agent Whitmore," and then he presented his credentials to Agent Logan.

Agent Logan after studying them for sixty seconds, handed them back.

Whitmore pulled a side chair over to the bed and asked, "How are you feeling?"

Keith Logan responded in a voice stronger than he imagined he could, "Doing well. I suspect they are taking excellent care of me."

"Good. Can you tell me what happened?"

Laying back slightly and looking up and to the left, Agent Logan narrated the events of the day. "Agent Widmer and I were running surveillance on a black market weapons sale when one of their lookouts opened fire on us. We tried to evade but ran headlong into the main group of them and we continued to take fire. Agent Widmer and I were hit and we knew that we didn't have long. We sent out a distress call. Moments later a mobile crane came through the end of a warehouse and crashed into the group of people shooting at us. I was unable to stand, and passed out when I tried to do so. I woke up here and found out Agent Widmer didn't make it. That's all I can remember."

"You didn't see who was driving the crane or how many other people had become players?"

Firmly Agent Logan said "No sir. I did not. There may have been two or three, but I was having a hard time seeing anything. All I know from my mother is that someone called her and told her to come here."

"Does the name Thomas Wicker mean anything to you?"

A frown and a genuine look of puzzlement crossed Keith's face, to which he responded, "No sir. That is not a name I believe I have ever heard. Can you tell me who that is?"

"Perhaps if I give you some of the details, others will fill in," Agent Whitmore said as he began his recounting of the facts available.

As Agent Logan listened to the known facts, he realized that the name Wicker was false, that that person was undoubtedly a name Jones had conjured up. It was most certainly Jones who had called his parents as he had asked and gave her that false name. He was not about to betray that kind of decent behavior by naming him or the name he had given him, Calico. When the narration had finished, Agent Logan looked at Agent Whitmore, and met his gaze squarely. "Aside from what happened after I passed out, everything you just said matches with the events I know. I can't add anything else. This Thomas Wicker must be involved somehow in the events of that day, but in what way, I cannot say. I must confess, I am somewhat puzzled as to how this 'savior' arrived and dispatched all unfriendlies in the area. Why he would set fire to all the vehicles, if he did, makes no sense. That would take at least a few minutes of time, and every second would be best spent escaping. The name sounds British, but that may be intentional. It strikes me that the name is so utterly banal as to make it impossible to trace. Perhaps Wicker had another meaning or is an anagram?"

"We have run most permutations and one of them we actually enjoyed was 'At cow he smirk' as if he is laughing at us."

This caused Agent Logan to grin, and remark "I would doubt that."

"But the more ominous ones were:
WAR Chemist OK, WAR Cometh SKI, WAR

SECT HO KIM, WARM tech is OK, WARM COKE SHIT, WATCH ROSE KIM. There are over seven thousand permutations, twenty two thousand if you allow other military anagrams. We have Langley cross referencing."

"Isn't that a bit too much?"

Whitmore pulled a chair over, sat down and looked at the man before him recovering in the hospital bed, and said firmly but gently, "One agent is dead, another nearly so. There were seven bodies burned beyond recognition, four vehicles and a mobile crane destroyed and a warehouse severely damaged. All this occurred in a friendly country with our involvement. Then a person, or persons unknown, saves you and your dead partner, torched everything, and seemingly vanished like a fart on a windy day. No intelligence agency can so much as find a bit of evidence as to who he or they are. I can tell you that MI5, MI6, Scotland Yard, Interpol, and four other agencies are now interested that someone could waltz in and pull this off, leaving no trace whatsoever. It is frankly, one of the slickest extractions we have seen. Particularly because we can't find any agency that admits this was their op. We lean to believing that either one of them is lying to us or that someone is watching us, which scares the hell out of us or that he was watching your quarry, and that you missed their surveillance."

Whitmore considered Logan's response, as well as his body language and facial expressions, and concluded he was getting complete and truthful recollections. "What is most difficult to fathom is that Agent Widmer was likely dead before he was moved from the scene. It seems that this person or persons moved him KNOWING he was dead, but chose to not leave his body behind. We have yet to ascertain why," and with that little tidbit, Whitmore was wanting to observe the expression that this revelation might cause on Agent Logan's face. What he got was what he expected, which was a look of surprise and confusion.

Logan blurted out with an intense sound of curiosity, "Really? That makes no sense. Why move someone who was already gone; at least, why move him with me to the hospital. In the interests of cleaning up the event, perhaps, but you can drop a body off anywhere. In the interest of expediency, the hospital might have been the fastest, but expediency would dictate that you left the dead where they lay not moving them about in broad daylight."

Kingston Day 252

The man seated at the front of the room at the head of the table was Deputy Director Hanstram. He was normally a very even tempered man, but most of the staff had none the less leaned to avoid him. He spoke loudly to the room, "It is now 9:00. I trust all of you have had a chance to review the alert bulletin. For those of you just getting a kick from your morning coffee, I'll summarize. Yesterday in London, a routine swap of weapons for cash and intel went badly wrong. All of the weapons were destroyed; the Albanian mercs were killed as well as one of our agents. One survived, but is in critical condition and has not as of yet woken up to be debriefed. Additionally, their vehicle was destroyed in what appears to be arson, the Albanian vehicles also encountered a devastating fire, leaving no traces of who caused this mayhem and an eight wheel mobile crane and a warehouse wall were destroyed. An apparently single British agent delivered the deceased agent and his partner who was still alive, to Royal Mercy Hospital in London, in violation of all protocols. It did however, likely save our agent's life. MI5, MI6 and Scotland Yard, have no idea who the agent was, and they all deny it was one of theirs. The name given to our surviving agent's mother was

Thomas Wicker. Does anyone have any idea how a British Agent was able to arrive just in the nick of time, dispatch all the targets, and rescue our agent and destroy almost all evidence of his identity?"

"You said one agent did not survive; is that significant?" analyst Harrington asked.

Deputy Director Hanstram said, "Yes. It appears that the deceased agent, Agent Widmer, was already dead before he was delivered to the hospital. We believe he was brought along to move the body, not to try to save his life."

"Whoa! Are you saying he was dead and then moved along with the agent who survived?" Harrington asked.

"We believe, based on the extent of his injuries that he died almost immediately after being wounded. There is no way he would have survived the injuries long enough to have been moved from the site of the event to the hospital."

"That makes no sense! Why move a body, particularly for another country?" Straker inquired.

"Unknown. It violates protocol. It suggests several possible motivations. Professional courtesy, most likely by the agent of a friendly power. It suggests respect from a fellow agent, whether of the same agency or another. It suggests honor for a fallen comrade not unlike the respect shown by the Luftwaffe to American and British pilots during the war. It suggests a desire to clean up a mess and make it easier for us. It also suggests someone who just couldn't tell the difference between a dead man and a live one or didn't have the time in the heat of the moment to check, and to be safe they transported both agents to the hospital. When the security officer asked the driver who brought them to the hospital, he was told that it was Crown's business. That could be either misdirection or an honest answer to allow them to leave and maintain their anonymity. If I brought two men to a hospital and I had a cover to maintain, I would say whatever it took to get out of there as fast as possible. But that implies that they have something to protect which means coming there was a risk. So why take the risk?" With that, Deputy Director Hanstram finally took a breath.

"What we do know is that the agents sent out a general distress call. It was picked up by other assets of ours but before any of them could respond our agents were recovered and moved. Whoever made the grab was not one of ours. All in place assets were verified to be elsewhere. So did this person or persons unknown just happen upon the scene or were they monitoring our frequencies?" He continued, "I would like the two of you to look into it further. You had some success last week with listening in on that Russian. Perhaps you could apply yourselves to this. Do a routine search of CCTVs, cell phone traffic, blogs, SMS messages and all other frequency bands. Find out who moved our agents and why." He stood up and exited the room without saying another word. That pretty much indicated the meeting was over, and while it appeared to be discourteous, he had given his orders and expected them to be carried out. No further discussion was needed.

Harrington told Starker, "Let's go run the scans and see if we can pick up any patterns. If there was money involved, it has to have come from somewhere. Maybe some of it survived the fire."

Starker contemplated what would be required and then a spark of an idea crossed his face, and that caused Harrington to ask, "What?"

"Why don't we have Aardvark poke around. He's already on the ground and doesn't appear to be shy. Perhaps he can ferret out a few facts," Starker mused.

"You aren't confusing a peacock with a first class ground asset are you?"

Starker responded with a surprised look, "No. I just think that his abrupt manner might force answers to the surface. I don't seriously expect him to find anything but he just might scare them from the tall brush." Both analysts laughed a bit at the thought of their novice going into the thick of it. They walked out of the room in a better mood than when they went in.

Nigel Day 253

Bloody hell. I just got my eyes closed and the damn mobile has to ring.

Nigel felt his mobile on the end table and answered, "If you aren't a blonde pushover then sod off."

"Good afternoon Aardvark," came the voice of Kingston. Actually not a voice but a computer modified voice that other than being enunciated clearly. It was completely unidentifiable. "We have been reviewing your operational results. Please listen carefully. Five days ago, a CIA team was ambushed in London."

Nigel sat upright so fast he almost got dizzy. *What were they on about? Did they know he was involved? Had Agent Logan given him up? There would be fifty ways they could track this to you.* Nigel said before they could continue talking, "What has this got to do with me?"

"Please allow us to finish. One agent was killed and one was badly wounded. A person or persons unknown brought both agents to Royal Mercy Hospital and left before he or they could be questioned. We will be sending you all the operational details we know."

Nigel took so long sorting out his thoughts that Kingston checked to see if he was still there. Nigel's brows were furrowed as he asked, "I'm not clear, what is it you want me to do? There is no event to attend, no attention to draw, rather out of my realm of activities."

Kingston continued, "Actually not. Management has been impressed with your results to date. We are hoping that by using your talents and customary demeanor, you may flush out the party or parties that we are looking for."

Nigel thought about the proper response to give and then decided that an affirmative response was not only called for but a certain amount of enthusiasm was also needed. "Right. I shall await your instructions and endeavor to return a favorable result. I've wanted a bit more involvement in operations and this is my big opportunity. I only hope that I can provide something useful."

Kingston finished the exchange with, "Your op details will be downloaded in five minutes. Key is the most widely distributed pop song in history. Kingston out."

Bugger, just what was the most widely distributed pop song? Now wait, these questions are constructed to your psychological profile. Some people would get them, some would not. In five minutes as promised Nigel's mobile beeped to indicate an incoming transmission. Nigel had still not worked out who the answer was. *White Christmas? Louie Louie? The intent was to be obtuse and misleading. How widely could you distribute a pop sing? Number of languages? Worldwide hit? Number of genres? What was greater than that? Beyond the world? AHHH!!! Johnny B. Goode by Chuck Berry was on one of the Voyager spacecraft! Surely that was the widest distribution, like what twenty billion miles? Can't get wider than that.* Nigel typed that in 'Johnny B. Goode.' The program on his mobile indicated a correct response by replacing the clock on the screen with the operational details for his next op. The details were more or less correct except that they had no idea who had rescued the boys. And more interestingly there was no mention of the money. It occurred to Nigel that he might score some brownie points if he could return the phone under a plausible story. To sell it he would need to make it believable, and although he doubted they would ever check. If they did he would need to be seen in the area.

As part of being a good operative, culling any information was always good practice. So he removed the back of Agent Logan's phone and inserted the memory card. He powered up his laptop and connected a USB cable to the phone and then he placed the phone in a shielded box and powered it up. He was able to clone the information from the phone to his laptop in about ten minutes. He then reached into the box and powered the phone off, making sure to remove the battery. This phone might be able to be tracked if left on or possibly put into a stealth mode even though the phone was off but the battery was installed. He would look at the information later.

Nigel spent most of that day driving around the area in a rented car, going to every pub, charity store, dive and low rent establishment he could find. He made sure to ask most people he came into contact with that he was looking for information about yesterday's events in the industrial district. After spending the day talking to all the riff raff he could find and making as large a search as he could, he returned to his regular flat and called Kingston.

"Kingston here. Go ahead," came the digitized voice.

"Aardvark here. I have in my possession the mobile of one of our agents." After a large pause, Nigel said, "Allo?"

Kingston responded, "How do you know it is one of our issue phones?"

Thinking fast, Nigel spat out that he had walked the entire area that day, searching for information when one of the kids who ran around the streets offered to sell him a mobile he had found, cheap because it didn't work. "I realized when I turned it on that it was an encrypted phone and without an encryption key, not only could I not determine anything about it but that it was likely one of ours as the little urchin had recounted how he found it behind some rocks near where the cars had burned up. I had to give a tenner for it so I will be expensing that."

"Can you power up the phone?" Kingston demanded.

"Stand by," and he pressed power till the LED turned green at the top. "Powered on," he said.

Twenty seconds later the screen sprang to life, scrolling rapidly through log files and then the pictures on the chip. Nigel smiled with a little pride as he recognized the pictures he had taken just the other day with this very mobile. The picture timestamps would confirm that the pictures were genuine so this would be considered quite the intelligence coup.

"Aardvark, you magnificent bastard!" Kingston called out after the data was downloaded, "You did find the phone of one of the agents! Well done! You have succeeded where no one else had. We did not even know that a phone was missing. This result will not go uncompensated. What would you like?"

"I'd like better assignments. These spotlight affairs are rather boring. I'd like something with more red meat."

"Difficult to do but we will look at the upcoming opportunities. In order to get you advanced, we will need to bring you in for more training, and budgets are tight. But we do mean to get you something for this truly respectable result. We will contact you about any additional work we can assign you to."

"Just want to be useful. I feel like I have more to contribute," Nigel offered.

"We will contact soon. Stand by. Kingston out," and the call dropped.

For the first time in several days Nigel was hopeful that he could move up in the company. This flashy shake and meet stuff was fine, and he had discovered he had a taste for it. The money was good, the scenery changed, and he had a real knack for pulling it off. Spies usually needed to blend, but his skill was becoming who his audience thought he was. Not having done much acting before, Nigel used the skills he had developed over a lifetime to ingratiate himself to the different people he met at these public events. The events themselves lent a certain 'air' of a person to play the braggart and visible person that he appeared to be. As with all hierarchies, the more you took on, the more you made, and he needed to make more money. The stash he had recovered from the gun merchants wouldn't last forever and he wouldn't be able to hide it through legitimate channels anyway. He could though, use it to make himself more successful at his craft.

While waiting for the return call, Nigel turned on the telly to get the latest scores from the game. Manchester United was doing well this season and he was hoping to get highlights from the last game. It was just before the player interviews that his mobile lit up, indicating that there was a call. "Allo," he said.

The voice on the other end was the computer generated voice of Kingston and it said "Aardvark, we have decided to grant you the opportunity to attend the Prime Minister's daughter's wedding. There should be ample opportunities to push your computer executive persona, and make additional contacts that might serve us later. We have arranged to have you attend as a guest of the Scottish Development Council. You will need to shake fifty hands and pass out at least as many cards. Details will arrive in one hour with all the contact information, times, dates, etc. Any questions?"

Excited about the opportunity, Nigel did have one question. "Usually all my operational details arrive via encrypted file. Yet this time, we spoke in the open about my assignment. Seems odd."

"Actually," Kingston answered, "we haven't had time to construct a riddle encryption for you. We will by the time your mission parameters are complete. Kingston out."

Enslow Unemployed Day 91-120

    Enslow put the phone back into its cradle. He had just told Major Hurst that he would need to talk to his wife about the offer. He knew she wouldn't like it but the news from his friends and peers was very depressing. The economy continued to decay and virtually no one he knew was even getting an interview. Good people with great work ethics and not one bit of interest. Enslow could hear his inner voice telling him he should take it as long as Ella approves. It could be months before anything else turns up and it was already the beginning of the year's fourth quarter, when whatever job openings existed were going to be locked down or closed. It would likely be four months later, in the middle of February when things might, might open up. That would put them within a few grand of all of their savings spent. Not a good place to be. He could get a part time gig like Bill Wester got at the HandyMart, but that would only pay enough to cover utilities and some food not the car payment, house payment, insurance, etc. It was at times like these that Enslow had learned to trust that things were going to work out. So many times in his life, he took the only option open or the least desirable one because he couldn't wait for a better option, and life would throw some interesting things at you, things that worked out very much in your favor. In college, he had taken the least desirable job because it was the only one he was actually offered, and in addition to learning some real world computer problem solving skills, he had met the great love of his life, Ella. She had been a student assistant in the department where he became the applications developer. Enslow was often very obtuse when it came to things that were obvious. Obvious things like a pretty girl who laughed at anything he said, and always smiled at him. He was slow, but not blind. One day he noticed her noticing him, and the rest was history. That history had now gone almost twenty years and he owed it to her to continue to be her partner and provider, as much as he could, to their house and family.

Major Hurst had said that he could give him twenty four hours to think it over, and would need an answer by 3:00 p.m. sharp. Apparently Enslow had passed the security assessment, and would likely pass a full investigation, so in this case, a provisional clearance would be granted and he could report to Fort Benning for one week of basic weapons instruction. He would not be expected to ever use a weapon, but in the event things went really wrong, he was expected to pick up a weapon and defend himself. None of that was sure to please Ella, but Enslow would stress to her that it was a good thing, that he would actually be safer because he could defend himself. His inner voice told him that was not likely to win her over, but it was the best explanation he could come up with. The money, though, was the key. Since he was going to be stationed on a base, he would have everything he needed, and would need to spend very little of the money, so he could send it all home. One year of this would allow him to pay off his mortgage; two years would allow him to put away some real cash for living, retirement, kids college expenses, etc.

Ella would be home very soon and Enslow found himself getting nervous. He had already made up his mind that he had no choice but to go, but would abide by whatever decision Ella wanted. After twenty minutes of anxious waiting, Enslow heard the familiar sound of her Buick pulling into the driveway. A slam of the car door and the sound of her pretty feet walking up to the door and there she was.

"Hi dear, how was your day?" Enslow inquired.

Ella instantly could tell, whether it was his voice or a nervous look in his eyes, that something important was about to come out. "It was fine. Just the usual people with their usual conversations. What's going on? Something up?"

No fooling her. Enslow decided to take the straight approach and just tell her. "I got a call a little while ago from Major Hurst. He said he would like me to be on his team. I have until tomorrow to accept or decline."

Ella looked down at her feet, and she took off her coat and hung it on the coat rack then she put her purse on the kitchen table. With a slight exhale she turned and said "Is that the military job in Afghanistan?"

"Yes, it's the defense job overseas, likely to be Afghanistan."

"I am not comfortable with you taking it; I will worry every single day. But I know how hard it is for you and I understand it is probably the smart thing to do to take it. If you don't someone else will and we could be left with nothing." Ella said while meeting Enslow's gaze.

"Why the change of heart? You weren't in favor of it before" said Enslow.

Ella's shoulders dropped just a little, and Enslow could see she was a bit troubled. Then she spoke. "I found out today that the Winsteds down the street, have been out of work for nine months and will likely get their house repossessed."

"Really?" a somewhat incredulous Enslow asked.

"Yes. I was talking to Denise today at the market. On the way home she told me that they are out of money and out of options."

"Well, it will take some time to do that and maybe they can work out a deal. But that is what I don't want to happen to us."

Enslow said "Alright, I'll call him back and accept. I just want you to know it isn't my first or second choice, but I think it's my only option at the moment."

Ella looked into Enslow's eyes, hugged him and said "I know."

Nigel Day 254

Nigel's mobile made its particular chirp that indicated it had received a text message from Kingston. He picked up his mobile and read the screen, which asked "I met a man on the road to St. Ives who had seven wives. Each wife had seven cats, each cat had seven kits. How many cats were on the road to St. Ives?" Starting to do the math in his head he realized that was the wrong answer. So before the timer ran out to zero he typed in the answer: "Fucking cats." The screen cleared and now presented him with his mission details. He was to be prepped in his nice suit, not the tux, and arrive at Lindley Castle at 3:30 p.m. sharp in two days. He was a consultant to the Scottish Development Council, a part of the Ministry of Trade, and he was to shake fifty hands. Primarily, his mission was to observe. Nigel gathered from the instructions that there were to be other operatives there. Since it was the Prime Minister's daughter's wedding, undoubtedly there was going to be an enhanced level of security. Perhaps this was a test to see how well he handled additional scrutiny. In any case, it was a more high profile assignment. Not that he understood anything about it. Go to a wedding, go to a dinner, go to the party, meet people and be seen. Hardly cloak and dagger stuff. Still, it was exciting. He would be in the same room as the Prime Minister and a lot of upper crust types. Although, he hoped it would not take all night. Nigel had been neglecting his mates and wanted to be at the pub for their regular Saturday darts. The operational details left him two days to prepare. He needed to get the car in order and made a note to tell Suresh he would need it to be done in black. Seemed like a good color for the wedding. It might be a good idea to blend as far as the transportation goes.

Staggering to his feet, he walked over to the wall where he had Suresh's number and rang him up.

"Hello?" came the familiar sing songy voice.

"Allo Suresh?" Nigel asked.

"Yes. Good to hear from you. Haven't seen you for several days and I was hoping everything was all right."

"Thank you for asking. All is well but I do need a small favor."

"Well with you, these favors are never quite small. What would you like?"

"As you know, my mother drives that

Mercedes you built for her. Lately she has been feeling like silver is not quite 'her' anymore. Could we do a color change to black? And in the next day?" inquired Nigel.

"Certainly. Would you like to drop the car off or shall I come get it?"

"My work has got me just completely buried. I will not be able to get it and bring it over, so could you come get it? I will pay you for your time. I expect you still have the duplicate keys. I will leave it on Marksbury by the bus station. Can you get a cab there and pick it up make the change and return it?"

"I certainly can. In the interests of your mother, I have an additional safety item I would like to add to the car. It will only cost three thousand pounds."

"Three thousand? If it wasn't for my mother and her safety I'd tell you where you might take that offer. But you know I hopelessly adore that mad old cow, so go ahead and install whatever it is and tell me about it later. I need to drop the car off for you. I'll leave the money in the false panel behind the seat. Please take my gratitude for seeing to this so quickly."

"Oh you are quite welcome sir. It is I who should be thanking you for allowing me to express myself through your mother's car and perfect my skills. I will have the car done by morning and returned to the same spot. Good day sir."

"Good day to you too, Suresh. Please say hello to your wife for me." Then the connection went dead.

Nigel was left to wonder exactly how Suresh was going to spend three thousand pounds of his money and on what. Since the events of the previous week, he little cared. He had more than enough money to spend, and as Suresh had so aptly demonstrated, he had an eye for this and understood Nigel's needs better than Nigel did. Whatever it was, it was likely well worth the price. *Well, you have a lot to do, so let's get on with it.* Nigel was back in his regular flat, having swept it for listening devices and found none. Either the CIA team that rummaged through his belongings wasn't too professional or they were not really that interested in him or the whole event was just a notice to him that they were watching him. The woman who Agent Logan did not like was still out there, and for all Nigel could tell, still did not know who he was. For that matter, he had had time to go over the things that Agent Logan had said to him in his mind and they had been gnawing at him ever since. If they were CIA, and he believed they were, why were they following him? He wasn't an operative worthy of that kind of attention and even if he was, why would they follow one of their own? That thought gave Nigel pause to consider. Did he really know who Kingston was? He really only had their appearance when they recruited him and an in-depth knowledge of who he was and his personality profile, but other than appearing American, were they really? The communications were always via a digital voice and that was easy enough to do. Their manner of speech was spot on, and indicated they were at least from America. Though that didn't mean they were not working for some other side. Their connections to all things UK seemed not too worthy of concern, since the UK and America were more or less good friends, it would make sense that they had access to the things that they obviously did. Then why would one CIA team follow another? Perhaps something was not quite right at the agency or at the least, something was not quite adding up in a way that made sense to Nigel.

Those kinds of thoughts made his head hurt. It was well above his pay level. He had been hired to do this job, and was given considerable variance to do it how he wanted to. He suspected that they did not know about his safe house and surely did not know about the modifications he had made to his car. Nigel did not know why that brought him comfort, but that they did not know things, and that he was doing everything he could, meant he was as prepared as he could be. If the last several years of his life had taught him anything, it was that you needed to be better prepared. Having a house off the grid and a car with tricks up its tail pipe and some extra money (a lot of extra money) made him feel like he could get out of trouble at least as fast as he might get into it. The plan was that he would likely never get into trouble. His role was to be a distraction so that other people, who could 'blend' could carry out their functions. It occurred to Nigel that he may just be a bit too much in the dark about things, but that perhaps that was for the best. The less he knew, the less he could tell anyone, particularly if he was detained and questioned. Actually, he could tell them very little. He had no real names to give, only a couple of phone numbers, but those were undoubtedly dead-end drops that really would never amount to anything. *Wonder if they are setting you up to take some kind of fall?* Who better than someone who could say nothing, do nothing, and had multiple IDs just lying around. *Well, that might be, but the longer you do this the more you will earn, remember that.* They weren't infallible; witness the events at the warehouse. What a cluster foxtrot that was. Whatever the plan was it was rubbish, until he came in like John Wayne and rode in on that crane. Their whole operation was tits up till he came in and resolved it for them. Shrugging his shoulders, he walked back to his bedroom and changed his clothes to take the Mercedes to the station and drop it off for Suresh. Nigel grabbed five thousand pounds and put it in his coat pocket to put into the seat for Suresh. As for the extra it never hurt to have some extra cash in pocket. He picked up his keys and locked the door on his way out to the car. In about thirty minutes he had made it to the station and parked at the west end, leaving four thousand pounds in the seat compartment. The overage was for the color change. He locked the car and walked south to the bus stop, where he boarded a comfortable and familiar icon, the red number 215 bus and rode it to eight stops away, where he then after looking around, hailed a taxi cab and went to a spot three blocks from his flat. When he had walked all the way back he opened his door, and went in to make a spot of late lunch.

Nigel pulled out his mobile and after entering the code read the mission briefing again. He realized he had neglected to scroll the message where it listed the name and likeness of another agent, whom he would be contacting at the wedding. The man appeared to be mid twenties, medium dark hair, good height and had a strong jaw line. *Probably a waiter.* The mission parameters said he was in fact, a waiter. *Stupid cock.* Like that took any originality. A young kid who was playing the part of a waiter was his contact. Score one for the old guy.

As had been his habit, Nigel was often too keyed up before one of his assignments, so he took to doing a bit of exercise, just some pushups, some small weight lifting and some time at the gym to use the machines. This time was no different. He needed to burn some time so he changed into his workout clothes and headed to the gym. Mindful to not overdo it or stress anything, he just found it a great way to burn off the adrenaline of waiting and worrying about the next couple of days. One thing Nigel noticed was that he had begun to lose that middle aged gut, and was slowly shaping up into a more handsome figure of a man. He still had sore moments from the recent injuries he suffered, but they had been healing for over a month and he found that the mineral bath and exercise had helped him keep loose, rather than letting the injuries remain sore and tight.

Nigel decided that to be as interesting a guest as he could be, and he would do some assimilation on the history of Castle Lindley. He went to his laptop and logged in, went to the ever trusty browser and typed in Castle Lindley history. The castle was built on the site of a monastery from around 1250 A.D. and that in turn had been built on the site of a previous church. This church had been built on the remains of a temple that had been destroyed in some of the fighting that occurred from the raids of Boudicca, the Iceni warrior queen. She had had enough of the Romans. The final straw for her was when the Romans raped her daughters to teach her a lesson. A classic example of overreaching and not knowing who you were messing with. Boudicca went on a rampage, slaying thousands of Romans and burning down London itself. While she excelled at fighting in a savage manner with overwhelming numbers, was defeated by a large well trained Roman force. Her final end was never known, in all likelihood she was left to rot on the field on which her soldiers fell, as the Romans were not too forgiving to opposing forces. Some say she committed suicide by poison, others say she fell in battle. In any case, after this battle, her story ended. Nigel had often wondered if she was the source of the idea that gingers were ill tempered. Not that dealing with any number of red headed women wouldn't communicate that idea. Boudicca was renowned for her magnificent red hair that went all the way to her waist.

The castle had also had its share of ups and downs, as the fortunes of war and families show the ups and down of their times, but what was most notable in the last three hundred years for being abandoned for almost two centuries. It had always been in the family's possession, but it was just not lived in or used. In the middle of the eighteenth century, the family ended up making substantial amounts of money in the India trade. The castle was restored to more than its original grandeur, and was lived in from that point forward. The family patriarch had invested his money well, and each succeeding generation demonstrated their excellent stewardship of the family fortune. As a result, their net worth grew each and every year. Their wealth was not as large as that of modern industrialists, but the family continued to cultivate the image of benevolent benefactors, by annually giving to charities favored by the royal family. Add to that a never ending stream of appointments to diplomatic posts, and it was easy to understand the prestige offered by having a high profile wedding here, as well as the reciprocal prestige offered by the wedding occurring there for the family.

Nigel had no special suit for the wedding, at least as far as a specifically equipped garment like his tuxedo. Not expecting to need any gear and perhaps feeling more at ease in his role, he determined that just a fashionable set of threads would suffice. Using his mobile, he called Byrd & Thayer and asked for Rupert.

After a brief delay, Rupert answered the phone, "This is Rupert, and how may I be of service?"

"Hello Rupert, this is Gavin Brown, I was there recently for a tuxedo, which was just brilliant, great fit, truly a wonderful tuxedo. I have a small problem. I have been invited to a high profile wedding, and I will need a respectable suit. The suit I was expecting to wear has suffered an indignity and can't be worn. Will you be able to equip me?"

"I am certain we can sir, I have looked up your measurements and we have several suits we can adjust to fit you. Will the wedding be evening or morning?" Rupert inquired.

"The wedding will take place in the afternoon, followed by dinner and then a celebration afterwards."

"Very good. When is the wedding? Soon I suspect?"

"Yes, as I said, I found that my suit would be unavailable, so I do need it in less than two days."

"If you can be here before 5:00 p.m., we can take the measurements, and have it finished by tomorrow. Will that be satisfactory?"

Nigel nodded his head as he said "Quite. I very much appreciate it. I will see you before five. Thank you." Nigel clicked the call off. He surveyed his flat looking for an acceptable shirt and after finding it and putting it on, went outside to call for a taxi. Finding one, he raised his arm and it stopped. He opened the door, and as he entered said "Byrd & Thayer Fine Tailors please." As he closed the door, the taxi sped off. In less than thirty minutes they arrived. Nigel paid the driver and walked in where he found Rupert waiting.

"Good to see you again, Mr. Brown, I took the liberty of selecting three possibilities for you to look at. I think given the occasion, the suit from Barkins & Sons would be an excellent choice."

Looking at the three options Nigel agreed, "Yes it is most striking, formal, yet solid feeling." He said as he rubbed the sleeve between his finger and thumb.

"I thought you would like it. Appealing enough for formal occasions like weddings, funerals, and official functions yet it moves and breathes well and looks workday enough to blend in with the executives or at other functions. If you will step into the fitting rooms, I'll have our tailor take the measurements and we should have it ready for you by, four o'clock tomorrow?"

Smiling as he talked Nigel said, "That would be just wonderful. I really like what you selected. You do know your clothes."

"Oh I should hope so sir. It is the single preoccupation of my life. Clothes make the man. Who could take you seriously if you were standing there in an off the rack suit? A suit says so much before you open your mouth. It speaks of your income, your occupation, your status in life, all of that can be said with your suit before you open your mouth to speak to anyone."

Nigel agreed, "I think it allows you to not open your mouth. Silent communication can be substantially more effective than anything you say. It is so powerful and often overlooked in the modern age."

"Brilliant!" exclaimed Rupert, "I think you summed it up perfectly."

"No, you summed me up when you chose that suit for me. Well done."

"You are too kind sir, but I appreciate it. Now if you will step this way, we will get the changes we need." Rupert directed Nigel to the fitting room where a very old stooped over tailor made some quick measurements and then smiled as he left. Nigel exited the fitting room and went back out to the counter where Rupert gave him a claim slip for the suit. Nigel said thank you, went outside, and again was able to get a taxi, but this time he went to another destination and got out. He then walked several blocks as if sightseeing, trying to make sure he wasn't being followed. It was really more for his practice than any real concern for his safety. Just to ensure that it would be harder for anyone else following him on CCTVs, however, he turned his jacket inside out, as it had an interior lining that looked decent enough unless you looked too closely, and he pulled out a small hat he had had in one of the pockets. He then took another taxi to get closer to home, reversing the jacket once again and removing the hat. Feeling confident that he wasn't being followed, Nigel returned to his flat, and sat down for a night of football he had recorded. He knew Manchester United had won the match but he still liked watching, particularly if he needed to participate in a discussion of the game.

Feeling like he should have a drink while he watched he went to his kitchen, opened up a bottle and returned to his chair to watch the rest of the match. One bottle turned into two and then turned into four. Before he had even finished watching, he felt sleep approaching in its unrelenting war against consciousness, so Nigel signed the forms of surrender and closed his eyes.

Nigel Day 255

He had a good night of sleep, sitting there in his chair and for the first time, the wounds he had suffered six weeks ago didn't bother him. He slept as well as you can, being poured into a large padded chair. He awoke to the sound of his mobile beeping at him. With blurry eyes, he took in the number calling. It was Suresh.

"It is too bloody early! Is there a problem?"

Suresh reassured him, "No sir, I was unable to sleep so I was able to make the modifications to your car faster than I thought."

"You never did tell me what the modifications were. What are they?"

"Given that your mother may not see as well as some people her age, I added a sensor trigger alarm to the car, where it will record who has approached it and it records those images to a small laptop I have secured into the boot. So if someone were to approach your mother to see if she might be a worthy victim, you will have a visual record of it. I have tied it into the digital surveillance system we previously installed in the car. I also have added a black skin as you asked."

"Thank you Suresh. Was there enough money for the modifications?"

"Yes, you paid me very well. Will you be wanting me to drop the car off as we discussed?"

"Yes, that would be most helpful. I will tell my mother that you completed your work early and she will be most thrilled."

Suresh finished, "Then thank you. I hope all is well with you. I will leave Aldawolfa in the place that we discussed. There is one more thing. I have password protected the laptop in the trunk. It is the spice you detest so much. I just thought it would be easy for you to remember."

"Aldawolfa? What is Aldawolfa?"

"In German it means Noble Female Wolf. I decided after laboring so much the car needed a name. With all the modifications for your mother, it seemed appropriate. As it is a German car, I felt a German name would be more in character. I would have suggested an Indian name myself, but your mother's generation while not fond of the Germans, is likely less fond of my kind."

"Hardly a concern there. Mother is more than

impressed. She knows a good man can come in any size, shape or color," Nigel assured. "You are a clever lad, Suresh. Thank you for getting it done early. Be well my friend. Goodbye."

"Goodbye sir." The connection terminated.

Well that's a bit of all right; he got the car done early. Nigel decided that he didn't like taxis. He was getting rather fond of the chameleon Mercedes, or Aldawolfa. It was still mid morning, Suresh wouldn't likely have the car back in place for another hour so Nigel went to the kitchen and cleaned up his empty bottles from last night. With a bit more effort, he had the kitchen looking well enough, so he went to the sink by the mirror and took a quick shave. Then going to the wardrobe, he selected a causal outfit for the day. This time he made sure to have some extra money and an extra phone. He didn't expect to need it, but he was growing accustomed to planning ahead and having a few additional key items. He locked up the flat as he left and walked almost all the way to the station, and having gotten there early, he kept walking past, then around the entire area, ducking into little shops and buying a coffee or bag of crisps. When he judged the time to be correct, he made his way back to the station and just as he expected, he found Aldawolfa, but with a shiny new black skin. Taking a few seconds to admire the color, he decided that unless you looked very closely, it was a very passable finish for an older car, and that you could not tell that it was in fact a removable skin. *Say what you want about his taste for curry, that man does wonderful things with cars.*

Nigel opened the boot to find the laptop that Suresh had installed. It was a typical big box laptop. Nigel found Suresh's note and logged on to the laptop. He was impressed to find, but ultimately not surprised, that Suresh had rigged up a cheap power inverter to the car's battery that kept the laptop running for an extended amount of time. Reading the note left to him, he saw the instructions for accessing the camera software. Clicking on the desktop icon he was able to bring up the recordings. Oddly voyeuristic he realized. Several people had approached the car. Several lost people looking for their cars. There were some kids and an altogether monstrous dog that you would not normally see on the streets of London. There was a couple that had embraced in a rather passionate kiss while leaning up against his car. He erased all the recordings using the menu selection and closed the lid to the laptop. Then he closed the boot, walked up to the front, got in and started the car. Easing out into traffic, Nigel drove back to his flat and parked the car in its assigned spot. He exited the vehicle and armed the alarm and the video for good measure. He then went back to his flat to prepare to lay out his new suit for tomorrow.

Enslow Employed Day 121-135

Enslow accepted the position and passed all the background checks. Then he had to pass a general physical exam to verify his being free from chemical dependencies. His credit was investigated. He heard from two former co-workers and even an old high school teacher, that they had been contacted and asked questions about Enslow, his character, etc. One thing you can be sure of is that they are thorough. When Enslow had accepted the position, Major Hurst had mentioned he would be going to Fort Benning Georgia for twelve days for general military training. While not a member of the armed forces, he would be working closely with their personnel and would need to understand some of the basics of their culture, the chain of command, the language and acronyms they used as well as some small and medium weapons training. They (the contractors) were not expected to fight, but if you got into trouble and the soldier next to you was unable to fight, you were expected to be able to pick up the weapon and to know how to use it and return fire to save your own skin. Enslow had never shot a rifle much after his childhood when his dad and mother divorced. He had no problem with guns in general, as long as they were in responsible hands. He had had arguments over the years with well intentioned, but grossly uninformed people in office situations who felt that the police or soldiers would always be able to restore order or defend you. In the combat areas, that might not be a certainty and Enslow wanted to make damn sure he got home. So if he had to learn how to shoot from some of the best shooters in the world, he was determined to be a good student.

Enslow had just packed his bags earlier, got his plane ticket and said goodbye to his wife and kids. He never really imagined how hard it would be to look into those lovely brown eyes and say goodbye. Somehow she held it together and didn't break. That gave him the strength to hold it together too. What he didn't know was that she cried all the way home. Ella understood that he was going into harm's way for her and the kids. As a husband, as a provider, it was his responsibility to do whatever he could. In the modern world, it was frowned upon to look at it that way. That didn't change that Enslow was still feeling like that was his role and that he need to play it. Ella understood that. She didn't like it, but she knew that he needed to feel productive again. While she never let on, she knew just how little of their savings was left. There were no jobs that would pay what they needed, and this was really their best option. So she let him leave. Not that she would worry any less, but she was somewhat comforted by the fact that he was going to be assigned to a base, rather than the forward operating areas, so other than mortar barrages and the usual dangerous nature of having so many things around that go 'BOOM'. Her husband would be relatively safe, relative being the operative word.

The plane ride was uneventful. When they arrived, the ten or so guys on the plane that were also contractors all followed the driver who turned up at the airport with a sign saying "MilaDyne Contractors". The assembled group then took a small bus. They then drove for almost one hour to Fort Benning, where they had to pass an ID check at the gate. Finally, they arrived at their temporary quarters. On the plane and in the bus, one guy would just not shut up. He had an opinion about everything. Not that he disagreed with him on many of his positions, Enslow just wanted to sleep and then get on with it. His constant chatter was beginning to put him on edge. All annoyances will pass and this one thankfully did as well. Enslow was assigned quarters in the third building and Mr. Yackety-yak had quarters in building four. Enslow secretly believed that was not enough distance, however, and that if this guy bored some other poor bastard; Enslow would be able to still hear it through the walls of two buildings.

Enslow had read some of the tweets and blogs of other contractors, and had brought as little as possible. Key items were show inserts, lots of good quality underwear, a killer 'Full Monty' laptop with two terabytes of disk memory and almost eight gigabytes of RAM, a VOIP phone for making cheap calls, and a nice athletic digital watch good for one hundred meters depth. Not that Enslow expected to be anywhere near any water but a watch so designed could likely remain free of encumbrances from dirt and dust which Enslow expected to be everywhere. His hard drive was loaded with all the MP3s he could beg, borrow, rip or steal. He also brought several dozen movies that were his favorites by making AVI copies of his discs at home. When he had free time, which he expected to be very little, he could at least see and hear familiar things.

The first day of training was what he expected, which was an explanation of how the various services were constructed, their rank and insignia, their command structure, and their history. There was a lot of new information here, but none of it was surprising. For instance, while this was real life, not a Hollywood movie, it was clear that elements of all the popular war movies had some elements of truth in them. Not that all military men were blood thirsty raping murderers, but there was a chain of command and it was followed. It had to be. Some people were going to die, but if commands weren't followed, more people would die. While it was a sad day when services members fell, you could only pause to honor them, because the work went on and there would be others. The drill sergeant who was assigned to work with them was very much like that movie caricature of a drill sergeant. He was a loud, firm, hard attitude man whom you were bound to respect because if you so much, for a single minute, did not follow what he was telling you, he would make an example of you in front of everyone.

It was during one of the morning exercises that Mr. Yackety-yak, who was behind Enslow, snickered at something that Sergeant Spaulding said, and this caused the good sergeant to spin and walk with unbelievable speed back to where Enslow was standing. Thinking that Enslow was making fun of him, he proceeded to get within an inch of Enslow's face and scream at him.

"Do you think I am funny?!"

To which Enslow barked back without thinking, as loudly as he could, "Sir No sir!"

"Then why were you laughing at me?"

"Sir, it wasn't me sir."

"Then who was it? Give me their name and I will shit can them right out of here. This ain't no game. You must learn everything I am going to tell you or you could die. And while that might not be a loss to mankind, it would be a black mark on my career because I am responsible to train you to survive should you be caught in a bad situation. I will ask you again, who laughed if it wasn't you?"

"Sir, I can't tell you."

"Can't or won't?"

"Sir, I can't. I don't know sir."

"I can't make you do any pushups or KP, you are not a soldier but I am disgusted by your attitude."

"Sir, I am sorry you feel that way, sir." shouted back Enslow, "but I deeply respect you and those who serve, sir. I wish to atone for the sin of someone else sir. How many pushups would you like, Sir?"

"You are soft Mr. Funny Man. I bet you couldn't do twenty regulation pushups."

Enslow replied, again as loudly as he could, "Sir, I will try."

He dropped and gave about seventeen before he started to falter. Sergeant Spaulding said, "That's enough son. You are trying but you ain't going to make it. You ain't got it in you."

Enslow Stopped briefly and replied, "Sir, would you suggest I quit, sir?"

"I ain't suggesting anything. As a civilian I just know you can't make it. I would have had one of my young bucks' do fifty."

"Sir, then I will do fifty, with your permission sir."

A smile crept across the face that they had never seen smile. "Then go to it."

Enslow wished he had kept his big mouth shut. This wasn't his fault. He could tell for almost ninety percent accuracy it was that guy who couldn't shut up. He felt like he couldn't point fingers at anyone though. In this place, he knew honor meant a great deal and ratting out someone was almost worse than the offense itself.

After doing thirty-five agonizing pushups, Enslow was unable to continue. He wasn't in shape, he wasn't an athlete, and he wasn't a young soldier. When he was unable to continue, Sergeant Spaulding told him to stand up.

"I didn't think you'd make it. But your attempt took heart. I know it wasn't you who made fun of me. But I wanted to see what you were made of.

You keep trying like you did and keep your head down, and I think you will do all right. Every one of you could learn something from this man. He ain't a quitter." Then Sergeant Spaulding turned on his heel and walked off. A certain programmer, who stood there that day, arms aching like they hadn't in years, stood a little taller.

Enslow and the rest said nothing more about it and they walked back to the mess hall for lunch. After lunch they were again in the company of Sergeant Spaulding, who was instructing them on the proper way to hold a weapon, to load a weapon, and the basics of shooting; all without the aid of a real gun. They were going to spend all their time on a virtual range, where the conditions like light, wind, and distractions could all be mixed and modified. It was really a big modern version of that duck hunting game, except that your targets scream and splattered. The fake rifle had a pinball servo installed and it would kick with each shot. Nice attention to detail.

This was the routine every day with little variation. They got up early, they took classes, they exercised, they ate, they took more classes, and then they practiced these large video games up until the last two days. Sergeant Spaulding said to a surprised group, "It is with some concern that I have stuck my neck out and arranged for you all to practice with live rounds. You will follow all the protocols you have been practicing, and you will observe all safety precautions. Failure to do so, will at the least result in your reassignment to stateside activities, and the most could harm or kill one of us, something I am very much against happening. You will follow me in a single file to the shooting range, where you will be assigned a rifle for the rest of the day, and you will be assigned fifty rounds. Do NOT load your weapon until instructed to do so. AM I CLEAR?"

Enslow had apparently affected the men, as from that day of his pushups; the men prefaced their statements and responses with 'Sir'. They also finished every sentence with 'Sir'. So the group responded in unison with, "Sir, Yes sir. We understand. We will not load our weapons until instructed to do so, sir."

They proceeded to march to the shooting range, and were each assigned a rifle and given a box of rounds to fire. The rest of the afternoon was spent with groups of ten firing twenty five rounds at targets under the direction of the ever vigilant sergeant. When the rounds were expended, the rifles were turned in and they had a quick group discussion on what they had learned. It was at this time the sergeant gave them a farewell speech, which for him was quite long, but to anyone else seemed like thirty seconds, because it was about thirty seconds long. They each thanked him and walked back to their quarters, then when it was time for dinner. They ate in the mess hall. Their last day was for packing up their personal belongings and then being assigned their gear, consisting of body armor, a more or less ballistic resistant helmet, their duffel bag, and their clothing. All of their personal stuff and their assigned gear had to fit in the bag. Enslow had the foresight to read up and prepare, but some of the contractors did not. They would have to leave some stuff behind. Some of them had not even brought their own laptop, assuming that they would have computer access. *Idiots, this was about as close as you can get to military service, without being in the service.*

When they were all finished, they got as much sleep as they could. Enslow used the last minutes on his throwaway cell phone to call Ella, and as he had every night, told her about his day. He would be out of contact for days at a time, so she need not worry. He would be able to download her emails and reply, but not always on the same day or even in the same week. He had taken a few prepaid envelopes so that she could have letters from abroad. It was nice to hold something a loved one had held, with an email it was really just ones and zeroes; it wasn't the same. When she sent letters to him, she could scent them with some perfume. The next morning, they were woken up at 6:00 a.m., having been allowed to sleep in late by military standards. They ate their breakfast mostly in silence. Enslow had not taken the time to talk to many of them and as a group they were all rather quiet. What they were doing was not something they wanted to do, but had to do. Enslow surmised that they were roughly his age or older and in the same financial place due to the economy. He knew none of them had done this duty before. He hoped it was because once you did a tour or two, you have enough money and didn't need to do it again. That was his hope. All his pay was going into their common checking account; their mortgage was on auto pay, as were all of their bills. He would be able to access the account remotely and wire himself some money to base, so that when he needed something from the PX he would be able to get it, like a soda, toothpaste or chips. He also had a heads up that when you travelled, the customs officials in Arab countries would play games with you to get a bribe, otherwise, you could sit in the airport all year and they didn't care.

The flight took just over thirty six hours with stops and layovers. It was on commercial flights or charters and when you finally got to the last spot, the military base where you would be working for the next year, your first thought was "Holy mother of God, what have I got myself into?" The air was dry and cold and dusty and it had a sort of gritty funk about it. You could also detect the smell of oil and grease from all the trucks and tanks and military equipment. The base was just as he imagined it, but worse. Enslow did not expect puppies and rainbows and the base did not disappoint because it was very impersonal and cold, almost brutal at every turn. It took some time for them to be assigned their quarters. Due to some expansion on the base, instead of being assigned one or two to a room, eight men were assigned to a larger room. They had cots on the floor and hammocks strung from the room supports. "So much for privacy," Mr. Yackety-yak mused.

"Look, I have been patient with you. I don't like it here either. I don't want to be here. I have to be. I signed up to do a job and be very well paid for it. Looking at things now, I expect we will earn every penny, but I swear to God if you keep up with your whining, I'll take you out myself, and I don't think a man here would lift a finger to stop me." Before a startled Yackety-yak could respond, one of the guys who till now had said nothing spoke up and said "Enslow is right. You have been a pain from the first day. He took the sergeant on to try to teach you to grow up and shut up. I was going to rat you out till I saw Enslow take the sergeant on. Impressed the hell out of me. So you shut up, do your job, and we will get along fine." He turned and continued to unpack his gear, then repack it, as there was little place to put stuff. A completely stunned pain in the ass just stared, mouth open a bit, and then he looked down at his feet and began to also rummage though his stuff quietly.

Enslow slept as well as a man who had travelled fourteen thousand miles in thirty six hours could. It would take some time to get used to the time zone here. It was almost a complete inverse from where he came from in the US. There was precious little time for lollygagging. They were expected to be at work in forty eight hours. Their orientation started with a two day class on installing and testing the BDS components and bringing them online. This consisted of unpacking, connecting, cabling, and configuring the computers, communications parts, and the satellite dishes used to link up with and download data from the BCC (Battlefield Control Center), nestled safely in Fort Benning. It was only the first full day and while Enslow was surprised at the relative quality of the food, he knew instantly by looking at the menu posted for the next two weeks that he was not going to like the food. Just the thing for weight loss. Eat as much as you like, but that was the secret eh? Eat as much as you like, so that except for the days where you were famished from everything you did, you were generally not disposed to eat too much. At least there was a good supply of fresh fruit and veggies, though not top quality, and there were a lot of them. Ella had told him he should eat more of these, and he knew this turn of events would make her happy.

After two days of orientation, they were

assigned to unpack and pre-configure twelve systems. Enslow's team consisted of three other guys. A big Texan oddly enough named Dallas McIntyre, a guy from Philadelphia named Orlando Fuentes. While he wondered why people would give their children geographic names, being named 'Enslow' gave him little room to mock others. Nothing was very macho about the name Enslow Spengler. Sounded geeky. Dallas sounded like a man's man name. The final member of the team was Mr. Yackety-yak, whom Enslow discovered had the entirely predictable name of Daniel Weiner. Might as well have named him Weiner-Weiner. When, after the day had ended and Enslow could detect that his other team members had tired of Daniel, told them how he wouldn't shut up, they all agreed that Yackety-yak was a good call sign for him. Being civilian men, they didn't have or need call signs, but they liked giving each other names. When Yackety-yak returned, they started referring to him directly as Yackety-yak, he objected. So they started to call him Weiner, where upon quite quickly he asked to be called Yackety-yak. Dallas had a cool enough name on his own, and no one thought Orlando needed a name, but he asked the group to think of one. After talking to him for a while and hearing his life story, the name that stood out was BoomBoom. It seems that as a younger man, he had a habit of climbing the tree outside his wife's second floor bedroom window and they would spend several hours enjoying each other's company. While one might think that was the source of the name, it wasn't directly. It seems that one night they were PARTICULARLY fond of each other, and made too much noise. So her father grabbed his shotgun and chased him out that window where he didn't wait for the luxury of climbing that tree, he just jumped, landed and rolled and took off with no pants. The 'BoomBoom' was the double shot that his now father in law let off at him as he ran. He insists that he still has a pellet or two in his cheeks. He was persistent, however, and not only maintained his relationship with his girlfriend, but won over her father. For twenty seven years, they have stayed together.

Hoping to bypass this process, Enslow merely smiled throughout the story telling. Then Dallas spoke up, "What should we call you?"

"I honestly don't know," said Enslow.

The group started firing rapid questions at him.

"Favorite actor"? "Cary Grant-everyone wants to be Cary Grant, even Cary Grant"

"Favorite car?" "Chevy"

"Favorite Movie?" "Captain Blood with Errol Flynn"

"Favorite color?" "Blue"

"Favorite food? "Bacon"

"Beef or Chicken?" "Beef"

"Dogs or cats?" "Fucking cats."

"Favorite subject in school?" "Recess"

"Favorite President?" "The one who gets us out of this mess."

"Favorite song?" "Fire on High – ELO"

Seeing that wasn't yielding any clues, Dallas finally said, after a minute, "I got a hankering to call you Wichita. We know that's in Kansas, and we all know you're from Kansas, so we can swap one fer the other, but it lets us talk bout you in a stealth."

Enslow thought about it and said, "OK, Wichita it is, I sort of like it. But that leaves us with a problem."

BoomBoom said "Like what?"

Enslow elaborated, "Well while the name Dallas is cool, and the guy Dallas is cool, it doesn't mask him in the same manner. No one will ever know who BoomBoom is, unless we tell them, but since his name IS Dallas, it is too apparent who we are talking about."

Yackety-yak spoke up, "You know, Wichita is right, my last name is Weiner, and I can't tell you how often I've had that name shouted at me or said behind my back."

Dallas quickly said "You could hear us? We didn't know it was your name man."

"Thanks," Yackety-yak assured.

Enslow spoke up, "You know, there is the story of the Indian brave who went to his father the chief and asked him, "Great Father, how was it that you decided on names for your children?" The old chief said, "When your sister was born, I emerged from the teepee, and the first thing I saw was a Spring Flower, so I named her SpringFlower. Your brother, RunningBuck, was named after the first thing I saw after he was born, which was a magnificent running buck at the top of that ridge. Why do you ask such questions TwoDogsFucking?"

The assembled men all laughed very hard, but Dallas suddenly stopped and said "Hey, I ain't going to be that TwoDogs fella. If you think I am gonna wear that name, your face and my fists is gonna dance."

Enslow assured him, that was never my intent, but you can see how important a name is, it must be given much thought."

"Well think all you want," Dallas went on, "but I wouldn't touch that with a ten foot pole."

BoomBoom's face lit up, "That would be a great name!"

"Don't make me smack you, I ain't going to be called TwoDogs or anything like it," Dallas said quite firmly.

"No," BoomBoom said, "TenFoot."

"I ain't got ten feet. I got ten toes" a confused Dallas replied.

"TenFoot like Ten Foot Pole. If anyone asks what TenFoot means, you can tell them it's for ten foot pole. If they still want to know what it means, tell them to ask their sister. It will shut them up."

After considering it for a minute, Dallas agreed, "Yep, I like it. You boys done good."

That was how the first work day ended for the men. They had come together as strangers in hard times, taking a dangerous job they didn't want, but had found a way to bond and become friends and to make a stand. In the next couple of days, other contractors got very curious who these guys were that they had never met Wichita, TenFoot and BoomBoom. Yackety-yak was sort of obvious, and once they worked that out, it was easy enough to figure out who the rest were. Not wanting to be left out, and needing the bit of escape the idea offered, most of the other contractors also assumed call signs. The base command structure didn't like it, but the men assured them that all paperwork would be filled out properly, but that should someone overhear a discussion they didn't need to hear, having these names would allow them a bit more security. Some of the names that were regularly being bandied about were TinCan, OneShot, Pegasus, Jammer, Wheels, Quadcore, TravelingMan, Rhinestone, and the almost too easy Joker, Riddler, and Mr. Freeze. There was one woman on base, a liaison for the company. She never left the base. She was not pretty, but had a beauty that could best be described as 'handsome'. She did not participate in the call signs, but everyone referred to her as Ripley.

In the third week there was a problem with a forward operating base's computer systems and one of them was chosen to go. 'Yackety-yak' drew that duty. He reconfigured and repaired all the associated systems and made it back safely.

Almost. The convoy he was riding in was ambushed, and three troops were killed along with two contractors, one of them was Yackety-yak, and the other was a guy called Snoopy. Yackety-yak didn't go easy. According to the radio intercept, he went screaming. First at the leg he had lost, then as they drug him away. Perhaps he had the last laugh though. It seems that as they were assaulting him, they got distracted by the rescue convoy or someone searching for him, and he managed to detonate an explosive vest near five of the insurgents. He lived long enough to tell the rescue troops what had happened and ask for a priest. The meal that night was quiet. Not that they really liked Yackety-yak, but he was one of theirs, and he didn't deserve this, and he didn't want to be here. It could have been any of them. From then on, instead of just riding in the Humvees, they also used their eyes to scan the road ahead. In a popular movie an actor once remarked to his partner, "It's your ass Cochise, what do you wanna do?" Well, it was their ass now and they were going to take as active a participation in things as they could. They all wanted to go home.

Nigel Day 256

Nigel got up around 9:00 in the morning feeling really good for the first time in weeks. His wounds had largely healed and were no longer sore, not even after moving about all day long. He had always been suffering one pain or another so he was really quite used to it, but just as he always had done, he took fewer pain pills than the doctor recommended. *What doesn't kill you only makes you stronger. And right now what I need is a stronger cup of coffee.* Nigel had taken to brewing a local store brand, but at double strength. Horrid taste, but a bit of cream and sugar, and it was just what a man needed, one cup and ready for action. He went to the bag from the cleaners, and selected a good white shirt to wear this afternoon. Having checked how long it would take to get there, he calculated he would need to arrive by 2:45 for the 3:30 wedding. You didn't want to arrive too early or late, certainly couldn't disrupt the festivities on the bride's most important day. So if he wanted to get there by 2:45, which would allow a little time to inconspicuously mingle, he needed to be in his car and underway by 12:45. That left him about three more hours to get ready. Seeing as there would likely be upper crust types there, Nigel felt obligated as a loyal subject to be as presentable as possible. He took longer than his usual amount of time to shower, and for the first time in years, actually followed the shampoo directions to wash, lather, rinse and repeat. He even stopped off earlier and bought some conditioner for his hair, but a manly one, not something that made him smell like a Nancy boy. Then he shaved with one of those larger magnifying mirrors, where your nostrils seem twice as large, and given that he had not trimmed his nose hairs in a while, thought that he should secure a hedge trimmer. After spending almost thirty minutes shaving and weed whacking, he slapped his face with a brisk aftershave. *Now mate, you look almost presentable.*

Nigel decided that a spot of jam would be just the proper breakfast, but old habits die hard, and while he did toast up a bagel and smother it in jam, he also found time to fry two eggs bangers. As he was loading his plate, he realized that he hadn't intended to make such a large meal, but sat down to enjoy it. When he had finished, he tossed a piece of the bagel near the rubbish bin, but only then realized that the rodent roommate was in his other flat that was off the grid. He still wondered if maintaining another flat was a good use of money but he needed at least one other place. Does the CIA really play multiple levels against each other to hide, as that other CIA team had ransacked his place? Why didn't they know he was on their team? Did they really need to be that cloak and dagger? Maybe these questions were above his pay grade. His duties were quite specific, and he had in all likelihood, been pushing things too far with his interpretation of what they meant, but Kingston had not made him stop, so he intended to keep doing what worked or seemed to be working.

Given the high profile nature of the event, and not wanting to attract too much attention or at least the wrong kind of attention, Nigel did not take a weapon. He seriously doubted that he needed one and there would not only be good security there, but that was not in his mission parameters to be armed. Looking though, at the absolute beauty of a .45 caliber handgun, he couldn't resist taking it. He wouldn't be carrying it, just leave it in the car in the concealed space in the seats. He did take an extra phone battery, his car charger and five thousand pounds in fresh notes in a variety of denominations. He also took his ear comm and a backup. These things had a battery life of about four hours. He had been used to turning it off to conserve the battery, but Kingston didn't like being off-comm very long, and owing to the event today he decided to take the backup comm, which would give him about eight hours. He wished the suit had some built in bling like his service tux, but that stuff would likely be revealed by a pat down or scans. He rather expected both. Now pat down could be fun, especially for a sailor who has been at sea for a while, but his luck always got him either the masculine brut or the masculine brute-ess. Neither of which were to his liking.

Nigel kept feeling that he was putting off something he had wanted to do. Deciding that it would be best to get it over with, he also wanted to prevent the inner voice from bitching, which it would surely do sooner or later. He reached into his go bag and removed an unaffiliated mobile phone and powered it up. When it had signal he called Royal Mercy Hospital and asked for Keith Logan's room. The switchboard woman insisted there was no one there by that name which irritated Nigel. He said "This is his neurologist, Dr. Calico. I am looking for the CIA agent who was brought in almost eight days ago. Nice bloke. Mother was a pain in the arse. Know him now?"

The switchboard operator informed him he was not listed as an attending physician and Nigel said "Look. He isn't supposed to even be here so if I know about him then I am on a bloody list somewhere. While you look for it put me through. I need to confer with my patient." The momentary silence was replaced by a dial tone and then a phone ringing. In three rings the phone was answered by the familiar voice of Agent Logan. "Hello." he said.

"Keith Logan?"

"Yes?"

"Good to hear you up and about, this is Dr. Calico."

A momentary pause and a now friendlier Keith Logan Said "Hello Doctor. Good to hear from you."

"How are you feeling? Making a recovery?"

"Yes, thanks to you, I shall make a full recovery."

"No worries. Happy to help. It's my job. I do have a question, though."

"I am all alone so ask away," Keith said.

Calico asked "Once upon a time you chased me on the M4. Why?"

Keith Logan replied without delay, "We were sent there to look for an asset who was off book, meaning he was not logged in our active agent's lists. We had no idea who it was or who they worked for. We detected some chatter to and from you and thought you might be that asset. We were unable to uncover a duty profile for you but we found your official cover. We were gathering information on you and you spotted us. We believed you to be a low level courier without intensive training. Your ability to detect and evade us indicated you were way above the courier we thought you were and decided that you must be the off book asset. We thought you were British, but the chatter was originating back to Virginia. We never did know who or why you moved up on our lists. We were going to do a full grab and interrogate you. I fell afoul of our team leader and was reassigned. One of my other team members let me know a couple days after that about your evade in London. That confirmed it for the team that you were likely a high value asset and when we could get no confirmation from Langley we knew you were valuable. We hoped to find out if someone in our government was running you or if there was a UK program working against our interests. I was able to pull your complete file by getting a favor form a buddy in MI6. What I read was startling. I couldn't tell where fiction and fact intersected or separated. I decided that it was just about the best piece of pure hogwash I had ever read. Then my new assignment went bad. Suddenly there you were riding in like John Wayne but instead of a horse you chose construction equipment. You took out all the hostiles and brought us both back."

"So what do you think now?" asked Nigel.

"I still don't know what the truth is but I suspect that the man who dragged me back from the abyss might be more than his profile. Certainly more than I thought. I think you can count on Maria not understanding the man she is dealing with. Should you need to that could work to your advantage. She is not usually the kind to overestimate a target. If she is still tracking you she has my pity. Did you know that based on what happened, they are looking for THREE men?"

Nigel chuckled a bit, and said, "Well, maybe they just aren't used to dealing with real men."

"I think that would also describe her if you catch my meaning. You haven't asked if I gave you up," Keith added.

"A man like you is a man I will always trust. A good Marine wouldn't lie to me. You said you would cover for me and that's all I need," Nigel offered, in a sincere, but solemn tone. "Who was your team leader?"

"Her name is Maria Vostro. A cast iron bitch if there ever was one. Has all the warmth of a scorpion and the tenacity of Sigourney Weaver from all her Alien movies all rolled into one. Not someone you ever want to piss off. Ever," Keith warned Calico. Then he added, "Although, between you and her, my money is on you."

"Any way to get her to back off? She is likely to impede my objectives," Nigel observed.

"Two ways. One. Kill her, which I admit has a certain allure. Two. Get her orders changed. That's it. She is like an estrogen terminator. She absolutely will not ever stop. Truth is I felt sorry for you at first. Then I thought she had found a worthy adversary. Now I feel sorry for her or anyone else who crosses you. I don't honestly know whose side you are actually on, but I hope it's ours. Given what you did for me and my partner I'm pretty sure it is ours. Watch your back. If I can ever help you call me. I owe you. Whatever you are into you will need all the friends you can get."

Nigel took a couple of seconds to respond, and finally said, "You don't owe me. It was my privilege to assist you. I'd do it again, but apparently I will need to always make sure I have a crane."

Logan said, "Call my mom to get a new number for me. I don't know where I will be or how this will all play out for me. Tell her the same name you gave her. She will know she can trust you. God Speed Nigel." Nigel pressed the power off button, pulled the battery then stepped on the phone and chucked it into the rubbish bin.

Nigel grabbed his service mobile and clicked to the files he had recovered from Logan's phone and found a number listed for Maria. He might have to just give her a nudge. If she couldn't be scared away then maybe he could get her to blow the gig. The most important part of all of that was that they were from Langley. They were legitimate CIA and they could find no record of him except for the published fiction attributed to him. How is it that a low level asset like him whose primary function was to attract attention was 'off book'? He might have to ask Kingston about that. Something didn't add up. Whatever the truth was he was going to remain a target of this harpy.

It was now almost 11:30, so he got dressed and pocketed all the objects he had laid out. It was just as he was trying on his jacket that his mobile rang. He fingered the button and said "Allo?"

The familiar yet vague voice he had become quite accustomed to responded with "Kingston here. We have a small change in plans. No operational changes, but we have received word that your favorite Russian will be there. It seems he has had quite a grudge against you since Paris. Just be alert. With the security there, there will be no need to be armed. Your contact there will, as part of standard protocol, be carrying a weapon. So do nothing. We just wanted you to be ready."

"Roger that. Will take no weapon. Confirming," said Nigel, "Will he be bringing Miss Jiggles?"

"Actually she was recently uncovered as a deep cover Israeli operative. She has been sent home."

"Really?" a startled Nigel said, "She had me completely fooled. I thought she was just a nice arm warmer. Never would have seen that."

Kingston responded, "We didn't know either. Had we known we would not have told you. You needed to be who you were and the avenging male standing up for the pretty girl played perfectly. Would you have played it differently if you had known her true status?"

Nigel considered their question and realized he just might have. "Yes, it's possible. Tell you what. Make sure I have what I need and don't give me any bad surprises and don't set me up to fail. That's all I need."

Kingston said "We run clean ups. No worries. Please make sure you leave on time. This is your first class A event."

"I'll be leaving in forty five minutes. I have all my prep work done."

"Good luck Aardvark. Kingston out." The call dropped.

Nigel went over the conversation in his mind. It

was entirely possible due to the masked voice that he was talking to different people each time. Probably nothing, but it just caught his attention. Nigel made his way out of the flat and locked the door. Then he activated the security system he had installed after that last CIA visit. Knowing that they would know and knowing that he didn't want to call the locals on 'family' he had it set up to activate three webcams. This way he could see what was going on and call him. In the event it was a local hoodlum he could elect to call a Bobbie. He momentarily had to scrutinize the cars on the street, at first thinking his Mercedes was still red. Recalling the black color change he quickly found it and put his jacket in the back seat. He then placed the .45 in the seat's hidden compartment and got into the front seat. The security system indicated only three approaches and no intrusions. He didn't bother to play back the video. He was leaving early to make sure he had enough petrol and found a station on the way. This was the most nerve racking part of the trip, when he realized he would impact the whole operation if he got any petrol on his pants or hands. Nothing said 'common' to the upper classes like the smell of benzene on you.

The drive was dull and boring and just as Nigel expected. He took the opportunity to practice his detection skills by mentally tracking the cars and occupants and noting when similar cars were nearby within several minutes. No signs of pursuit were detected by Nigel, so he started stalking other cars, often from half a mile away or more. He was using the digital zoom feature that Suresh had installed. Not that he saw anything suspicious or worth stalking, but it was at least good practice. The picture seemed to bounce, which was expected. The idea occurred to see if Suresh could replace the cameras with high quality camcorder internals, and add some image stabilization to the system. Seemed like a cheap way to achieve better results.

Nigel found the road leading to the estate and pulled onto the grounds at exactly 2:40 pm., and gently he nudged the Mercedes to the parking area that had been set up on the grounds. The freshly mowed grass smelled more like alfalfa than he would have expected. As he exited the car he detected a slight smell of manure and then it made sense. Somewhere nearby were wee beasties and this was probably part of their range. Horses made sense, but it also might be cattle. If it were cattle, he hoped it was his favorite, the Scottish Highland cattle. Cattle were generally only suitable for eating, but these bovines were adorable. Rather hard to imagine something as big as five hundred kilo could be adorable. A lad of about twenty came over as Nigel got out and said "Good afternoon, may I have your key?" as he handed Nigel a ticket.

"Here you go," and as he handed the valet his keys he also passed him a tenner.

Looking up at Nigel, the boy said "Thank you, sir," and took the keys and the bill and drove off in Nigel's car to the east end of the group of guest's cars and parked it. Nigel walked toward a carpet on the ground denoting a pathway that they were obviously expected to walk to the main hall. As he got to the door Nigel noticed the weight of the door and the stonework. *Obviously not new construction, but it looks very well maintained. Must be a lot of money here.* He walked in and there was a lovely girl with her hair down about her shoulders, all bright eyed and pretty, who said in a northern accent, "Hello sir, may I see your invitation?" He handed it to her and after reading his name and who he was there on behalf of, looked at her list twice not finding his name. Rather than be rude she kept checking the list. Worried there had been some monumental cock-up he spoke up "Miss, I am a late addition. Is there a second list for changes?"

Her eyes looked into his when he spoke. She smiled and said "I feel so silly. There is a second list, but I don't have it here. One moment, sir" and she picked up the phone and dialed some number. "Millicent, this is Sally at the front. I don't have the late changes you mentioned. Can you look and see if there is a Nigel Synclair Jones from the Scottish Trade Ministry on there? There is? Brilliant, thank you." She hung up the phone. Nigel noticed that her fingers, while graceful, were really just a little too long. Sort of freakish, extra terrestrial freakish. "Thank you so much. I need to tell her to send it down. You were on that list. My apologies, sir. You'll find the guests gathering in the main hall. Please sit in the rows behind the blue flowers. If you would like a drink, the bar is open just down the hall. After the ceremony dinner will be served outside on the west lawn and a later celebration will be back in the main hall this evening. Enjoy yourself, sir." Nigel nodded and smiled, and said "Thank you" with as much of a Scottish brogue as he could manage without over 'dewing' it. He did walk to the bar where he ordered a single malt. He tipped the bartender who refused the gratuity. "Nonsense" he said "I have never ordered a drink in my life without recognizing the hours you spend on your feet." The bartender smiled and said "Thank you, sir" rather than argue with free money, although he was being paid quite well.

Nigel took the opportunity to walk around and shake a few hands and talk for a few minutes to five or so gentlemen and one intimidating looking woman who was a weight lifter, a forklift driver or a cattle rustler. In spite of her menacing appearance she had a gentle voice and was actually very sweet. After listening to what each of them had to say Nigel just told them that he had recently signed on with the Scottish Trade Ministry and was looking forward to helping out Scottish industries. Just as their questions got specific, he told them he would like to talk to them later, but that it might be time to take their seats. They all suddenly became aware of the time and as a group they made their way out of the bar area and walked back to the main hall and took their seats. As Nigel was selecting a row, he saw an old friend. It was Konstantinov. Nigel tapped him on the shoulder, which seemed to upset the bodyguard next to him.

Nigel was all smiles and stuck out his hand and said in as genuinely a warm voice as anyone could "Hello friend. Good to see you!" The Russian was all too quick for appearance's sake to smile warmly to and shake hands with Nigel, but he made quite sure to grip Nigel's hand too firmly. Without showing any indication of pain Nigel said "Я вижу, вы оправились от вашей мастурбации травмы." The ensuing chuckle from the bodyguard drew a quick scowl from Konstantinov, but he regained his smile and said "Yes, it is good seeing you. I have been hoping to spend some 'quality' time with you. Perhaps we could meet later?"

"If you feel up to it bring your friend. I could use a good workout," and then he sat down in the row just behind and to the right where he could observe the Russian and his bodyguard. *Really, you brought a trained killer as your date to a wedding? What a girl.* He took his seat, unfortunately near an old woman who smelled of too much lilac, but such were the fortunes of war. As Nigel waited he

examined the crowd in a very leisurely way so as
not to appear very interested, as many of the
attendees were doing. The front rows were for
family and appeared to be filling up at even rates.
One could infer that both families were very happy
about the joining. At precisely 3:25 the Prime
Minister, who was in the front row, received a
quick message from someone who looked quite
terrified. A look of alarm spread across the face of
the Prime Minister, who looked around nervously.
Did someone back out? Now that would be a bit of sport,
wouldn't it? Much to Nigel's surprise, however, the
Prime Minister and pretty much everyone in the
room, the organist struck up "God Save the
Queen." All eyes and heads turned to the direction
the Prime Minster was looking and after a couple of
people entered Nigel's jaw actually dropped open
in disbelief. Before he knew he was doing it he
found himself rising to a standing position. The
entire assembled crowd was also in the same state
of hypnosis and they also found themselves
compelled to stand. A sudden sound of clapping
ensued, not thunderous, but appreciative and
sincere. The older woman, wearing a dignified and
pleasant looking dress made her way into the main
hall and after stopping to nod at the Prime Minister
tried to take a seat in the second row. *My GOD!*
The Queen herself has decided to attend! Nigel was
momentarily stunned and realized that he needed
to mimic the actions of everyone else so that he
didn't stand out. When the applause had died

down the music being played changed to a more traditional wedding selection and the groom and his men entered, followed immediately by the attendants and lastly the bride herself. There was no need to stand as no one had yet sat from the entrance by her Majesty. The bride deserved a lot of respect for her stamina. The dress was obviously quite heavy and to have the Queen of England actually there was likely more excitement than most women could bear, but she was holding up magnificently.

The ceremony seemed short by Nigel's estimation. He had never been to an upper crust wedding and he had never been in the company of her royal highness the Queen. After the usual biblical readings, songs, exchanging of vows, the music started and the bride and groom walked down the aisle to their future as man and wife. Next were the bride and groom's parents. The Queen and her attendants, however, declined to stand and walk out. Everyone understood. The next rows cleared and then the next until everyone had left. Nigel rather imagined that the Queen did not want to be seen walking with the common folk, and she did not need to be on display on the day that belonged to another woman. He also assumed that given her years, the spectacle of her falling or tripping would be quiet unseemly. When Nigel could get clear of anyone too near, he pulled out his mobile, pretending to talk and used his comm. The computer voice answered "Kingston. Identify yourself."

"This is Aardvark, route me."

After almost thirty seconds, the voice replied "Sorry. No one is available. Please call in one hour."

"The Queen of England was here and that wasn't in my mission statement."

A pause of twenty seconds and then even with the computerized manipulation of the voice it was easy to detect surprise "THE Queen of England?"

"Yes."

"Standby Aardvark. Routing."

Another computer modified voice identifying itself as Kingston, *(weren't they all Kingston? Seriously, it's like every agent of the FBI is agent Smith)* came on. "Aardvark, her royal majesty THE Queen of England is in attendance at the wedding?"

"Yes," Nigel informed. Again with a long pause and the voice said, "Life is often made up of opportunities. To withdraw now might work against us. You being at an event she is attending raises your profile. That is your function. Stay on mission. Stay on comm. We will monitor until you leave. We will be off comm for twenty minutes until we gather our team. If you need us, ask."

That was rather interesting. How good was their intel, if the Queen is attending and no one knew. Since he was there and got through the security and no one had much noticed him, his painted history must be holding up well. Nigel wandered about shaking hands and meeting people as his mission called for. In just over an hour he was up to 40 people. By concentrating on groups he was able to hit three to six people at a pop. It was getting close to dinner so Nigel went back to the bar for another drink. The same bartender was there; saw him approaching, and after a quick flurry of hand motions had a duplicate of Nigel's his previous drink order waiting. Nigel smiled, passed him another bill and thanked him "Good lad." It was while walking with his drink that he came face to face with his dear friend Konstantinov. "Good to see you again, mate."

The Russian smiled "Yes. It is good to see my friends. I was unaware you spoke Russian. "

Nigel smiled and looked up at the ceiling for a second, squinted his eyes as if concentrating, but was actually trying to cover for Kingston who for the first time tonight was on the ball. They recited very carefully, phonetically in Russian, "Kak interesno bylo by, yesli vashi faily, soderzhashchiesya vse, chto vy hoteli?" (What fun would it be if your files contained all you wanted?)

Konstantinov replied, with a canary swallowing smile "I will see that they are updated. We shall see you soon."

"Yes," Nigel smiled back, "Let's have lunch. I'll treat." This only elicited a scowl and a small "grrrr" from the bodyguard, but no real reaction as the Russians moved away through the crowd.

A waiter came over with a tray and said "It's best not to piss off the Russians Nigel."

"Ahh, anything from our friends across the pond?"

"No. I thought with the Queen arriving they would have been a more active comm chatter."

"I have them on at the moment."

"They know about you and the Russians?"

"It would seem so," said Nigel.

The ersatz waiter was all the while writing on his order tablet as if taking an order. He finally said, "For dinner, would you like Coq au vin or the Boeuf au poivre avec Cognac"?"

"Which one is beef?"

"The second one."

Nigel said, "Then I will bloody well have the beef. Do I look like a Frenchy?"

Not liking the treatment, the onsite contact moved off to work the rest of the event. Nigel hoped he would not take his attitude personally, but decided that he would not. The kid was supposed to be a professional. He talked with another five people and having met most of his salutation quota, moved back to the main hall to start dinner. It was assigned seating, so he was directed by one of the staff to his proper table. The tables were arranged in staggered rows so that you could not walk a straight line between them. This seemed silly, but probably was done that way to appear more attractive. Nigel sat down at his table of twelve people and introduced himself to the six that were there. Nice folk, but other than being pleasant and listening to their idle chatter, Nigel found himself sitting there trying to look excited. He knew he was going to struggle with boredom. He did not anticipate much of anything being very much exciting. He found himself scanning the room for the waiter or any waiter and even trying to see if Konstantinov was close by. It occurred to him that he had probably tweaked 'his old friend' enough and that he should not go over and talk any further. Kingston had also seemed to go silent. Nigel excused himself from the table and went to the men's lavatory where he found that although the battery was still good he was going to need to switch to his backup comm. When he had switched over, Kingston confirmed that he was back on line. He returned to his table which now had three more people, and it looked like there might be some no shows leaving some chairs mercifully empty.

Suddenly there was again a stirring and murmuring from the crowd. The Queen was making her way to the lead table up front where she was given a microphone and she began to speak. The crowd instantly went silent as if you switched off the telly.

"Good evening. Many years ago at my own wedding, a young palace guard was injured by a horse in the procession. After my wedding, I went to the hospital to visit him. He was badly injured and eventually succumbed to his injuries some weeks later. His son grew up to be a fine man and is sitting before you tonight. He is your Prime Minister. I have never spoken of this publicly, but the man's chivalry and love for his country was such that when I told him I was so sorry for his accident he replied, "Tis but a scratch. Please do not concern yourself over it your Majesty." I was so moved that this young man was so in love with his service to his country that he did not want me to worry. I learned of this wedding some weeks ago and decided that I should attend and publicly thank this family for their service at that time and the service they provide to this very day." The Queen turned her head, looking straight at the prime minister and continued, "I thank you, your government thanks you and your people thank you. May this union be successful and happy."

The crowd, most of whom had never seen their Queen in person or heard her speak, as she seldom made public pronouncements, sat there in complete silence. For seconds there was not but a sound. Then a loud sound could be heard by all. It was unmistakable. Somewhere in the front of the room possibly near the Queen, someone farted. It was a loud boomy explosion from someone; no one may ever know who. The look of amusement that some people shown on their faces, turned to a ghastly horror. You could see what they feared on their faces. They think that at that moment of silence that it was her Royal Majesty who blasted. A panic seemed to set over the crowd. It was awkward. Nigel stood up, his feet moving of their own accord. He seemed to have no control to abate his progress across the few rows that separated him from the front tables. He made it to the clear space just as various security people noticed him too. Still under an influence he did not understand, he kneeled.

His voice called out loudly but respectfully. Not at full volume, but loud enough for most people to make out. "Your Majesty, I beg your forgiveness. I am the offender. I have brought shame to this occasion and I fear my act has brought shame to the Crown. I offer myself for any indulgence you may wish." Nigel kept his head down.

A kindly voice called out to him "Arise. It is of no matter. Please resume your place and enjoy the night."

That voice was the Queen's! She had addressed Nigel personally, something she seldom did. "Think nothing of it."

Nigel raised his head and replied with great humility, "Thank you, mum" and he turned and walked out, appearing to be a highly shamed and embarrassed individual. Indeed, the show was so convincing that Konstantinov was considering the man he had come to loathe. *A brave man, a man of honor. Perhaps I should know more about him before I kill him.*

Kingston was buzzing on the comm, "What the hell was that? You are supposed to be seen, not be the whole show! You may have jeopardized us. We wanted to up your profile not steal the whole focus. Your assignment is over. Return to your flat. We are going to re-evaluate your role."

"I don't know what came over me. I could not look up there and see her stand there with everyone thinking it was her. Bad for her, bad for the wedding, bad for the UK. It was the right call."

"It wasn't your call to make. GO home. Kingston out."

Nigel realized he had just stepped in it big. He needed this job and he had just gone cuckoo. A real agent was meant to blend. He was supposed to draw attention, not become an international incident. No two ways about it. His career was rubbish, he was rubbish. He was just a daft middle-aged fool who was playing spy while real people did the work, the dangerous work in secret. He was just playing the clown. Perhaps he could find additional work in this industry. Apart from a spectacular misjudgment it seemed like he was pretty good at it. *The real trick though, was how are you going to keep the twenty four million dollars you liberated? Not a crime to take it, it likely wasn't traceable, those kind never like money that was traceable, but you would have to be careful, it would attract attention.*

These and other thoughts swirled through his head as he went to the valet and handed him his ticket for his car. In a few minutes they brought it up. He handed each lad a tenner and drove away. He also switched off his comm and threw it in the back seat. *Stupid cock, putting yourself front and center. Like a stupid bloody Aztec sacrifice begging to have your head cut off! They probably could have shot you just for walking in her direction. God you are thick!* Nigel grabbed his mobile and powered it down. He removed the battery. *No sense talking to them. It won't be good news. What you need is a good drink, and lots of them.* This made sense to Nigel. When you are in trouble you go see your mates. Instead of going home he drove to the Badger and Canary, his favorite pub. He had only been going here for the last six weeks, but there was just something instantly comfortable about it. Rather run down and a bit dodgy, but there was sincerity about the place, like a stray dog that wagged its tail when you said something kind to it. In less than two hours he made it just shy of 8:00. In the corner were Evan and Sam.

"Oy! You bastards better have a pint for me!" he shouted at them.

They smiled broadly, "Where have you been? Don't you look nice! You been to see the Queen?"

A sudden panic broke over Nigel, "What have you heard?"

Looking completely confused, Evan said, "Nothing, are you all right? You look buggered."

"I have had about the worst day you can imagine. I embarrassed myself at work today. I bet I'm going to lose my job."

Sam said, "It'll be all right. We're mates. I'll put in a word for you. We can get you a new job. But I bet it will be ok. I know people and you are one of the good ones. First night I saw you I said 'Chris, that guy is all right.' And all you did was lose a game of darts. But you paid up and bought us drinks. We'll stand for you. Should we call your boss? I mean it, we'll do it."

Nigel was impressed with the affection these two men he really didn't know much about had for him. Just a couple of nights a week it was just some blokes having stupid talk about football, politics, cars and girls. Harmless pointless stuff that had always made Nigel feel like he had a home. He was so far away from his in order to do this job. It was nice to have a place to belong to. Men were hunter gatherers. It was coded into their DNA. They liked to collect stuff. Some men collected cars, some collected conquests of the fairer sex, and some collected money and power. Nigel was more of a gatherer than a hunter. This new role as hunter was new to him. It had been such a long time since he felt he was really good at something, and he thought he had found it. Apparently he hadn't. "Right then, you boys have given me perspective. I'm going to go in to work tomorrow and tell those smarmy bastards to sod off. Who the bloody hell do they think they are? I work hard and all they can do is find fault. I may have messed up a bit, but my intentions were noble. I am going to get me a better job. You want to know why?"

Evan and Sam looked at each other, smiled that their friend was getting back his mojo. "Why?" they shouted in unison.

"'Cause I'm a good bloke! I work hard. I try to control costs. I am looking out for my company. I'm looking out for my mates, and I'm looking out for my country. If they can't appreciate what a dedicated man can do then they don't deserve me. They can just let my job go tits up. I'm a bloody brilliant bastard!" Nigel boasted, and raised his glass, "To me, supreme bastard!"

"To you!" Evan and Sam responded with abandon. They raised their glasses, but never letting an opportunity to raise their glass go wanting, about ten nearby patrons raised their glasses as well. All drank their drinks to the end of their glasses, "AHHH!" they shouted.

The rest of the night was a long and completely drunken affair. Chris, Sam, Nigel and two other people he never quite got the names of or couldn't remember spent the next several hours drinking Nigel's wad of cash he always carried. Being too drunk to drive Nigel took a cab home where he ended up collapsing on the floor. Thinking that the floor was perfectly acceptable place to lie, he wadded up his smoke and scotch scented jacket and fell into a solid drunken sleep. The time was 1:30 a.m.

Enslow Employed Day 136-150

Ella,

Very little you can imagine will prepare you for life on a military base as a civilian contractor. It is always busy, always noisy, and the general lack of color makes it dull looking. No motion picture or television show really reflects it. There is sometimes friction from the younger soldiers. They make very little and the contractors make a lot. And the contractors are older, and slower than the young soldiers. But that all goes away off base. When you are in a convoy, these young men and women put their lives at risk to see that you get to where you need to be. The skills that the contractors have are what ensures that they and their fellow soldiers will stay as safe as possible. Wars are still fought much as they always have been. The idea, to paraphrase General George S. Patton, is not to die for your country or cause, but to make some other son of a bitch die for his. Battlefield intelligence derived from satellite, UCAVs, remote sensor packages, and good old fashioned human surveillance and communication with the locals, puts so much advantage into the hands of the western forces. But it still isn't easy. The enemy is ruthless, cunning and cruel. Their own safety or the safety of women and children means very little to them. They use this to their advantage.

One woman shot her own child, and brought it bleeding and near death to a forward base. As the doctors rushed to help her, she removed a grenade from her garments and killed herself, her baby, and three medical personnel, injuring ten more. It is hard to put into words how you should feel about it.

But I am doing well. I have lost 22 pounds, and can lift as much weight as when we were married. The staff doctors here have fixed my ingrown toe nail that was always an issue. I had a crown replaced and I have grown a beard (see attached picture). I'll shave it off but it is nice to not have to shave every day. They actually encourage it as it helps you blend with the locals.

Not everything here is dire. The basic decency of people was reaffirmed for me when we were riding in a convoy last week and a little girl stepped out in front of us. That brought us up to full alert status, as it is harder to hit us when we are moving, so stopping is almost always forbidden. Every time we tried to shoo the little girl away, she kept getting in front of us. She spoke no English and couldn't understand us. One of my chauffeurs, Jackson Dupree, finally recognized her. He had gone through the week before, and saw her crying by a door, so he stopped. Her mother was inside and had delivered a little brother for her by herself, and had lost a great deal of blood. The woman's husband had died in a market suicide bombing the week before and she had no one to help her. Jackson called for a medical team and she was stabilized and after a couple of days, seemed to recover and went home. The platoon stopped by several days later and left them some blankets, some food, and a stuffed bear for the little girl. So today, when Jackson got out of the Humvee and smiled at her, she smiled back and took his hand and walked him about thirty feet in front of the Humvees and pointed at the ground. He called for another guy I like, Ramón Santiago, and he brought out a metal detector. Turns out an IED had been planted in the road the day before, and the locals were too scared to tell us. Our guys dug it up; disarmed the bomb and we resumed our mission to repair a satcomm link.

I miss you, Dee Dee and Augie very much. Due to new restrictions on data connections (I think we lost a satellite), I may not communicate as often. Tell the kids Daddy is doing well and will be home in a few months for a visit when I earn my first rotation. Tell Augie he gets to be the man of the house till Daddy gets home.

I got your last email. Tell your sister to mind her own damn business; you don't need her to weigh you down. Better yet tell her to come here, and I'll explain it to her myself.

Enslow

He pressed 'send' and sent his wife the letter. He was grateful he had bought the expensive laptop. It allowed him to play games, watch movies and keep up with everything. A few people had already had their laptops break or discovered that theirs were limited, and they should have bought what Enslow and some others had bought. It was all deductible anyway. Why worry about another grand when you are making this kind of scratch?

The base Enslow was assigned to was a NATO base, so there were Army, Air Force, Marines, and people from other countries. None were there in as large a number as American forces, but the ones that were there were generally as brave and hard working as any American troop. He came to appreciate how much national barriers broke down. We really were, for the most part, 'allies' with the foreign military forces on base. Enslow guessed the shared sacrifice was a bond from one service to the next, from one soldier to the next. For the last several weeks he had been getting the short end of harassment from some of the soldiers. Time after time the young men would mock and ridicule the 'old guys' who were not as tough as the Marines.

No fight ever broke out, but it was a constant refrain. Having the respect he did for these young men and women meant Enslow never criticized them. One time Enslow had been walking from the mess hall to their quarters, when a Marine, named Jackson Dupree, had been chasing a football and ran headlong into TenFoot. Once the boys realized one was from Texas and the other from Louisiana, a football argument ensued. Jackson was having none of it and was quite ready to start pushing around TenFoot. Thinking better of it at the last minute, even though the Texan was taller and bigger than Jackson, Jackson was a Marine and could quite likely squash TenFoot. So he said "What is your name, civilian?"

"Why do you want to know?"

Jackson said with a cocky tone, "So I can make sure they spell it right on your tombstone."

TenFoot replied, without blinking, "TenFoot."

Jackson came back with "You don't look native American. TenFoot What?"

"TenFoot pole."

"What does that mean, ten foot pole?" Jackson asked, not making the connection. Ramón Santiago, who had by this time come to see what the yelling was about, just grinned and turned his head away. He had guessed where this was going. His snickering was not noticed by Jackson.

"Ask your sister," was the Texan's reply.

A look of confusion was evident on Jackson's face as he tried to understand what he had just been told. The look of confusion turned to one of anger. One of the last things you should do is insult the chastity of a Marine's sister. For just a brief second Enslow feared this was going to come to blows but then Jackson's face broke out in a huge roaring fit of laughter. The kind of roaring laughter that comes from the gut, up like a volcano. Ramón Santiago was finally able to let out his howling. The whole assembled crowd now numbering around a dozen Marines and civilians hooted and laughed. Jackson stuck out his hand and said "Good to meet you TenFoot, I am Jackson Dupree. If you and your friends would like to play some football tomorrow with real men, be here about this time. Since you are all old men, we Marines will go easy on you. I could use a big man like you with some brains on my team." With that exchange over the Marines ran back to the bit of grass they had been playing on, leaving the contractors to continue on their way.

"I didn't think you were going to say it. He could have killed you. We just made that part up to be funny."

"You know," said TenFoot said, "When we were laughing about it, giving each other names, I didn't like it. But it seemed to so entertain you fellas. I just had to take it to please you."

"Well, we aren't done yet," said Enslow.

"What do you mean?" asked TenFoot looking like he had not gotten the drift.

"Wait till we tell them why we named him," Enslow said while jerking his thumb back to BoomBoom, "You know. How he earned his name."

Though it had only been two weeks since YakkityYak had died, the contractors so far from their homes had been able to grieve for a man they barely knew and start to laugh again. Enslow smiled to himself that YakkityYak would have enjoyed that exchange between TenFoot and the Marines. His thoughts were interrupted by an argument about the current college basketball rankings. Every day it was something. One day it was a comment about their age, their accumulated middle aged guts. Other days it was a small comment like, "Hello ladies." Wichita knew that he meant no harm; it was his way of teasing. He only did it because he liked the older guys. Jackson kept poking the contractors that they were not full men.

That honor was the sole province of the Marines. Maybe in their next life they could earn it, but in this life it was unlikely. It was all good natured ribbing, but Wichita always wondered if it was closer to the truth than a poke. Ramón usually stood to the side when they were being harangued. Wichita would admonish him to not count the old guys out. Age and wisdom usually beat youth and inexperience, but it was no matter. The relationship was set, and the verbal beatings would continue. It even extended to the mess hall, where the Marines would mock the civilians for their lack of stomach for what was called 'grub'. Wichita reflected that he really understood why it was called that.

Nigel Day 257

Nigel awoke with a start, his head still hurting. He was getting too old to drink so much. He had lost his professional ranking from his days at university and now hardly qualified as an amateur. There were several people in his flat, all dressed in suits. A man not quite thirty was standing over him and said, "Mr. Jones, please get up; we need to leave."

His mind now clicking in, he responded with a bit of indignity. "Who are you? How did you get in my flat? I am not going anywhere till I get some answers."

"There is not sufficient time for answers. You need to get up and get dressed. You need to shower and shave. I'll give you ten minutes for each."

"What's this about?" A still non-moving Nigel said from the floor and he suddenly realized he was likely in some trouble. You can't just approach the Queen and speak. He guessed that his manufactured identify fell through."Is this about yesterday?"

"Indeed it is," came the reply.

"All right, let me get ready," said Nigel, a bit of surrender creeping over him. As he made his way to the loo, the man who first spoke to him followed. It was all a bit too close for comfort.

"Oy, I have done this all my life, I think I can still do it unassisted, but if it is your heart's desire, by all means please join me!" Nigel spat out, now genuinely indignant.

"My orders are to stay with you at all times till I turn you over. I have done that my entire life. Followed orders. I am not going to cease doing it now. End of."

Nigel stepped into the shower and turned up the hot water. When it was ready he disrobed in front of this stranger and stepped in. He didn't need to be a tarot card reader to know he was armed. They all were and they all appeared to mean business.

"Do you mind at least closing the door?" Nigel inquired, "I'm getting a bit of a draft."

"It would violate protocol in this situation."

Nigel made a quick wash with the soap and washed his hair as it likely it was still full of smoke, a bit of beer, and who knew, even a little sick. It was a good night ending to a most disappointing day.

The dark suited man asked, "Do you have another suit?"

"Yes, but the one I took off was my best one." Nigel replied. Through the shower glass he could see the blurry figure speak to someone in the hall, but he returned in twenty seconds.

Nigel finished with his hair and shower in seven minutes, and stepped out, saying, "I need to clean my pipes. Have a slash, done it every morning since I was lad. Would you care to participate?" he said with an inviting smile on his face, but with little humor in his voice.

"Leave the door open partway. I will be listening," was the reply.

"Well then, if you breathe deep you can smell the daisies I usually drop out of my ass." Nigel bellowed. He figured that a gruff showing might be the best way to play it. As he squatted down and began to eliminate for real, he reached behind the seat, and took out his emergency comm. He always kept it there and kept it charged in the event he needed one and couldn't get to it or put it on in front of anyone. He clicked it on and snapped it into place behind his ear.

Wiping his backside and flushing, a naked Nigel walked out of the lav area, and went to the sink where he lathered up and began to shave. He finished that task ahead of schedule and went to his bedroom furniture where he took out a fresh pair of BVDs. Only after he put them on did he realize that two of the people in his flat were women. They didn't seem to care about him in all his glory so he paid no attention to them. After putting on a good pair of socks he turned to the first man who had followed him.

Nigel heard a slight pop in his ear. A voice indentified itself as Kingston.

"How would you like me to dress? Is my execution formal or casual?"

Kingston replied "What? What is going on?" but Nigel could not respond directly, so he continued asking questions, hoping Kingston would figure out the situation.

Showing absolutely no emotion the man said "We need to be formal. This type of function would go much better for you if you were as formal and polite as possible."

Picking up his suit and sniffing it, Nigel agreed with the earlier inquiry. "Well, this just won't do.

All I have better than this is my tux. Have you ever seen a man sent to his final reward in a tux? While we are at it, what is your name?"

"I never gave you one. It's Perkins."

Looking from face to face Nigel said, "Who do you work for Mr. Perkins?"

"I am with MI5. Would you like to ask me anything else?" The newly named Perkins asked.

"What is Perkins from MI5 doing in my flat pushing me around at such an early hour?"

A now concerned Kingston responded "MI5 is there? Standby Aardvark. We will activate a Red Flag response." Nigel noted that although the voice was computer generated the concern still showed through.

Perkins turned his head slightly to face Nigel and told him, "I am not able to inform you at this time. My orders are to convey you to a specific destination at a precise time and in a presentable state. I have complete confidence that I will be able to accomplish the first two elements but, the third is in doubt."

Pausing for effect, Nigel shrugged his shoulders slightly and said, "No, that will do for now. But if I require anything additional, I will inform you as to what that is."

Nigel got out his service tux, a clean white shirt and his black shoes. It took him all of another ten minutes to dress. When he was finished Perkins said, "We are leaving. Now."

"Where are we going?" Nigel inquired.

"Sorry. Need to know basis, and you do not need to know, but you need to go."

"Clever little twonk, you can rhyme," Nigel observed, as he left with the assembled minions of MI5. They made it outside where one of them locked the door to Nigel's flat and they walked down to three Jaguar saloons. Mr. Perkins gestured to the middle one so to keep Kingston as informed as possible Nigel confirmed aurally, "Three Jaguars? Why do I have to ride in the middle Jaguar? Are you certain?"

Kingston repeated in his comm. "Roger that. You are approaching three Jaguar sedans. Possibly in the control of MI5. You are entering the middle Jaguar. We are caught flat on this Aardvark. We have called a Red Flag on this, but we cannot get to you for thirty minutes. We will try to track you through CCTV. No satellite is overhead at the moment. Intelligence assets are being mobilized, but we can't get to you in time. You are on your own. Good luck. We will monitor for as long as your comm stays open. "

Nigel sat in the middle of the rear seat as five agents got in and surrounded him. The rest took up their seats in the leading and trailing cars and then they were off. In forty five minutes time they had made it to a garage near the Tower of London. The three Jaguars entered the complex through a very innocuous looking garage door.

Nigel guessed that given the distance and direction they had travelled they were likely a couple of blocks west of where they entered the garage and several stories underground. Nigel's comm couldn't work under this much steel. As they parked the cars they got out and Perkins gestured for Nigel to exit the vehicle. He asked "Can I ask where I am now?"

"Tower of London, detention level 6." Perkins replied.

"Tower of London, detention level 6? Am I being detained or executed?" Nigel asked, who by this time was getting a bit annoyed. Imagine, a spy being annoyed by cloak and dagger stuff, but there it was.

"No. You are not being detained or executed.

We are merely waiting here till it is time to go to your final destination."

Nigel raised his eyebrows, "I don't' like the sound of that. Final Destination."

Mr. Perkins informed Nigel, "I am only to bring you here and hold you. Another agency will arrive shortly. Please sit in this room." He gestured with his right hand, "Would you like some coffee? I know you had a staggering amount to drink last night and we need you to be alert. I have taken the liberty to bring you breakfast."

As Nigel walked into a nice room he noticed it really wasn't a cell of any sort but it appeared to be more like a nice executive conference room. He found a table set with a steaming breakfast of eggs, bangers, jam and coffee as well as orange juice. "Are the condemned allowed to at least specify their last meal?"

"What is your problem? Have we harmed you? Have you been shot?" A now slightly agitated Perkins asked.

"I have been taken against my will, forced to dress up, and taken across London to the Tower, where I am being held against my will. I'd say that constitutes a bit of harm. For you cloak and dagger types this must be just a normal bit of skullduggery, but for a private citizen this is rather a bit over the top and far outside of the usual affairs of my corporate life."

"It's no wonder you are so good at what you do. Arrogant and angry, all the time," Perkins said.

"And just what is it you think I do?" Nigel postulated, with an additional dose of arrogance since it seems to rattle Perkins just a bit.

"You sell overpriced computer goods and services to companies whilst actually sending a great lot of decent British jobs overseas. You are supposed to represent the Scottish Trade Council, but I suspect like all fat corporate pigs, you prefer to reward yourself."

Acting as if he was considering what he was just told, it was immediately obvious that his cover was not blown. They must think he did represent the Scottish Trade Council and that he was a computer executive. Relief swept over Nigel. Whatever was going on, he was at least not outed. His cover was intact. Either the boys in Virginia were better at their craft than he gave them credit for or MI5 was worse or he just got lucky. Nigel raised his eyebrows and pursed his lips slightly. After another ten seconds he told Perkins, "Seems you do know me. Better than me mum. She thinks I'm adorable. Well then, I will avail myself of this meager meal before me and await your next interruption in my life." Nigel was having trouble hiding his grin and hoped that Perkins would take it as more corporate arrogance. The food was actually quite good and while not a coffee drinker he found that he was becoming addicted to it and he really did need the boost. He was not as young as he used to be and a jolly good night at the pub was sure to set him back a bit. It was now 8:15 am, and the door to room 6 opened, and the men who entered showed identity papers to Perkins who acknowledged their authority. Perkins had the professionalism to address Nigel. "Good luck. I'm sorry we came off as gruff, but today is a very important day for you and if we did not get you there on time we would have been at fault. We don't normally do this sort of activity, but after we found your car abandoned we shifted into high gear to locate and acquire you. Best of luck." With that, Mr. Perkins left the room and walked down the hall.

The new 'leader' walked over and introduced himself. "I am Jeremy Bristol, one of her Majesty's personal events coordinator. We need to depart. We would not want to be tardy."

"I don't feel tardy," Nigel assured. Then they left. This time as they returned through the garage there were a pair of Rolls-Royce automobiles. Nigel had the door opened for him and he entered with only one person sitting near him, Jeremy Bristol. They drove out and back onto public streets. Nigel asked, "Can you tell me about what this is all concerning?"

"I'm sorry, sir, that is not in my responsibilities. I can tell you that you need to be on your best behavior. Say as little as possible, be as humble as you can, and you may just get through this with no regrets."

"Duly noted. I seldom have regrets. Except for a ginger lass in Edinburgh."

The car drove for approximately thirty minutes and pulled up to the side gates of Buckingham Palace. Now Nigel was feeling a bit of terror so he said, hoping the comm had re-linked, "Are we at Buckingham Palace?"

"We are."

The cars pulled up and went to a side portico that was covered and they all got out. As they did so Nigel noticed that their demeanor was one of deference, not confrontation. He walked through and they gestured to follow them, so he did. They walked down several halls to a smaller office area, but it was quite grandly decorated. After all, it was Buckingham Palace. At last they arrived at an impressive set of doors and the attendant standing there opened them. Nigel walked in to find himself standing before the Queen of England. He immediately bowed and held the bow while addressing her as "Your Grace."

She addressed him. "Hello Mr. Jones. It is so good to see you again. You know, after yesterday, apparently we had some trouble locating you. How wonderful we were able to and I must compliment you on your wardrobe selection. It is a bit too much really. I didn't want to make so much of this, but I must say I am not surprised. A man of your character and chivalry would appear in nothing less than respectful attire."

Nigel straightened up. All he could say was, "Thank you your Grace."

Kingston was back on line and had been since before the arrival at Buckingham Palace. "Aardvark, we have called back our teams. You are still on your own. What is going on? Your Grace? Precisely where are you Aardvark?" Nigel could not answer. It was not only impolite, but disrespectful and he also was quite in the dark. He had no idea what was going on. Anything he could say would be undoubtedly mistaken.

The Queen again addressed him "Throughout all of recorded history, and quite likely even before that, the spirit of British manhood has been one of heroic actions often carried out with little regard to personal safety or even life itself. The crown would not exist to this day and most certainly my family would not be here had not many, many British men answered the call to service. That call to service often meaning that they would make that most noble of sacrifices. Their sacrifice was not for personal gain, but for the good of all men and for the good of their country. Yesterday you perceived your Queen in danger. Not mortal danger, but it would be correct to say that a minor bodily function exercised at the most inopportune moment appeared to come from me. Before anyone could act you and you alone took it upon yourself to throw your dignity and your reputation into the abyss of public humiliation, all to save a nice old lady the embarrassment of a public display. For you see my dear lad, it was not I who committed the unseemly disruption, it was a member of my staff. But you took it upon yourself to protect your sovereign without any thought of personal dignity. Your selfless act of sacrifice was no less noble than that demonstrated by all British heroes throughout the ages. Though your life was not in physical danger you nonetheless rose to a challenge to your queen, selflessly, quickly, and with great humility. I have no doubt that were you in battle you would have acted as equally heroic as you did that day. You see Mr. Jones, heroes are not made, they are born. Deep within them is that quality and courage that instinctively allows them to act in the interests of others with little regard to their own safety. At the end of it all, when your name is put on that stone, what have you got to take with you, but your name and your reputation? Therefore, in recognition of yet another British hero, and a gallant servant to his country and his crown, I ask you to please kneel."

Nigel was having trouble breathing now. His heart was racing, his palms and feet were sweating out perhaps all of his bodily moisture. He silently knelt before the Queen and bowed his head. She withdrew a sword and said "For gallant service in defense of his queen and his country, for selflessness in the face of public ridicule, for coming to the aid of a woman he did not know to spare her public attention, I dub thee once, twice and thrice, Sir Nigel Synclair Jones. Arise Sir Nigel Synclair Jones. From this point forward, you shall be known as a Knight of the British Empire, a commander of The Royal Victorian Order and subject to all the rules and privileges that title imparts. God bless you, Sir Nigel Synclair Jones." She then handed him a ring and bade him, "Keep this with you at all times."

Nigel stood up, took the ring and bowed to the Queen and said, "Yes mum. God Bless you." The aide named Bristol escorted him out of the chamber and back to the waiting Rolls Royce. Another aide opened the door and Nigel got in. The driver said, "I'll have you back home in a jiffy, sir. I've been told that they have had your car returned there as well. It's a pleasure to drive you, sir. We should have you home in thirty minutes."

All Nigel could think to say was, "Thank you." The car pulled out from Buckingham Palace, onto the main roads and in the general direction of Nigel's flat. Nigel did not quite know what to think and marveled that he had a clear and empty head. Every time he tried to engage his brain to assimilate what had just happened he was unable to. He was in a stunned state and just could not reengage. He was staring out the window when Kingston finally spoke up. "We are calling off the Red Flag and securing the extraction teams. We will contact you in the next few hours to discuss this. Frankly we are at a loss for words." Nigel responded "As am I."

The driver said "Sorry?" and Nigel said, "Just thinking out loud, pay no attention to me." They drove on and shortly thereafter arrived at Nigel's flat. He waited till the door was opened, got out and shook hands with the driver. He then walked back into his flat having absolutely no idea of what really just happened or why. Life was full of amusement. One day you are down, one day you are up. One day you screw up at work and are going to resign and then the next day you are Knighted by the Queen. It was just a regular everyday occurrence.

Kingston Day 257

The phone rang and Harlington answered. "Field Analysis – Harlington."

"Bob, it's Scott. Have you heard?" Starker asked, speaking a bit low so as to not draw attention to the conversation.

"Yeah, I heard. Mr. Asshat Jones made a scene at the wedding party. I should have listened to my doubts but the world class fuckup had me fooled with his bravado shtick. We wanted him to draw attention, not create an international incident. I think we need to pull the plug. It's just gone too far," Harlington analyzed.

"Oh, I think that is an under estimation of the events."

Harlington seemed puzzled by the tone not the statement. "What is his status?"

"You are apparently not current. It has escalated to unchartered levels." Scott Starker said, his tone dire.

"What? In what way?" asked Harlington.

"Approximately five hours ago Aardvark's apartment was breached by MI5 and he was forcibly removed and then detained in the Tower of London," Starker replied, "and it only elevates from there."

"Have you informed Central Control?" asked Harlington.

"No, I wanted to make sure we were both up to speed. I didn't want any questions to surprise you."

"Decent of you, but I trust you. We are both in this up to our necks. This operation was both our ideas," Harington's tone showing a bit of concern. "Why the Tower of London? Did they go to the ultra secure level?"

"Yes."

"Is he still under British control?"

"Yes, and will be for life."

"Good God! Maybe a swap can be arranged later. He didn't sign on for this. We promised to keep him out of trouble."

"That won't be necessary," assured Agent

Starker.

Harlington asked, "Sorry? Not following. You said he was under British control for life?"

"Well, at the moment he is freely roaming London under self determination."

"Then how is he under lifetime British control?" a completely confused agent Harlington asked.

Straker began to speak with a completely confused, inexplicable expression and twisting of his facial features but all Bob Harlington could hear was the discomfort and elevated tenor of his voice. "Well, it seems that the palace guard received control of Aardvark, who took him to Buckingham Palace. He spent twenty or so minutes in the company of the Queen and after thanking him for his chivalry, Knighted him. From this point forward it would be proper to refer to him as SIR Asshat Jones."

The silence was awe inspiring. If a pin had dropped, you could have heard it. Scott Starker was quite sure that Bob Harlington had actually stopped breathing.

Bob changed positions in his chair and said after a long thirty seconds, "I have no response."

"Nor did I. Aardvark kept an emergency comm under his toilet seat and activated it when he was taken. He had no clean suit so they let him wear his service tux. We were able to track him with the GPS buttons from the tux. They only knew that the Queen herself wanted to thank him for the events at the wedding. They have not apparently broken his cover. Aardvark played it completely in character, and NEVER let on he was anything but what his cover dictated. I have no idea how he held on to it. But we'll debrief him when we can. I think he needs a day to process this. We need several. Anyway, our boy is still playing his role, but now he is a Knight of the British Empire who has automatic access to any number of places on Earth and instant credibility that even *we* can't create. The implications for us are enormous. We will need to get him to sign on for more than another six months." Starker sucked in a huge breath.

"We will have to bump this up the chain, and we will likely lose ownership. That's not good for us, and not good for him." Harlington said into the phone in hushed tones, "but this might be our ticket up the ladder."

Starker agreed, "Yes, but remember we are dealing with a fundamentally good man who is here because of us. No one will look out for him, but us. We need to keep doing it. We owe him. He wouldn't be in this if it were not for us. Our little pet project has gone beyond the parameters we set up."

Nigel Day 258

Nigel had had a very busy couple of days. After decompressing and letting it roll around a bit in his brain pan and also letting it roll off of his tongue, he was getting used to the sound of it. "SIR Nigel Synclair Jones," he would say in front of the mirror. "I'm sorry, it is not Mr., and it is SIR Nigel Synclair Jones. Yes I would like a private suite." After letting the emotional high settle down it was really just a bit of sport for him. *I should get some cards printed.*

Nigel had spent the better part of the day buying some food, washing the car, and getting his suit cleaned. He realized he needed another two or more suits so he had called Byrd & Thayer and asked to have another two made identical to his previous suits, one lighter gray, and one darker, perhaps almost black, but not looking like a mortician. As the day wound on, he called up Evan to see if they would like to knock down a couple of pints and told him he was buying. Naturally Evan was in favor and was quite sure Sam would stay for the duration. The time to meet was set for 6:30 and Nigel even offered to get some fish and chips. Again, Evan was open to the idea.

Nigel's car had been towed to his flat and after checking the internal surveillance was quite sure there would be no issues. With some amusement he did see three of the MI5 agents who had come to his flat inspecting his car. None of them even knew they were being recorded, but since they thought he was merely a computer executive, why would they? He dressed in casual wear this time, trying on some cowboy boots he had decided to treat himself to. He arrived at the pub just a few minutes early.

"Allo Chris," he shouted as he saw his mate, "Where's Sam?"

"He'll be along in a few minutes. Said his wife was being a bit under the weather." Evan explained and then he looked at Nigel's boots and exclaimed, "Aren't you just the High Plains Drifter!"

"You like them? Couldn't resist. Ever since I watched all those westerns, I have always wanted a pair, and after a promotion I just got, decided that I deserved them."

"A promotion? That's just brilliant. I knew you were the right bloke for the job, whatever it is. I was rather worried when you were so down the other day. Now it seems you are back on top of the world again. So will you still be here in London?"

"Well, maybe a bit less. Difficult to say, really.

They may send me around to some of the other countries. Someone has to impress the locals."

"Wear the boots. They suit you."

About this time their fish and chips arrived. Seeing the confused look on Nigel's face Evan said, "You said you were going to treat so I took the initiative to order them before you got here. Didn't want to be sitting there all hungry."

Nigel smiled and thanked Evan "Decent of you to be thinking of me. Glad you did. I am quite hungry," and he handed the server a crisp 100 pound note instructing her to keep the pints coming. Nigel didn't hear the door open or didn't pay any attention to it. A familiar voice said "I thought I'd find you here." It wasn't anyone Nigel was excited to see. It was the ever obscure Mr. Perkins from MI5. He continued, "May we have a word Sir?"

Nigel said "I just sat down to eat and tell tall tales with my mates. Can we do this later?"

"I'm afraid not. We'll provide some dinner for you if we take too long. Please get up."

Nigel grabbed a hot fish piece and stuffed it in his mouth. Seeing the concern on his friend's face he waived him off that everything was ok and then took a step back to the table to swallow half of his pint. He told Chris, "It's all right, just work. You go on and enjoy my largess. I'll pop back if I can, but don't wait on me. Keep the match day open. I want to see United on top."

Looking worried, Evan managed "All right, best of." He stayed in his seat. As they were leaving, Sam walked in and said "Oy! Leaving so soon, I just got here."

"Just some work thing I need to address. I paid for some food and pints. Stay with Chris. Back in a flash." Nigel said with a smile and he left with Mr. Perkins.

They walked out of the pub and got into the familiar Jaguar saloons that must be the standard transport. Only this time, Nigel noticed that the glass was likely bullet proof and the tires seemed heavier as if they were also resistant to ballistic intrusion.

After entering the door that was held open for him Nigel settled into the leather seats. As the car took off he asked Perkins, "What is it this time?"

"It seems we have a problem Sir Nigel," Perkins uttered with a serious look on his face.

"Oh, what would that be?" queried Nigel with

as much disdain as he could muster.

"Well, Sir Nigel, it seems we were not as thorough in our relevant check into who we present to the Queen. Our first query indicated that you were a computer services executive who travelled a lot. We were satisfied with that, but after doing some additional investigation; it appears that while a British national you are actually in the employ of a rival agency."

Not blinking and hoping that his face did not indicate any change, Nigel brought out a flask of Tequila and took a quick drink. The intent being that if any change in the colour of his face was apparent, the change would be attributable to the tequila. "What are you on about Perkins?"

"Sir Nigel,"(Nigel found this interesting that he was still using the title and that he thought he was a British national), "Depending on what you do for the CIA, you may or may not be in violation of various laws regarding national secrecy. At this juncture we can find no indication you have endeavored in treasonous activities. It appears to be a just a job."

Sizing up the situation, Nigel decided to play the helpful civilian role.

"Well, that's quite correct. I do work for them

and it is just a job. I was quite clear to them. I was never going to betray my country and I would not accept any assignments that would put me in a position to do so. Things are difficult in this economic climate both in Europe and abroad. I had the opportunity to make a few extra quid. Satisfied?"

"Actually, I am almost satisfied. No one would have performed that little drama you did the other day unless they were utterly dedicated to their country and their Crown. It was obvious that what you did was what you thought was in the best interests of England, and not yourself. I'll be brief. What we want is for you to assist us in some matters of national security. Being not only Knighted, but being a member of that prestigious order she assigned you to, would help us in some low level operations. What we want to do is send you out on some assignments when you are not otherwise engaged, and give you access to the resources of the Commonwealth. That may also help you in your career across the pond. We know things they don't know and they know things we don't know. What the concerns are of the US government are not always of concern to us, but you never know what one contact will lead to. Are you in?"

After considering the offer for fifteen seconds to make it appear he was weighing the opportunity

Nigel finally said, "As you know, if my country and my sovereign need me what else is a loyal subject to do? I am at your direction."

"An excellent choice. I want you to know you could have turned us down without any unfortunate effects. But hope we can be of use to each other and I hope should England ever need you, you will be there."

"When you put it like that, yes, you can rely upon me."

"I don't think there is any need to go to the office. It looks like you had a nice evening all planned. We can return you there. Any paperwork we will just send over. You haven't asked what it pays."

"Don't need to. While the job itself is almost reward enough, I just want whatever compensation is equivalent to the tasks at hand or at least in line with whatever others receive. I trust that can be arranged?"

"It already has," and the MI5 agent removed a small satchel from below the seat. "Here are your passports, credit cards, and other documentation, NHS card, etc. Look through it and if you need additional elaboration as to any specific points please call me at this number." He handed Nigel a card which Nigel put into his pocket..

"Oh, almost forgot. Here is a service phone for you." Perkins handed Nigel a new phone. "It uses L5 encryption like your American phone so you should be familiar with it. Your first assignment is listed in the phone's calendar. It will be standard arms training. We use a variety of weapons which you will not likely need to use, but it is part of standard training."

"Thank you. I look forward to whatever awaits me."

"Good night, Sir Nigel." The Jaguar pulled up outside the Badger and Canary and Nigel got out, taking his new leather satchel with him, making sure to lock it. He walked back into the pub where Sam and Chris's faces brightened up at his return.

Perkins signaled the driver to continue on. The black Jaguar drove off into the dark night.

Harlington/Starker Day 165

Agent Starker picked up the phone and called his fellow analyst, Harlington. When he answered, he said, "Wanna see something really funny?"

"Like what?"

"My wife was playing around on that site for Job Networking, ProNect, and someone who is an alumnus of her school that she didn't know, seems to be linked to someone so bizarre, she showed it to me last night. This guy is either crazy or one of the best fiction writers I have ever seen. Listen: Was assistant navigator for the Royal New Zealand Yacht Squadron during the 1995 America's cup race, notable for the televised sinking of One Australia. Pity."

"Huh?" Came the over educated response. "What is so great about this guy? Yachts?"

"No, I'll forward you the link. When you read this guy's profile, he holds an eclectic series of jobs, but it begins to dawn on you after reading that there is a sub text underneath. The guy is a master of espionage, and no one has caught him, he has worked in Baghdad, Istanbul, Cleveland…."

Enslow Employed Day 151-180

Wichita, BoomBoom and TenFoot were getting a reputation. A reputation for excellent work and being the best at what they did. If there was a tough problem, they were your men. That's what years of experience and talent coupled with the kind of motivation derived from excessive compensation and also a desire to do it right so that you can zip back to the relative safety of the base did. It made you the best at what you do.

Wichita would be the first to tell you that what was so obvious and such a complete mystery to the overpaid under talented corporate executives who precipitated the current economic crisis is that you get the behaviors you reinforce. You want people to hustle compensate them or give them a self interest in performance. In his case the motivation was the money and the safe return of your ass to the base. The three of them were fast earning the reputation as the go to guys for the southern half of the country.

The base commander came in and asked TenFoot, "Where is Wichita?"

TenFoot looked up, and after taking the four

seconds he always took before answering any question replied "In the mess hall getting his bacon. He'll be back shortly. What's up?"

Commander Aris spoke with his usual 'commander' voice, but rather than simply ordering he was instead asking. "There is a problem south of here. We have an SCL completely down, and the BDS can't sync. Eyes in the air show movement, and we need to be online. Can you three go?"

TenFoot looked a bit concerned and asked for clarification, "You asking, not tellin'?"

"Yes," came the reply, "it's likely to be hot."

"When do we need to leave?" TenFoot asked, seemingly not concerned. After all, it was just another trip out.

"Next thirty. Make sure and wear your vests." With that, Commander Aris turned and left.

Four minutes later Wichita and BoomBoom walked in laughing about a joke they heard from Dupree, but their faces took note of the expression on TenFoot's face. They knew something was up. Before they could speak TenFoot said, "Saddle up. We are riding out in twenty five minutes. SatComm link is down and they can't fix it."

BoomBoom offered "When it positively absolutely has to work you call the best and that's us."

Wichita nodded his approval "It's all the grey hair and we have the miles and experience to know what we are doing. Anything else?"

TenFoot looked them straight in the eyes and said "Yeah. It's hot. Wear your Sunday best."

Without missing a second all three men turned and grabbed the protective ballistics clothing, helmets and their tool packs, and walked out the door, heading for the chopper pad. They stopped by the mission hut to log their seat on the chopper and then they boarded it. While you might think they were flying one of the latest American designs, in fact, they were flying on a very old Russian Mil MI-8 – the 'Hip', the kind that had been in service for over thirty years. This particular bird was likely one of the first. Taxicabs way past their prime made this pig look good. These beasts were bleeding fluids from about every gasket. She spent three times as many hours in repair and maintenance than she did running. Not always unusual for a helicopter, but after that kind of attention you usually had some confidence in the results. Not with these birds. They were leased form a consortium of Afghani and Russian partnerships at inflated rates. The intention was that some money would enter the local economy. As is the usual outcome in these cases precious money actually ends up in the hands of locals, but instead it enriches a corrupt local government official or a local crime lord. Rather than earn the money with decent transports they instead bought aircraft well past their prime.

Often as standard procedure when going into more difficult situations, military escorts were sent. In this case they made a one to one pairing of an armed escort per techie. Jackson Dupree, Ramón Santiago, and Reggie Smith got into the chopper with TenFoot, Wichita and BoomBoom. All six had become closer due to their agreeable personalities and time spent tossing a football. Usually Jackson made fun of them for being old men or civilians. Even acknowledging that they were good men, they still weren't good enough and would never be good enough to be Marines. It wasn't personal; it was just something he could throw at them to badger them as all men do. Women like to chat and share. Men, especially real men, don't. They will insult each other or punch you in the arm quite hard, maybe even enough to bruise. It was just how they were wired, but today was all business. Every man was suited up and armed. Even the techies. Usually they didn't carry, but today each was signed out a .45 caliber with an extra clip. The transport choppers were not armed, but they did carry several M60 machine guns inside with extra ammo and an army Blackhawk was going up with them. The site of all this hardware and strength would have made Wichita nervous, but after only four months he was getting used to it. The single issue that stuck out though was that this was the most he had seen in a single trip. He just assumed it was a precaution because one thing you could count on with his employer and his client was that they didn't like surprises and wanted to be fully prepared for any contingency.

Wichita stowed his pack and sat in his chair as BoomBoom also got situated. Somewhat of a rarity, this time they actually had seatbelts. Not that the flights were bumpy, but after so many years of having a seatbelt in every car he rode in or every plane it was just uncomfortable NOT to have a seatbelt. It was nice that they had one now. Jackson and Ramón likewise got secured, but they also secured the weapons. In the next helicopter Wichita assumed that Reggie and TenFoot were also getting ready to lift. Wichita always enjoyed watching Reggie and TenFoot. Watching a kid from the projects who didn't know a white person by name till he was fifteen and a hard southern Texan become best friends in a short time was encouraging. Now if these crazy people in this part of the world could worry a bit more about each other and less about what some old decrepit proclaimer had to say, the human condition might improve. Reggie and TenFoot were proof that it could happen.

Wichita and BoomBoom were in transport 114, and TenFoot was in Transport 697. They both lifted off, and out the port window Wichita saw the Blackhawk also lift off. The cockpit door was open and he could hear the radio chatter. Much of it was in Russian, which was quite convenient because the pilots were Russian. Strange people, they didn't really smile and Wichita never quite trusted them. Something about how they never smiled and had cold eyes. Twenty minutes into the flight the call came in over the radio. There was a small firefight starting in the north and the Blackhawk was being re-vectored to assist. That left the two ancient helicopters to continue. After another ten minutes 697 radioed in that it was having to turn around. They were having fuel issues. Nothing more than that, but Wichita watched as the bedraggled helicopter made a slow turn to the east and flew back to base. Something didn't feel right. Their formation of three had turned into a single and they were all alone in the cold sky. This time of year, though, to be fair, the ground in Afghanistan wasn't much warmer. *These things were made to haul people and stuff but couldn't they install a heater that did more than buzz?*

Jackson had become quite detached during these flights. He stayed aware, but would sit there waiting for it to end, never looking out the windows or talking. Normally a talkative guy, he just relaxed and sat there. Except now. There was a distinct 'ping' noise. Then another. Then another and another. Two points of light opened up above his head and as he looked up at them he knew there would be a corresponding hole in the floor. Sure enough, when he looked there were not only two holes but another two as well. They were taking ground fire. Two shots had exited the roof, a third had penetrated a hydraulic line, and a fourth had penetrated his buttock and embedded into his spine. He just never felt it. As his control over his legs ebbed, he found it difficult to stay in his seat. Jackson looked down at his legs that now refused to follow his orders. He noticed a small trickle of blood that was making its way off of the aluminum bench seats to the floor. Before he could quite register it, the blood that was pooling on the floor was now being covered by a stream of red hydraulic fluid. An alarm sounded through the open cockpit door and while Wichita had only picked up a few words of Russian, one he had learned was pronounced 'der-mo', which meant 'shit'. It was apparently raining shit in the front of the now mortally stricken Hip. It was losing altitude and slowly beginning to wobble, which meant the pilots were losing control. One was on the radio frantically and the other was making a valiant struggle to maintain control. Wichita looked around the helicopter to see if everyone was worried or not and everyone was except Jackson, who was beginning to look pale. Wichita asked him, "Jackson, you ok?"

Jackson looked at him and met his stare and said, "No, I don't think so."

"We'll get down man, these guys are pricks," as he gestured at their Russian pilots, "but they are good."

"I've been hit and I can't feel my legs," responded Jackson as he was now quite apparently unable to sit up straight in his chair and had it not been for his seatbelt he would have fallen forward.

"Ramón!" Wichita shouted, "Jackson's been hit!"

Ramón swung his head so quickly it seemed as if it would pop off the little stalk that it was attached to, but it didn't. He removed his seat belt and leapt across the cargo hold to his friend, "You hit?"

"Yes. Can't feel my legs," Jackson said, "getting cold."

Without saying a word Wichita undid his belt and joined Ramón in unbuckling Jackson and laying him out on the floor. Ramón could see the wound on Jackson's left buttock and using his big knife cut open Jackson's combat pants, and then opening a med kit took out a compress and handed it to Wichita. Wichita said nothing, but placed it over the wound and pressed tightly, hoping to stem the blood flow. Ramón made his way to the cockpit and informed the pilots they had a casualty and while the Russian's eyes met Ramón's he said nothing and continued to try to maintain control over the wounded bird. Ramón pulled out his BC (battlefield communicator, essentially a satellite phone) and called in a mayday.

"This is transport 114; we are taking ground fire and have casualties, going down at coordinates 224X822. Need medical evac and additional transport."

Flight Control responded almost immediately. "Stay calm. Your escort will stay in place."

"Negative. Escort was called away twenty minutes ago, we are on own. One man down, losing blood. Three CTCs on board."

"Rodger 114, we have a UAV nearby, will provide cover till transport arrives. Dispatching Medevac. Standby for further updates."

To describe the normally affable Ramón as grim might have been too harsh, but he was clearly concerned about the situation. Their overall status started to decay as Wichita could now see additional warning lights grow across the control panel. Then the engines began to cut out. Helicopters don't usually 'fall' out of the sky. They can auto rotate when they lose power and that is what they were reduced to. The engine revolutions had dropped noticeably in the last fifteen seconds. Wondering what would happen next, Wichita got his answer. The ground came up and hit them. By most accounts it was not the worst landing ever, but decidedly far from a good one. They hit so hard that the rotor blades bent down and clipped the tail of the Mil-8, which, due to weakening of its structural integrity from age and poor maintenance, snapped off. The tail boom continued down and the still spinning tail rotor hit the ground and shattered sending shrapnel all over the place. One piece penetrated the fuselage and traveled through the cargo hold and embedded itself in the back of the co-pilot's skull. His death was quick and merciful. The pilot actually had an easier time of it. He was thrown from his seat into the upper part of the flight deck, snapping his neck quicker than a Missouri chicken farmer makes a quick meal of old clucky.

BoomBoom had stayed in his seat and was belted in securely, but hit his head badly on landing and suffered a concussion. Wichita had the easiest time of it. He landed on something rather soft, and suffered no injury. That soft thing was Ramón.

Wichita's weight plus a little bit of leverage broke Ramón's left arm. A clean break, but still a break. Jackson who was already on the floor and just got shoved around on the rough metal surface. He was otherwise not additionally injured. As the turbines spun down and the helicopter lost all electrical power it became quiet except for the sound of hot metal starting to contract and the moaning of the wounded. Wichita got off of Ramón and asked, "Are you ok?"

The grimace of the smaller man told him otherwise. "When you landed on me, you broke my arm."

Wichita said "I'm so sorry; I couldn't help where I landed."

"Not your fault, should have had you stay in your seat. Check on Jackson and BoomBoom." There was no need to ask about the pilots. The blood pouring from the front of the helicopter and the obviously snapped neck of the pilot in full view negated any need to ask. Wichita went over to Jackson and asked him how he was.

"I've been better. No worse for the landing. Still feel cold. Legs don't move and it's real hard to focus. How is everyone else?" Jackson asked.

"Pilots are dead, Ramón has a broken arm and

from here, I can see BoomBoom breathing, but he is out. What happened?"

Jackson replied, "We took some ground fire. Shouldn't have been so low. One shot got me and one or more hit something more vital. All that red stuff isn't me. Smells like hydraulic fluid."

Wichita bent down and with the light he could see that there were two distinct fluids. One synthetic and one was obviously from Jackson's insides. "Can I do anything for you?" he asked.

"Yeah, find Ramón's BC, give it to me. I'll run comm. While we wait, see if you can wake up BoomBoom. Take out the M60s from the locker. Mount one by the port cargo door, then get another and mount it in the starboard door frame. Load them with ammo. Remove the safeties. Watch for hostiles. They shot us down and obviously know it. They will follow us to see if they can make us into trophies."

Wichita helped Ramón get up, asking, "Can you stand?"

Ramón responded, through his pained facial expressions, "Yeah. Brace me. Get me to the door."

Wichita supported him. Even though Ramón was not a big man he was still a largely unhelpful one hundred seventy five pounds of muscle and gear. Wichita pulled and heaved and got him to the port cargo hatch. "Where's your BC?"

Ramón gestured with his head to the back of the hold, "Over there somewhere I think."

Wichita went to the back and looked around and finally found it after three minutes of going under everything and then found it in a crevice. After he handed it to Jackson, he went to check on BoomBoom. BoomBoom was still unconscious. One eye was dilated and the other not. Wichita had no real medical training, but he knew that wasn't good. Nothing he could do for him. That would need to be someone with EMT type experience. Best thing to do he thought was to leave him strapped in. Wichita took up station at the starboard cargo hatch and scanned the horizon. Jackson was in contact with FlightBase and updated them on their current status. Two dead, three injured, but they had enough eyes to watch for trouble. FlightBase told them the Reaper was ten minutes out and they had contacted a NATO patrol maybe 30 minutes away who was running with haste to their position. The MQ-9 Reaper was the successor to the original UAV, the Predator. It was bigger and larger and could carry substantially more payload and fuel than its previous version. It was almost always piloted remotely from another base out of country, but that did not make it any less deadly. Its ability to loiter for incredible lengths of time made it an extremely effective weapons platform for offensive operations. These characteristics, like range and fly time, also made it the ideal platform for protection when a crew was down. After ten minutes FlightBase informed them the Reaper was on station and orbiting. One thing that had always brought Wichita comfort was that on his first day the Base CO informed them that they need not be too concerned about getting help if they ever needed it. He said there was not a piece of the country that they couldn't own in thirty minutes if they needed to. True to his word, it was under thirty minutes. Kind of like a pizza delivery, but Wichita didn't care about pizza; he wanted to get to safety. He wanted his friends all there too. He found himself physically agitated, but mentally calm at the same time. His eyes scanned the horizon looking for trouble that had not come. After another five minutes a voice came over the BC who identified himself as Col. Wicker, British 3rd Regiment, and that he would be there in less than twelve minutes. Wichita thought that that was good news and that things were finally looking up for what had turned out to be a very bad day so far.

As he counted his blessings he heard Ramón shout "Pucker up!" and the pin go back on the machine gun. As if that was not enough of an announcement, the sudden burst of concussion from the shells going off and the clatter of brass

352

casings hitting the floor was the final part of the announcement that trouble had arrived.

Jackson shouted into the BC, "We've got company, FlightBase."

FlightBase responded coolly, "Roger that, 114. Identifying targets. Stand by." Thirty seconds later there was a very close explosion that shook the Hip, and almost boiled their ears. The Reaper had dropped a GBU-38, a five hundred pound bomb known to the public as a JDAM, less than a half mile from their position.

The BC called out "Bingo."

Jackson turned his head enough to see Wichita and smiled. Wichita smiled back. At this point it would have been nice for Ramón to smile in agreement, but he kept scanning the terrain for any additional unfriendlies. It was a familiar sound that got Wichita's attention. It was a metallic 'ping' and the opening of an air hole next to the hatch where he was standing. In a fast and methodical way that surprised even him he merely turned his head back to the outside and began firing. The shaking and jerking from the machine gun made his vision blurry so he relaxed his grip on the handle. It happened at exactly the same time as he saw four human shapes separate themselves into smaller shapes. Understanding instinctively that he had just killed four people Wichita nether shouted in triumph nor recoiled in horror. This is just what was. There would be time later to understand what had transpired, but when that time came he was likely to rationalize it. After all, he was a rational man.

A second explosion boiled up on Wichita's side of the helicopter, announcing another JDAM that was communicating with the unfriendlies. For just a second Wichita relaxed. Had he not, it might not have mattered, but whatever the reason; it might not have changed what happened. He felt a sharp burn in his thigh and saw a hole on one side of his thigh and then the other. The bullet had passed right through but as they say in the movies, it was a flesh wound. He did not fall, but hobbled over to the med kit by Jackson. He took out an emergency tourniquet and tied the leg with a med pack to the wound to slow down the bleeding. He needed to stay on station. Additional shots were starting to hit the Mil-8, but without being very accurate, as if they were being shot by kids, people who were poorly trained, or both.

The FlightBase spoke over the BC, "Gentlemen, we have a problem. There is a fault in the UAV targeting scanner. We can't see anything, we have to withdraw. The NATO guy is almost there. We have three Blackhawks in route, expect them in 45 minutes."

Jackson shouted out loud "Fuck me! Forty five minutes, this thing will be over before that." He hadn't said it to FlightBase, just out loud. The shots suddenly stopped and they could hear the sound of an engine approaching. It was Wicker, and a very armored-up Humvee. The British had taken some NATO Humvees and added extensive armor to them, making them into a 'Penetrator'. It was designed so that you could dash in and out quickly with enough armor and firepower that you stood a much better chance of survival. Often they were used in high speed interdictions where they would run in and shoot up a 'safe' house of the insurgents or one of their convoys. They used them for rescue missions, scouting, whatever the need was. They would just dance in and dance out. This time the dance was over. An RPG fired from not too far away struck the front left tire just as the Humvee was coming up to the helicopter. It blew off the front suspensions, making the vehicle immobile. It was still useful as a firing position to defend the 240 degrees of field view that they had, with the rest blocked by the helicopter. Because of its penetrator role, this Humvee came with the fabled M134 Minigun, capable of shooting two thousand rounds per minute. Instead of three or four people, this special Humvee crewed only two, a driver and a gunner. Jackson had told them it was influenced oddly enough, by the 1960's TV series RAT Patrol, about fast moving American Jeeps that harassed the

Germans in the deserts of WWII. There would be no more fast running today.

Col. Wicker called out "Everyone still here?"

Wichita called out, "Yeah, but we have been better."

The insurgents were roughly covering a patch of ground on at least two sides, from 100 to 500 yards away, and constantly moving, dodging behind rocks and taking shots. Number of combatants unknown. The Humvee's Belgian driver ran over to the Mil-8 as Wicker watched that no one got close enough to take another shot. Halfway to the helicopter, a distance of only thirty yards, he went down. A clean shot to the right leg that broke the femur. Out of the six men now only one was unhurt. The driver was on the ground and exposed, but they didn't finish him off. Wichita thought to himself, *Probably waiting to see if we go get him, and pick us both off.*

It was a sudden understanding that either he or Wicker would have to make a run. In less than a second he made up his mind that the lucky guy would be him. Wichita called out "Wicker! Set up cover fire. I'll go for him."

"Roger that," Wicker called back and let loose a volley from the minigun. Ramón also started shooting in the general direction of the bad guys, but while he could not shoot them directly he could lob shells up high and have them rain down on their approximate location. Wouldn't kill them unless he was lucky, but that might make them scatter. An age old question men have asked is whether it is better to be lucky or good. What the answer was here probably didn't matter, but the effect was exactly the best outcome. The insurgents did in fact, scatter and often became the receptacle for the bullets from the minigun. Wichita ran over to the driver. Every step causing him a great deal of pain. He found that if he hop-stepped he could manage the pain and go the distance to the driver. Wichita went to the ground, and the two men used what limbs were otherwise intact to scuttle like crabs to the relative safety of the helicopter. That left Wicker alone in the Humvee. Because it was armored it was probably a better place to be. Wichita just could not get all of them in there and even if he could Jackson really couldn't be moved again. What the crash didn't further damage, a move might. They may have already damaged his spine beyond repair. Although dead was worse than damaged, he realized.

"Can you stand?" he asked the Belgian, who gave him a look of disbelief and realized that was stupid. "What I meant was can you shoot?"

"Oui Monsieur, I can shoot. I am a very good

shot, Sniper qualified, but my rifle is in the Humvee," replied the Belgian.

In normal times Wichita would have considered mocking that French sounding accent. Today, he didn't notice it. All he noticed was another set of hands that could shoot back to defend the group. Before the Belgian could take another heartbeat Wichita was racing over to the Humvee to look for the rifle. Dodging behind the disabled vehicle he shouted, "Where is his rifle?"

"In the front where a passenger would be," came the reply. At least that's what he thought Wicker had said because most of it was cut off with another burst of ammo from the minigun. He looked in the front door which was hung open and saw a rifle with a really sci-fi looking sight on it. He unclipped it from its mount and grabbed what looked like an ammo box for it and dragged them both back to the Hip, trying to stay lower and be less of a target. He got the rifle and the ammo back to the Humvee driver and then handed them to Humvee driver without saying anything, and then ran-hopped back to the Humvee.

"Anything I can do?" he shouted.

"Yes, keep your bloody fool head down and quit mucking about. They'll pick you off for sure!" Wicker shouted at him annoyed.

"We need to get the Humvee closer to the chopper. Single target, but more protection," Wichita shouted at the Brit.

"Rubbish Idea. She won't move. Front suspension blown off. She won't even wobble around. But a good idea. That helo isn't armored and its skin is too thin," observed an agitated Col Wicker.

Wichita felt agitated himself and was thinking hard. *There has to be a way. Maybe he is wrong about the Humvee. It has a powerful engine. No. He might be right. Look under and see how much metal it is dragging.* Wichita looked under the disabled mess that was their best protection when a coiled drum caught his attention. He shouted back to Wicker, "Can you run the winch from inside?"

A confused Wicker looked like a lost schoolboy who had just told his teacher that two and two was five. Then his eyebrows went up and his face brightened considerably. "Yes. Hit the switch to the right of the steering column. Play out the cable then grab it and run like hell. I'll cover from up here."

Wichita looked to the right and couldn't see it, then realized the toggle marked with a big 'W' must be it. He pushed the switch up and heard the electric motor of the cable drum start to turn. He jumped out and landed badly on his injured leg. His vision faded from the sheer molten pain. An infinitely long 30 seconds passed and his vision returned. Judging that this time was as good as any other he made his move. He reached down and grabbed the hook, pulled it out from under the front of the Humvee. Wichita raised his right arm and hand, holding up his thumb till Wicker saw it and responded back with his thumb. Wichita ran and hobbled as fast as he could toward the crumpled Mil-8. He heard the minigun light up in short bursts that sent streams of death to any who dared raise their heads. Their enemy was not completely stupid because the sound of the ammunition kept them hidden and Wichita was able to make it. *So much for me. I'm getting lucky.* The pain from his wounded leg slowed him down, however, and he felt rock chips pelting him. He didn't have to stop and analyze it to know that it was likely AK47 rounds aimed at him and popping rock chips all around as the bullets rained in toward him. Angels favor fools and small children and since he was not the latter, he was most likely the former. He made the thirty or so yards to the Hip and got to the side cargo door where he saw that his friends were in worse shape than he left them. BoomBoom had not woken up. Ramón Santiago was looking very pale and seemed to be hanging his head a bit. The Humvee driver, whom he thought would offer some additional firepower, had collapsed, likely from loss of blood.

"Hang on boys! We are going to combine our forces!" he shouted. Only Dupree said anything and that was "Sure, Civi, just don't stay out too late. It's a school night. The real men will be here soon." Wichita wasn't sure if Dupree was all there, but making fun of him (again) for being a civilian maybe meant he was. The real men meant soldiers, likely Marines. Wichita circled the cable around the central door frame and the front hatch and hooked it on the cable. As he turned to leave the Hip, his right hand was hit either by a small round or a fragment of a larger bullet. On his right hand he now had a red open spot in it where the metal had passed though his hand. Some wounds are worse than others and this stung sharply and was burning a bit. He grabbed a nearby roll of duct tape and with his teeth pulled off a strip and taped his hand front and rear. Suddenly realizing he was on to something he looked over at Dupree and said "Where's your knife?" Dupree was unable to move very well. He pointed at his immobile legs and said "Right thigh."

Wichita went over and took the combat blade from Dupree's hip sheath and then cut into his own pants leg. The med pack was starting to leak more blood where he had patched his leg. He took the duct tape and pulled off about six feet. He used it to more permanently affix the medpac as well as seal the wound as much as possible. Then he jumped out of the helo, making sure to land on his good leg this time, and started to run/hobble back to the Humvee. Almost at the midway point, he felt two HARD hammers hit him in the chest. He fell over backwards. Lying there trying to get his breath, he felt his vision blur. Wicker had likely not seen him as he was busy shooting a full dispensing of rounds at a group of insurgents who had taken that moment to charge their position. Wichita's lungs seemed to be unable to expand. The pain was becoming enormous and forcing him to blackout when his lungs suddenly assumed their regular function, and at twice their standard rate of expansion and contraction, forcing as much air as possible in and out. Wichita momentarily felt relieved to be alive even for a few more seconds and felt his chest for blood that was surely pouring out of him. He drew back only his dry dusty fingers. *I'm hit, but the vest stopped it. I'm ok.* That little fantasy had a shorter life than the moment where you go through a speed trap and think you are fine till you see the flashing lights come on and the patrol pullout after you. He struggled to sit up and knew something was wrong. There was intense pain in his right side. Where the rounds hit he may have a broken rib. If he did he had to avoid moving too much or he would risk a puncture. If he didn't move much, he risked taking another hit. Turning and extending his legs and arms in the least painful positions, he stood up and continued his way back to the Humvee. Just as he got there he felt another bullet hit his other leg and another round go into or through his shoulder. But he had made it. When a man is in this situation it is hard to say why some can move and others can't. Ordinarily adrenaline can make someone who is scared have extra strength. Other people are so stoked up on their own fear or fear for their lives that they are able to accomplish things that they normally wouldn't. Like lift a car off of their child, or pick up a boulder.

Today there would be no superhuman demonstrations of strength or miracles of human physiology. Save one. Now Wichita was getting pissed. *These fuckers couldn't just kill you clean, no. They had to keep shooting you till they whittled you down to bits. I didn't start this damn war. All I want to do is make my money and go home and you fucking bastards just can't leave me alone!* He stood up as best he could and reached in, and looking up at Wicker, shouted as much as he could, "Hang on!" Wichita hit the switch on the winch to the down position. He crawled into the driver's spot as the cable retracted and then tightened. The cable then went tight and the winch started to sound a bit strained, but the front of the Humvee started to turn about forty five degrees till it was pointed at the helicopter. Then with the aid of the three good wheels and a surprising amount of rolling from the damaged one it started rolling and dragging itself to the helicopter. After two minutes it had reached almost the side of the wreckage and Wichita flipped the switch to off. The strained electric motor sound died off as the winch stopped. They had made it to the helicopter and at least they could be together. If the rescue party came soon they would find everyone in one place. If they didn't get here soon, then all the bodies would be together. Wicker climbed down from the gunnery position and only then did he see the holes from the hits that Wichita had taken.

"Can you shoot?" He shouted, looking into Wichita's eyes to see if he had enough fight.

What looked back at him gave him confidence and just a bit of fear. The eyes that looked back at him were tired and blood shot. They were also VERY COLD. All warmth that you would expect to see in the eyes of another man was gone. It had been replaced by a bitter rage. That rage was black and dark as any rage he had ever seen. That was a good thing. This man was hurt, but he wasn't giving up. He might go down, but he wasn't going to lie down.

"I want to shoot every damn one of them," Wichita said. What made it so eerie was Col. Thomas Wicker would later doubt that he ever saw Wichita's mouth move. Whether those words were ever spoken, they were received. Wicker helped Wichita up to the gunnery position, loaded fresh ammo and put his hands on the trigger. A wink was all he needed to turn and go. He made his way across the four feet or so to the downed helicopter and went to the forward cargo door where Ramón Santiago was now slumped over his gun. Wicker gently pulled him to the floor and put him next to Jackson.

"Is he dead?" asked Dupree.

"No. But he's done. Until we get medical help he won't wake up."

It seems the only people conscious were Wichita, Wicker, and Jackson. Jackson could only call in updates to the radio. His last update was that help was still eight minutes out. The insurgents were beginning to mass and the relative amount of fire coming in had increased. A sudden burst of the minigun caught his attention and he turned to see fire rain in the direction of the insurgents. The bullets came in short bursts rather than a full barrage. No doubt Wichita was trying to ration his ammo. Wicker likewise selected his targets carefully. He chanced to look over and just as his did he saw almost a hundred men coming over the ridge and firing their machine guns. The minigun now never seemed to stop, but carefully and methodically swept from side to side across the ridge and just in front of it. The advancing men seemed to hesitate and fall back when the minigun went silent. *Damn. That's it. I'll do what I can, but we are finished.* Just as Wicker lit up with the ammo that he had, the whole ridge erupted in fireballs, dirt and a mixture of human remains.

The radio crackled to life and the voice said "114, this is Echo Victor, you boys still with us? Over."

Dupree pressed his transmit button and shouted out, "Rodger EVAC, we are still here. Over."

"Stand by for transport. Over."

A smile passed over Jackson's face. He was going to get out of this. Wicker jumped out as the first Blackhawk set down and the second came down on the other side of the demolished helicopter. The third stayed aloft looking for targets, but whatever targets there were decided to retreat. The field medics began the job of extracting the wounded and stretchering them to the Blackhawks. When they went to the Humvee, Wichita was not responsive, but was still at station, seemingly scanning the horizon. His face was extremely pale and a stream of blood had run from his nose and his mouth, staining the front of his clothes completely. They shouted at him to come down, but he did not move or respond. They got to him and tried to pull him down, but he still wouldn't budge. It was only then that they saw that he had used the duct tape to secure himself to the gun and had duct taped his hands to the handles and trigger. "Knife!" shouted the med tech. By this time Jackson was on a stretcher and they set him down to remove Wichita from the Humvee. They cut down and pulled Wichita from the Humvee. They asked him his name and he said 'Wichita", but it was more of a whisper and trailed off. Wicker went to him as he was being attended to and said, "You were brilliant. First class job. Where did you learn to shoot so well? I thought you were a civilian?"

An even weaker Wichita turned his head slightly, and said in a faltering voice, "I just got angry."

Wicker placed a hand on his chest and assured him, "Jolly nice angriness!" Wichita was then picked up by the medics and loaded into Blackhawk 1, next to Dupree and BoomBoom, who had been loaded moments before. As they lifted off, sweet darkness descended over Wichita and his head slumped to the side. Noticing that only one man was conscious, the med tech asked him who the man was in the stretcher.

Jackson looked him straight in the eye and said proudly "He is a Marine."

Enslow Employed Day 181

It was four days till Enslow woke up. Someone had put a stuffed bear next to him. In the bear's arms was a roll of duct tape. He saw the bear and for a moment didn't understand what his eyes were telling him. *Why was the bear holding a roll of duct tape?* The nurse noticed him moving and looking around, and came over.

"Hello. How are you feeling?" she asked.

"I'll tell you as soon as my lawyer tells me we got the son of a bitch."

"Who?"

"The bastard who ran me over in a truck. That's what I feel like. How am I?" Enslow asked, still a bit groggy from the drugs he had likely received as part of surgery.

"The doctor will discuss it all with you, but you are going to be fine. Everything will be just fine." She smiled that special warm smile some women, and particularly nurses, seem to have. It takes a special woman to be a nurse and considering the special problems faced by military personnel, a

VERY special woman to tend to the fallen.

"Thanks. I am really quite hungry. Can I get something to eat?" An inquiring Enslow said as he looked up.

"Just as soon as the doctor says you can. Right now you are getting all you need from the IVs." She pointed to the drips going into his arms.

"Don't you believe it sister. Unless there is bacon in those bags I am not getting everything I need." a much more awake Enslow assured her. "Can you tell me about everyone else? BoomBoom, Jackson and Ramón?"

Her slight change of expression told him that something wasn't right, but her response is what he expected.

"I can't give you other patient information. But I know some of them will visit you shortly." With that she turned and walked away from his bed, back to the duty desk just at the end of the room currently about half full of other patients.

It was over an hour before a young looking doctor came over and said, "Hello. How are you feeling?"

Enslow responded with as strong a voice as he

could since he didn't like being coddled, "I feel pretty good. I looked at the spots where I thought I was shot, but you seem to have patched me up with no open holes. I expected more pain, but I feel pretty good."

"Well, that's the pain killers we gave you. The ballistic injuries we cleaned out and closed. The rib will take about four to eight weeks to heal, but you seem to be doing so well after only a few days. We expect you to heal on the fast side of that. I have to tell you it was a stroke of genius using duct tape. You would have likely bled out or passed out if you hadn't taped your wounds shut you would not have lasted as long as you did. Your being able to function likely saved your life and the lives of the men you were with. What made you think of that?" the doctor asked, with a slightly amused look on his face.

"Well," Enslow started, "I was out of work for a while and had no insurance and like an idiot, I cut my finger deeply on the table saw. Didn't really have the money to go to the emergency room so I splinted it with small pieces of wood and used a cream antibiotic. I immobilized it all with duct tape. Changed the tape regularly, but it seemed to be a cheap and effective way to fix my finger. When I got hit in the transport I grabbed a roll that was there and used it. Didn't think much about it. I had to stop the bleeding and keep moving."

Nodding his head in understanding, the doctor said, "Smart, just smart. In fact, I have asked that every Jeep and Humvee and every helicopter keep a roll of it always. It is just too useful and your experience proved it."

"Doctor?" Enslow asked.

"Yes?" came the response.

"How are my friends?"

"Your friend 'BoomBoom' is fine, mid level concussion but is doing nicely. Ramón Santiago is also doing well. His breaks will heal. They were pretty clean. His other wounds weren't too bad and he is responding to treatment for his blood loss just like you."

"What about Jackson Dupree?" Enslow asked, noting that he wasn't listed in the discussion so far.

"He has suffered a substantial amount of trauma to the spine, and may never walk again. Best case is months of therapy. He was transferred to Walter Reed yesterday. He left you this bear." He nodded his head at the toy.

"Do you know how I can get hold of him? I want to thank him," Enslow asked, in a concerned voice. He was sad that his friend was so badly hurt but grateful that he was alive.

"I'll bring you the email address. All his email will be forwarded there and he will have access to a computer so you can write him."

"You know he never once complained all the time he was lying there on that cold helicopter floor? Tough bastard."

"He did leave you a message for when you woke up. He said he was sorry."

"Sorry? Sorry for what?" Enslow asked, not seeing the gleam in the doctor's eye.

"He said he was, 'quote, 'sorry for the poor bastards that made you angry'. He doesn't think they liked you when you were angry."

A wry smile, turning into a chuckle and then a quick burst of gut laughter, erupted from Enslow, only to be cut short by a sudden pain from his broken rib. The doctor smiled and stood up and walked away grinning. Enslow was just in awe. Here was a guy, newly married life possibly changed in a dramatic way due to injuries suffered trying to protect him, and he still left him a joke. *I must someday pay him back, I owe him a debt.*

Enslow Employed Day 182

The next day seemed to start like the rest. First a sponge bath then finally some real food if you could call it that. Regular visits by the nurses and a lot of time to just sit. Enslow was not sure how or if he should tell his wife. She understandably would be worried, but he was going to be all right and not too worse for wear. He still had the basic problem that his world had not really changed. He still needed the money the contract offered. He had asked and since this was a work related injury he would be fully paid. The doctor was here rather than being stateside and everyone else for that matter that knew was here so no one could let the secret out. In the end, out of love for his wife, he was going to commit the sin of lying by omission. She would be happier and he would tell her after he got home. He knew he would be happier also knowing that he was not causing her additional worry. Around two-thirty the nurse came to see him with a wheelchair.

"What's this for? I can walk." He scolded the nurse ever so slightly.

"That may be so Mr. Spengler, but you have

two visitors and I have been instructed to take you to a conference room where you and they can visit."

"Who?" Enslow asked, perplexed at the hassle of it all.

"I'm sure I don't know and privately I don't want to know. Whoever they are they are way above my pay grade and I know not to ask any questions," she said in such a reserved manner that Enslow thought she could pass for any old librarian he had ever met.

Having no choice he got up and checked that his gown wasn't going to get too drafty and got into the wheelchair. He was wheeled almost to the end of the ward and then through a hallway and down another. Enslow guessed by the diminishing amount of noise he heard from around him that this part of the building was either deserted or had become so in the last several minutes. He was wheeled into a small conference room with a table and two other chairs and a pitcher of ice water and some glasses on the table. Other than that it was empty. The nurse left as quickly as she could, leaving Enslow to sit there alone.

The wait took about ten more minutes. Enslow knew enough from his military interactions that no matter how long it took he needed to sit there and wait. He was being paid and if they wanted to pay him to sit he would sit. Fine.

The door opened and two men walked in, both in nice suits. Dark suits, not military either. The first one spoke, "Hello Enslow," he said while extending a hand, "I am Scott Starker and this is my partner Bob Harlington. We have come all the way from Virginia to see you. We understand you had a difficult time of it recently. Can you tell us about it?"

"Before I answer that, and I will, can I ask why you came all the way from Virginia?" Enslow asked, holding his ground.

"Not at this time," replied the one called Starker.

"Am I under arrest for some reason?" Enslow asked now rather concerned. He had done nothing wrong, but it is quite possible he was being set up for something. The whole trip had been a big cluster fox trot and it was quite likely someone was looking for a patsy to pin it on.

"You are not under arrest. We just want to understand what you went through and your thought process."

Enslow did still not trust these two, but decided he would comply. "Not much to tell. I was on a routine FNR and we ran into trouble. In the course of the trip all of the members were either injured or killed. We managed to hold off the aggressors until a superior force arrived."

"That is more or less consistent with the report we read, but it differs," Starker said, looking genuine but a bit detached.

"How does it differ?" asked Enslow, not annoyed but less than helpful in tone.

"As the team began to wither under the assault, you rose to the occasion. Even though injured, you pressed on. Weren't you in pain?"

Enslow replied, "Hell yes! But my life was in danger. Stopping to whine would not have helped. In the end no one else could move as well as I did."

"What we believe is that an ordinary man rose to the occasion in front of him and did what was required." Harlington spoke for the first time. He went on, "We interviewed the rest of the team and we heard that you did whatever was required. You went back and forth while injured, you dragged a wounded man back to safety, and then you single handedly figured out a way to drag the Humvee closer to the chopper to increase the amount of armor and weapons."

"Didn't really think of it in those terms. There were problems to be solved and I was the one who could solve them. Had to think so fast it was more instinctive, really. I was injured and in danger. The adrenaline boost from the situation may have been the deciding factor in what transpired," replied Enslow in a coldly logical tone, sounding much like the most famous Vulcan.

"So you don't have anger management issues?"

Enslow shook his head slightly, "Not unless you are trying to kill me."

"From what we have read," Harlington told him, "you appear to be a hero."

Enslow looked at him with almost no emotion, except humility, "I'm not a hero. The real heroes are the ones who choose to do this."

"Then what are you?" asked Harlington.

"I'm just a man who situation required action. I had to deal with whatever came my way," Enslow replied matter-of-factly.

"Would you say that you have the ability to adapt to situations and based on the stress levels, employ elements not usually present in your personality?" Starker asked, with his eyebrows furrowed and oddly turning up at the ends.

A now confused Enslow studied the two men for thirty seconds and finally said when he had formulated his question, "Gentlemen, you have come a long way to talk to me and after what I have been through, I find that I would like to cut to the chase and ask what are you actually here for?"

The two men looked at each other and smiled. Harlington spoke before Starker could, "Your candor and forward nature just then is exactly what we hoped we would get out of you. Before you say anything else, please answer one more question. Who is Igor Stanislov Gregor?"

It had been almost three months since Enslow had thought of Igor. He smiled and said "Igor is the result of my boredom. I was unemployed and spending a lot of time on social networking sites. As part of teaching the newly unemployed how to use social networking I had a test character to walk people through the process of filling out a site. Usually I would erase all the data I had put in. One time I was just bored so I added to it."

"Where did you get the details?" asked Starker.

"I really don't know. They just spontaneously flowed."

Starker asked, and leaned slightly forward, "How long did it take to do that profile?"

"Honestly? Less than two hours. It just flowed organically. I gave it very little conscious thought. Why does any of that matter?" Enslow asked, again becoming concerned, but now quite confused how an event of survival and a bit of silliness could be connected.

Harlington stood up and walked around the room and spoke, "Mr. Spengler. We represent an agency of the federal government. In our jobs we recruit people with certain talents, not always developed, that can serve our country. Based on the fact that you are highly intelligent, calculating, clever and spontaneous, and able to tap into a wealth of information in your head and act on it instinctively, we believe you could be of use to us and your country. Couple that with a good level of ability to observe the environment you are in and make optimum strategic decisions, we feel you might do well in a new career with us."

"You offering me a job? I already have a job and it pays very well."

Harlington spoke without looking at the one called Starker, indicating that this was all part of the presentation, "We know. What we are offering you is actually more money and less personal danger. You will be able to bring more money home to your family, and serve your country."

"Would I have to kill people? I don't think I could do that," said Enslow said.

"You already did. Best count we can get is that you killed over fifty men that day," Starker said.

"That was different," a defensive Enslow responded, "They were trying to kill me and the men I was with. It was self-defense plain and simple."

"Does it bother you? Does it bring you regret?" Starker asked with little emotion.

"No, as I said, it was what I had to do. They came after me. They put themselves in harm's way. I only defended myself. But thinking about it, I would have to say, no, it doesn't bother me. I can sleep and have no regrets. You didn't answer my question. You asked me one and never gave me an answer," Enslow replied.

Starker looked at Harlington and then said, "We don't expect you to kill. What we have in mind is the type of work you may be very well suited for. What we need is a peacock."

A mystified Enslow replied, "Peacock?"

"Yes. What we want is someone to send to parties, other events, and have you be seen and heard to attract attention. We will have other assets there to perform the actual work. It's an old magician's trick. If they are looking at you they won't see what the other hand is doing. You are in no danger. You don't need to be. You won't have to do any of the heavy lifting, but you will make it easier for the covert operatives to perform their tasks more quickly and effectively. Understand?"

Enslow absorbed what was said and it made perfect sense. In all the spy movies the hero was always suave and debonair and banged the supermodels, and performed some heroic action to save the world. The real world of spying was likely much more information centric and to get that information you would have to be able to perform outside of people's glare. He reflected to them his concerns, "So no killing, no bomb planting, no harm to others, just be the center of attention. Thinking fast on my feet, and work without fear, is that what you believe I can do?"

"Yes."

"What do you require of me?" Enslow asked, who was thinking this might be a good gig; more money, less danger and a chance to live in a civilized location again.

"We will train you as a level 1 operative. Give you as much training as we can. Basic surveillance, etc, and set you up with a new identity, bank accounts, and a place to live. You cannot tell a soul who you are or who you really work for."

"Shouldn't be hard. I don't know who you really are. You haven't said anything I can verify. How will I pull off this alternate identity? I am not an actor."

"Really quite simple," Starker offered, "What we do is a mind rinse."

"Brain washing?" Enslow asked, sort of startled.

"No no, that's a complete personality. We call it mind rinsing to illustrate that it isn't as deep or complete. It is more of an immersion in a new personality based entirely on elements in your own make up. No new traits are introduced. For instance if you don't like liver and onions we can't make you like them. If you prefer Mozart to Bach we can't change that with these techniques. If you have a specific like of something you will still like it."

"How do I get back to being me?" Enslow asked, rather intrigued about the process.

"You never really leave. You are always who you are and you always know it. While you are in character it gets quite easy to stay in character. To leave and return to complete normality only takes a few days. Some of our agents get quite good at it and can completely revert back in a few hours, speech patterns, everything," Starker told him.

"Will I always know my name?"

"Yes, but you will call yourself your character name. Your name is Enslow, but your handle is Wichita. You answer to both, but it depends on your environment as to what you answer to. Do you think if you were back stateside you would even flinch at the name of Wichita?"

"Maybe a little, but it would pass quickly, I bet." realized Enslow. He summed up what he was being told, "So I would make a bit more money, I would be in no danger, I would not have to shoot or kill anyone, and I would have an expense account. But I can't tell anyone, likely not even my wife. You would spend some time training me as to the rules, methods and protocols to follow. All of this would only take a few weeks while I am healing and since I can't do much during that time it would be a big advantage to me, I bet."

"That about sums it up. Is there anything else

you need to know?" Harlington said as he smiled.

"What have you left out? There is always a catch. What happens if I commit a crime in the line of duty, etc.?"

"Well, we hope you will work within the confines of the law of whatever country you are living in. You can't rob, kill, rape or steal in the line of duty unless we specifically authorize it. You job is almost solely going to be up front, in plain sight, no cloak and dagger."

"When do I leave, and what do I tell my friends here? They would likely ask, and my wife would likely ask them."

"Just tell them you are transferring to Europe for full recovery and then you tell them you have transferred there permanently. Just don't give them too much information. Tell your wife you are working on the back side of the supply process and that occurs in England. But we need an answer now."

"Why now?"

"Quite simply. This position requires split second judgment. Without it, you could get into trouble. So I need an answer."

"Then I am in," Enslow replied, "Now what?"

"We start the process rolling. We'll arrange your transport tonight, and you will arrive at your training location in less than twenty four hours. We will send your stuff. Your training and physical recuperation will start, and in less than thirty days we will give you your first assignment. You will be on probation for at least thirty days after your training is over. We need to know that you can cut it. If you can't we can arrange for you to come back here. Your contract will be for 6 months with an option to renew every six months. That's the deal. You still in?"

Taking all of a half second, Enslow said firmly, "Yes."

"That's great," Starker replied as he opened a briefcase he had ignored for the entire meeting. He took out a small contract and handed it with a pen to Enslow. He said, "Please read and sign the contract. As you can see it is lacking most of the mumbo jumbo you usually see in a legal document and it is considerably smaller than most government contracts. It simply restates what we have told you and states your responsibilities and outlines the pay amount, pay schedule and accounting guidelines for expenses. More finer points of details will come with each mission you are assigned, if any, and you are agreeing in this document to abide by whatever these parameters are. Clear?"

Meeting the eyes of the two men, Enslow said, "Yes, clear." Enslow reread the contract, and saw that it was precisely what they had said, so he signed it and handed it back to Starker.

Starker smiled and nodded to his partner Harlington, who picked up and handed a small attaché case to Enslow. "Here are your study materials and what you will need to get started. Also there is some bank information and ten thousand dollars in cash for starting expenses. You will stay at the training facility for up to thirty days and then you will need to secure a car, living quarters, etc., and integrate yourself into the community. This ten thousand is part of your expense account so watch it wisely as it is taxpayer money. Do keep receipts for what you spend. We may never see you again. What happens is you are assigned a controller or controllers who communicate with you and assign you missions and you communicate back with them the mission outcome and seek their help for those little problems that arise, etc. When you complete your training you will be given new papers, verifiable history, credit ratings, education, etc. Good luck Enslow."

Enslow said "Thanks" as he shook their hands

and they walked out of the room. Shortly thereafter an orderly came in and took him to another room where his clothes were waiting and he got dressed and waited for the next part of the journey, which happened in less than thirty minutes when a 'company' man came in and helped him get into a Humvee that took him to a waiting C130 on which Enslow was the only passenger. The plane taxied down the runway and lifted off, heading south toward Pakistan, most likely where Enslow assumed he would then take off for Dubai and then Europe. From there he didn't know what was going to happen, but he was safe and was going to be paid better, and this job sounded fun. No shooting, no IEDs, no heartache. Enslow opened the case he got and looked inside. It had a passport with his picture on it and some background documents. Reading them caused Enslow to grin. Much of the history was either word for word what he had written several months ago or was obviously based on it and bulked up. Probably it would make it easier for him to play the part. Looking back at the passport he noticed the name was different. It was not Igor. It had Enslow's picture but the name under it was Nigel Synclair Jones. *Well, aren't you just a cheeky bastard!*

###
Nigel will return in: "A Basic Damn Fretting"
###

Maria Day 292 –A Basic Damn Fretting

Maria Vostro walked down the hall to the meeting she had been called to. She both relished new assignments, and loathed them. The newness of an assignment, a new team to dominate and a new chance to prove herself was always exciting. This time would be different; however, she knew in advance that she was playing clean up. Agent Logan had not only failed her before, his last assignment went bad almost from the beginning. His partner got killed. *Honestly, who can screw up a simple surveillance and get someone killed?* A person or persons unknown had pulled their asses literally out of a fire, but no one knew who or why. It seems that the whole fiasco had elevated the need to determine the who and why, but also who was doing the gun shipments to crime organizations. Many of the guns were of western origin, others were AK47s made who knows where.

She entered the conference room where there were three other people. Her new boss, Director Hanstram, a man in his late fifties she did not know, and a woman of mixed conception, Asian and Caucasian, given the cheek bones, maybe Polish.

"Good morning Agent Vostro," Director Hanstram said, "This is analyst Stewart and analyst Takanashi. They will be providing you with the current status of you mission."

"Pleasure to meet you," Agent Vostro said.

"Nice to meet you," analyst Stewart said. Analyst Takanashi merely smiled.

Director Hanstram stood up and walked over to the wall, where he tapped it and suddenly the lights dimmed, and a map of Europe appeared. He pointed to England, roughly around London, and began his mission overview. "As you are aware, a few weeks ago, Agent Logan and his partner, Agent Widmer, were ambushed and Agent Widmer was killed. Agent Logan is making a nice recovery. What you didn't know till now, was that Agent Logan's phone was recovered by one of our operatives, and it had pictures of the dead Albanians. Their bodies were destroyed by the fire, and dental records were never able to positively identify them. We have not shared our pictures with MI6, but we have been able to identify the men. They are known low level couriers for a loose organization of Eastern European scum who participate in various criminal professions such as gun running, drugs, prostitution, assault gangs, racketeering, shakedowns of immigrants, pretty much any unsavory activity where there is a profit to be made, and they don't usually care who gets hurt. This time however, a group of them was killed by the previously mentioned person or persons unknown. Analyst Stewart has some new information that we believe may help us track down their associates, and possibly tie up some loose ends with respect to Agent Logan's ambush. Mr. Stewart, if you would enlighten us."

Analyst Stewart stood up and walked to the display wall as Director Hanstram sat down. A picture of a middle aged man appeared on the screen as analyst Stewart tapped a button on a remote he was holding. "This is a Russian we know by the name of Konstantinov. He holds a diplomatic title from the Russian government, even though we think he is really Ukrainian. He has been involved in a number of illicit activities for many years. He likes flashy women and the roulette wheel, but he has little real luck with either. We intercepted some email from other known Albanian crime groups, and it appears that Konstantinov was brokering a gun transaction when it all went bad. The guns were not his, but he is responsible for them and the money for them. Forensic analysis of the vehicle fires indicate that most of the guns were on site and destroyed by the fires, and that the money may have been, I repeat, may have been destroyed. The fire was so hot, that we believe it may have vaporized, but some of the forensic analysis reveals a deficiency of certain markers that would be present from the burned remains of a great deal of cash. The reason beyond that is that other surveillance indicates that Konstantinov is going to be held responsible for the guns and the missing money, whether it burned up or not. The accounts we know he uses, show the money being moved out, but no appreciable matching funds moving back in. He is being followed by spotters to see if he is playing games concerning the money. We believe that it either was not in the vehicles, or did in fact burn up, but only at a 90% confidence level. The Russian ABC intelligence command does not seem to like his self enrichment, so we believe he is using his cover to play these aspects on his own, and they do not constitute an official program of either the Russian government or her intelligence agencies. Not even rogue programs. This appears to be an effort he is running on his own."

Maria let the information soak in. After analyzing it, and before anyone else could speak, she said, "We may not need to pursue him, if he is dirty, or if he is in any way responsible for that debacle, then someone else may take care of him for us. However, another rat will likely take his place, so if we were to get the best of all outcomes, then we would like to use him to get to the higher levels of these organizations."

While what Maria said was obvious, it also

underscored why she was selected for this assignment. She was coldly calculating, and able to drive to the heart of the matter. Deputy Hanstram grinned slightly, and replied to her, "Yes, I had wanted to present the rest of the information, but perhaps that would be a waste of time. Everything else is support information. Let's just do that. Your mission is to set up a watch on all things related to Konstantinov, ascertain whether he is a major player, and who his contacts are. Determine what his level is in the organization he plays and any higher ups. You are authorized to use level 2 forces and interrogation. This mission will also be a joint exercise with MI5. Because the attack in the industrial district occurred on their soil, the British claim jurisdiction. Considering that one of our agents was killed, they have extended a professional courtesy to allow us to participate. But the agent they assign will be in control. You will take your orders from that Agent. He will meet you at Heathrow in twenty three days. He will be outside the departure area and will be holding a newspaper in his right hand and a coffee cup in his left. He will know you by your appearance and that you will be wearing red shoes. Ask him if he knows how Liverpool is doing. He will respond that they are doing well enough, but without Manning they will never make the cup."

"What is the name of the agent? Age?" Maria inquired, noticing that he had not been identified.

"At this time," Director Hanstram replied, "Your contact is Braemar. You will leave in three weeks. In the intervening time, I would suggest you spend some time in Hardware; we have some new surveillance tracking items, as well as some recent advances released in the previous quarter."

Internally frowning, but outwardly expressionless, asked "Will I have Agency backup?"

Director Hanstram responded with his usual administrative flair, "No. This is primarily a British operation, and we are being allowed in. Do take efforts not step on their toes. They are generally gracious hosts but they can be pushed too far. One other thing to add, if you can determine anything more about who rescued Agent Logan and Agent Widmer it would be a nice bonus. This concludes our discussion. Good luck."

As that was a clear signal to say nothing further and leave. Agent Vostro stood up and gathered the folder that had been in front of her, and left. As she walked down the hall, she was already planning her departure.

Glossary

Aldawolfa- Old German for Noble Wolf (female).

Arse - Ass.

Anti clockwise - British for counterclockwise.

Banger - Sausage.

Birdwatcher - slang used by British Intelligence for a spy.

Bladdered - Drunk.

Bonnet - Front compartment of a car, usually covers the engine. In US is called the hood.

Boot - Rear compartment of a car. In the US called the trunk.

Boudicca - Queen of the Iceni, who rebelled against Rome in A.D. 60. Her uprising against the Romans slaughtered over 70,000 people and burned London to the ground.

Box 850 Slang for a British intelligence agency that is derived from their original mailbox number.

C130 - The Lockheed C-130 Hercules is a four-engine turboprop military transport aircraft. It is capable of using both paved and unpaved landing and takeoff surfaces. The C130 known as the Hercules has been in continuous production for over 50 years and is in use by at over 60 countries.

CCTV- Closed Circuit Television. In use all of London.

CTC -Civilian Technical Contractor.

Cobbler- A spy who creates false passports, visas, diplomas and other documents.

Faff – Waste time.

Floating box - A method of surveillance where a team of operators establishes containment box around the target wherever he/she goes.

GBU-38 – A 500 pound JDAM

GCHQ Britain's sigint agency, Government Communications Head Quarters.

GreyFriars's Bobby - Legendary dog of a night watchman who refused to leave his grave for 13 years after his owners' death.

Grotty - Dirty, rundown.

HIP - Mil-8 Russian helicopter.

HUMINT - Intelligence activities involving people rather than electronic eavesdropping or communications interception.

HUMVEE - All wheel drive military vehicle in use by the United States and many Western countries. Replaced the iconic Jeep for general crew transport and light duties. Often armored and armed with various weapons.

L-PILL - A poison pill used by operatives to commit suicide.

JDAM - The Joint Direct Attack Munitions is a modification kit that allows unguided bombs to be guided by GPS signals from orbiting satellites.

L5 - 4096 bit encryption algorithm

Legend - The faked biography of a deep-cover agent.

Loo - Toilet.

Lorry - Truck.

M2 - The M2 Machine Gun is a .50 Caliber Machine Gun.

M60 - The M60 was introduced in 1957 and was in wide spread use, but has been replaced by the M240 in U.S. service

M240B - The M240 Machine Gun uses a 7.62mm NATO cartridge. The M240 has been used by the United States Armed Forces since the mid-1980s by infantry, ground vehicles, and aircraft.

Merci beaucoup -'Thank you' in French.

MI.5 - Britain's security service. K Branch is responsible for counter espionage, F Branch performs counter subversion, C Branch performs security of sensitive government installations.

MI.6 - Britain's foreign intelligence agency.

MQ- Reaper - UAV. Deadly armed remote piloted vehicle. Can be armed with a variety of bombs and missiles. Uses different scanners to acquire and eliminate designated targets.

NOC - A spy with Non-Official Cover. A fake or real private sector job used by an agent as a cover.

Peacock - Someone who is designed to attract others attention while the real work goes on.

Poncy – Too self important, too pretentious.

Quid - Another name for money.

Slash - To urinate.

Tenner - Ten pound note.

Tower of London - A The Tower of London has been used as a prison, an armory, a menagerie, a treasury, the home of the Royal Mint, and the home of the Crown Jewels of the United Kingdom.

Wet work – Describes the type of work where someone kills targets.

Wheel artist - An outdoor surveillance specialist operating in a vehicle.

Wilderness of mirrors - A spy operation so complicated that it is no longer possible to separate truth and untruth.

Window dressing - Ancillary materials that are included in a cover story or deception operation to help convince the opposition or other casual observers that what they are observing is genuine.

Zero-out – The range at which a weapon's sights will produce a direct bull's eye hit. Handgun sights are generally zeroed-out at 25 yards. A sniper rifle scope is usually zeroed-out at 100 yards. Nuclear weapons just zero you and everything out.